I0589938

DEVIL'S GATHERING

BOOK 3 OF THE DEVEREAUX CHRONICLES

Debbie Boek

This book is dedicated to all of you that have been so supportive and encouraging as I travel down this new and adventurous path. Every positive comment, every review, every acknowledgement, means the world to me and gives me a little more faith in myself. I couldn't have made it this far without you. Thank you.

Copyright © 2019 Debbie Boek

All rights reserved.

ISBN: 0-9600775-0-2
ISBN-13: 978-0-9600775-0-2

ALSO BY DEBBIE BOEK

If Not For The Knight

Sommers' Folly

Devil's Bait

Devil's Retribution

5 STAR REVIEW FOR DEVIL'S BAIT

Devil's Bait was a great book! I could not put it down. I am not an avid reader so a book really has to catch my attention in order for me to get through it. I finished this book in two days. Absolutely LOVED it! You will too! I am waiting for the sequel!
    --K. DeGroot

5 STAR REVIEW FOR DEVIL'S RETRIBUTION

I just finished Devil's Retribution. Wow, I thought it was better than Devil's Bait, even though I didn't think that was possible! Awesome job Debbie!!
    --P. Martin

Visit the author at:
debbieboek.com
debbieboek.blog

WINDY SHOT

"A blast in a coal mine which--due to improperly placed charges, the wrong kind or quantity of explosives, or insufficient stemming--expends most of its force on the mine air; it sometimes ignites a gas mixture, coal dust, or both, thus causing a secondary explosion, which may or may not spread throughout the mine; a shot that blows out without disturbing the coal; a shot that is not properly directed or loaded; a blown-out shot."

CHAPTER 1

The creature stood on the knoll, its red eyes staring down into the valley, locked on its prey. The voice was still chanting, echoing in its head, and a low, deep growl of frustration emanated from its chest. The wiry, black fur along its spine stood on end and its lips were pulled back in a grimace, exposing long, sharp teeth.

Unaware of the creature watching them from above, Caleb and Leona wandered slowly back towards their house, enjoying the brilliant shades of red and orange shimmering over the valley as the sun set behind the rocky bluffs. The temperature was dropping as the sun went down and Leona pulled her shawl tighter around her shoulders.

Caleb reached out to grab his wife's hand, but found that she had stopped suddenly and was staring almost trancelike up into the hills near the old abandoned mine.

"What is it?" Concern made his deep voice even more coarse than usual.

When she continued to stare mutely up into the hills, Caleb turned in the same direction, trying to find what had caught her attention so profoundly. But, try as he might, Caleb was unable to detect anything out the ordinary.

He reached over and took both her hands in his own, trying to rub some life into them, but they remained inert and motionless.

"Leona, Honey, what is it? You're acting like you're off your nut, what do you see up there?"

She didn't respond, the sun was continuing to lower in the sky and Leona strained her eyes to catch sight of it again, but to no avail, it was now lost among the shadows that were forming.

Caleb moved directly in front of her, his large frame blocking her view, forcing her to focus her attention on him. Looking up into her husband's intense gray eyes, the haze finally cleared from Leona's mind, she bit back a sob, wrapped her arms around him and rested her head against his broad chest.

"You're scaring me, Leona."

"It was the dog," she whispered, starting to shiver violently.

He pulled her in tighter against his body, and asked, "The Black Dog?"

She didn't answer, but he could feel her head nodding in the affirmative as her tears burned through his shirt.

He stepped back and held her at arms' length so that he could look into her beautiful pale blue eyes as he spoke.

"Leona, there is no Black Ghost Dog, that's nothing more than an Urban Legend. If it was real, I would know it."

Leona searched his face, already knowing what she would find there. She and Caleb had been down this road before and he wouldn't accept that the dog was real ten years ago, so she knew it would be even harder for him to acknowledge it now.

She would not back down from the hard, steely gaze of his gray eyes. Leona had no doubt in her mind that the Black Ghost dog did exist and what it was capable of. It had killed her father and now it was coming for her.

Caleb knew what a logical person Leona was, not at all prone to foolishness, so it was disturbing to see how deeply this was affecting her.

There was a quiver around her eyes and her mouth was open slightly as she inhaled quick little breaths, trying to relieve some of her apprehension.

"Honey, you probably saw a stray or a coyote up there. It was no damn omen of death, so get that nonsense straight out of your head, right now."

Leona's face began to relax and a sad smile sat on her lips. For a few moments she had been overwhelmed by the knowledge of what she saw, and by the terror that had flooded her body as a result of it.

Her life had taken many unexpected twists and turns and because of that she learned to roll with the punches. Her pulse was now slowing down and her heartbeat was returning to a normal rhythm, allowing her to think clearly again.

"It's here and you know it, Caleb. I realize that you won't even discuss what happened with my father, but what about Michael and Clint?"

"What about them? Michael got bit by a snake and Clint got kicked in the chest by a horse. Both freaky, unusual incidents, but not supernatural in any way, shape or form."

"But they both saw the dog a day or two before they died."

"Says who?"

"They told me about it right after it happened."

"Why didn't you bother to share that information with me until now?"

"Because I knew what your reaction would be. At the time, I thought the same thing as you do, a coyote or a stray, nothing to worry about. Until I saw it myself. It was a huge, black dog, not a coyote, and it was staring straight at me. I could feel it's eyes boring into my very soul."

"Being a little melodramatic now, aren't you?"

Her smile had long since faded and now her eyes snapped in anger at his response. "No, Caleb, I am not being overly dramatic. I saw the thing and now I'm scared, very, very scared, so the last thing that I need is you belittling me right now."

She bit back a sob and Caleb closed his eyes and rubbed the bridge of his nose.

Slowly reopening them, he fixed his gaze on his wife and said, "Sometimes, woman, I cannot even begin to understand where you come up with the things you say and do. There's no damn Black Ghost Dog and it most definitely is not an omen indicating that you are going to die."

"I never said that it was."

"But that's what you think, right?" he asked, his gravelly voice even deeper than usual.

"When will the Devereaux brothers be here?"

Caleb had to think for a minute, she'd changed the direction of their conversation so abruptly that he almost didn't catch the question.

"I heard from Tim, he'll be here in the morning. Scott won't be here until sometime after that. He's bringing his new little piece of calico with him."

Leona frowned at Caleb. "You can be so disrespectful sometimes. I hope you don't intend to be that crass in front of her."

"Maybe I will, maybe I won't. I don't need you treating me like some old coot that doesn't know how to behave," he replied, feeling his own anger bubble to the surface.

"Then stop acting like one." Leona's fear was fading and the encounter with the Black Dog began to feel like it had been a figment of her imagination, but her annoyance with her husband was very real and growing exponentially. She turned and started striding back towards their house, the long gray braid that hung down her back swinging like a pendulum behind her.

"Why did you want to know when they'd be here?" Caleb asked, his long legs allowing him to catch up with her in just a few steps.

"Because, of all your friends, they are the two that I trust the most and I need to talk to them about this."

"About what?"

"The Black Ghost Dog killed my father, it killed Clint and Michael, and now it wants me. I am not going to let that happen without a fight and maybe they can help me stop it, since you obviously aren't going to."

"Leona,"

She stopped walking and turned towards him, her pale blue eyes filled with anger, hurt and frustration. "Don't say a word, Caleb. I cannot listen to any more of your condescending comments right now. You go meet up with your friends over at the saloon and don't worry about me, I'll take care of this myself."

Caleb watched her go, his lips pursed in frustration, battling within himself. He knew that he should go with her, be there for her and give her his support. But he couldn't bring himself to do that, wouldn't reinforce her silly notion that there was a mysterious black ghost dog haunting Windy Shot.

With one last look towards his wife, he turned, squared his shoulders and headed for the saloon so that he could visit with his friends, who had a little more realistic view of life.

*　　　*　　　*

It was a beautiful spring day, but Emma wasn't able to enjoy any of the sights and sounds as she approached the end of her journey. She found that the closer she got, the sweatier her hands became as they gripped the steering wheel, and the harder her heart pounded in her chest. The more she focused on it, the worse it got.

"For goodness sakes, girl, you've faced ghosts and demons and freaking Bigfoot, so get a grip on yourself. Doris Devereaux will be a walk in the park compared to them."

But her thudding heart didn't ease up until she reached the end of the driveway outside the house and saw Scott step out onto the porch, followed immediately by Callie, her beautiful, black German Shepherd.

It had been almost a month since their run in with Bigfoot, but Callie was still limping a little and her hind quarters were stiff as she walked down the few steps to the ground. Emma jumped out of the car and walked towards them, but her smile faltered when Doris followed them onto the porch. The older woman wasn't exactly scowling, but she definitely wasn't wearing her 'happy to see you' face.

Emma forced a broad smile onto her own face and hoped it didn't look as fake as it felt. She walked over to Callie, gently petting her head as the dog rubbed up against her leg. Emma was genuinely happy to be back with her girl again and it lifted a little bit of her anxiety. Then she walked forward a few more feet, straight into Scott's arms.

He kissed her warmly and she could feel her entire body relaxing against him, amazed, as always, at how calm and safe she felt when encircled in his arms.

"I missed you," he whispered. His lips tickled her ear and she could feel her face flush and her pulse begin to race as her body responded to his nearness.

Their eyes met and, for a moment, the world froze in place and it was just the two of them standing there. The birds no longer sang, the wind no longer rustled through the evergreens, and Emma's lips parted involuntarily in response to Scott's gentle touch as he pushed an errant lock of blonde hair from her face.

The world returned abruptly when Doris cleared her throat, a little louder than was necessary, from up on the porch. Emma gave Doris a sidelong glance, then turned her gaze back to Scott.

"I missed you, too, and I didn't even realize how much until this very moment. But it was a good trip, I always feel better after spending time with my kids."

Emma's daughter was away at college and her two teenage sons split their time between their father's apartment and their Prep School in the city.

Emma was recently divorced and her life was still in transition. Her relationship with Scott was fairly new, and they were in the process of finding their way together, so Emma had thought it best to go visit her children by herself, this time.

Soon she would have to deal with the explanations and the melding of these two parts of her life, her children and the man she loved, but not yet.

The divorce had not been easy for the children to understand and, until Emma was sure of the path that her relationship was going to take with Scott, she didn't want to complicate their lives any more than she had to.

These last couple of weeks that she spent with her children were very relaxing and fulfilling, but now it was time to work on this part of her life, the part that she wanted to share with Scott Devereaux.

First, though, she would have to deal with his mother. Scott and Emma had been separated for almost two years after they'd originally met and fell in love. That was Emma's decision because she had no choice but to put her children first and give her marriage one more chance.

The odds of her and Scott having a successful relationship would have been very slim indeed, had she not first proven to herself that the marriage was definitely over. If she hadn't done that, Emma would always have wondered if she could have done things differently and saved her children the heartache of their divorce.

The time that they had been separated was not easy for Scott and, although they had finally reconnected and were establishing a new life together, Doris couldn't forgive Emma for causing Scott so much pain.

Emma was a mother herself and appreciated the fierce love that Doris felt for her son. It was just a little daunting to know that, somehow, she was going to have to prove to Doris how deeply she felt about Scott, and convince her that she would never hurt him again.

Trust would have to be built over time and Emma had already decided that she would do whatever she had to in order to gain that trust.

Emma took a deep breath and lifted her head as she walked towards the porch. Her hand was gently encased in Scott's, which warmed her heart and gave her courage.

"Hello, Doris. It's good to see you."

Doris just nodded in her direction. "Come on in, I was just about to put together some lunch."

"Thank you," Emma replied, unable to miss the frosty tone in Doris' voice. Scott heard it too and gave her hand a gentle squeeze of reassurance. She took another deep breath and walked beside him into the house.

Doris had to be close to seventy, but she had the energy of someone much younger. She was a handsome woman, her silver hair was cropped short and she had the same dark, probing eyes as her son.

"Can I help?" Emma asked.

"No, just have a seat. I'm going to throw together a salad and get out the leftovers from last night's dinner. Scott get the iced tea and glasses, please."

"Sure." He winked at Emma as he walked over to the refrigerator to grab the pitcher of tea and set it on the table.

His eyes continued to wander back to Emma as he proceeded to fill three large glasses to the brim. His heart literally skipped a beat as he drank in her beauty, the sparkling green eyes, soft blonde hair and full, pink lips filled him with a depth of feeling that he had never imagined was possible.

Scott was in his forties and Emma was the first, and only, love of his life, and the feelings that he had for her were profound.

Although he was confident that Emma's love ran as deep as his own, he hadn't completely recovered yet from their lengthy separation. There was always a little niggling of doubt eating away at him when she was not by his side, particularly when she was spending time with her children and, possibly, her ex-husband.

"Damn it!" Scott exclaimed suddenly, as tea started overflowing one of the glasses, bringing his attention back where it belonged.

"Watch your mouth," his mother reprimanded, "and what you're doing."

Doris couldn't help but throw a nasty look Emma's way, since she was obviously the reason for Scott's absentmindedness.

Emma sat quietly, not realizing the thoughts that were churning through Scott's head, worried more about how she was going to win over his mother and wondering just how long that might take, and if she would have the patience for it.

Callie had followed them into the cozy kitchen and made herself comfortable on top of a thick comforter that had been arranged for her over in one of the corners.

Emma watched her fondly. Callie was getting up in years and her muzzle was now almost completely white. She seemed to have adjusted quite well to Doris' home in the short time she'd been here.

"Thank you for looking after Callie for me, Doris. Other than being stiff, she seems to have healed up quite well from her adventure with Bigfoot."

Doris' hand stilled over the tomato that she was slicing. She glanced at the dog, now fast asleep in the corner and, for the first time, Emma saw a genuine smile light the woman's face.

"She's been a good companion. Neither of us move too fast anymore and she seems content to wander around with me at my pace. We got on together just fine."

"It's true," Scott agreed, as he continued to wipe the tea up from the vinyl yellow tablecloth, "neither of them wanted anything to do with me. They were like long-lost buddies."

"Come on, Scott, you know that's not true. I love having both my boys around."

Emma just now realized that she hadn't seen Scott's brother since she arrived. Tim was Scott's younger brother and they shared many similar physical attributes, brown hair, brown eyes and strong, muscular bodies.

But they had their own unique personalities. Scott was exuberant, larger than life, and Tim was more of an introvert. He chose to think things through before charging full steam ahead, unlike his brother. But they shared the same strength of character and values, honesty, integrity and bravery being a few at the top of Emma's list.

Tim and Emma had some rough times, initially. He was not thrilled that his brother was messing around with a married woman, regardless of the sorry state of her marriage at that time.

Since her divorce and reunion with Scott, Emma was finding herself on slightly more secure footing with Tim, but she knew that she still had to prove herself to him, also. He was almost as protective as Doris and still a little wary as far as Emma was concerned.

Ironically, the one person that Emma did not have to prove anything to was Scott, the one she had hurt the most. They hadn't discussed what their future together would hold yet, but he showed how deeply he cared about her with every look, every touch, and Emma knew, without a doubt, how strong their relationship was and drew her strength from that knowledge.

Emma watched Scott as he moved around the kitchen and could feel her cheeks flushing when she thought of his full lips exploring her body and those strong arms holding her close. Realizing where she was, Emma risked a sideways glance at Doris and saw that she watching her curiously, so she shook her head, trying to clear it of those particular thoughts.

"Is Tim here?" she asked, taking a big of sip of iced tea to further cool herself down.

Scott shook his head. "No, he headed over to Windy Shot already."

"What's Windy Shot?"

"You'll find out soon enough."

"Always the mystery man, aren't you?"

"I try, we'll be heading out there as soon as we finish lunch and pack up."

"Why so soon, Son?"

"We're already getting a late start and I want to be there for the final farewells, particularly for Joey."

"Of course, I understand."

"I don't," Emma said, her brilliant green eyes clouded with confusion.

He hesitated, trying find the best way to explain. Scott and Tim were members of a small, relatively unknown group of hunters, where the game was anything paranormal. Emma was familiar with that aspect of Scott's life but since their relationship was fairly new, there was still much more that she had to learn about his world.

"We're heading for Windy Shot, Nevada, it's a Western themed resort that is owned by a hunting buddy of ours. Every year at this time we have a Hunter's Gathering where we catch up with old friends, find out what kind of critters have been active and, it also gives us an opportunity to say good-bye to the friends we've lost in the past year."

"It sounds intriguing."

"I've never been, but I've heard the stories and am pretty sure that is not the correct adjective to describe the event." Doris narrowed her eyes as she studied her son.

"Now, Mom," Scott said, walking over and wrapping his arm around her shoulder, "don't go getting Emma all worried. It's just a good old-fashioned reunion, that's all."

"Humpf." Her wordless reply spoke volumes as she slid out from underneath his hand and set the bowl of salad onto the table.

"Do you have everything that you need for the Bigfoot story?" Scott asked, pulling his chair over so close to Emma's that his muscular thigh rested tightly against hers.

"I have enough, I can make it work." Hunting monsters was not a financially lucrative line of work, and Doris helped support her sons by taking their stories and watering them down into a series of supernatural books for teenagers. The royalties from the books paid for Tim and Scott's travels, as they had for their father before them.

"All I'll have to add in is my own adventure with the damn creature. It took me almost two weeks to get my house back in order after that thing trashed it."

"But you were safe, right?"

"Yes, thank goodness I was out of town at a book-signing when it decided to drop by."

"And for that, we are all extremely grateful," Scott murmured, gazing fondly at his mother. "Come on, Emma, eat up and then we'll hit the road and see what adventures are waiting for us in Windy Shot."

Scott might not have been quite so excited, if he had even an inkling of what lay in store for them.

CHAPTER 2

"Hey, Gabriel, good to see you again."

"Yo, Tim, how you doing?" Gabriel replied, the smile growing wider on his face as he approached. "Hop in."

"Where's the horse and buggy? Did Caleb stop trying to be authentic for some reason?" Tim asked, folding his tall frame down into the golf cart.

"No, two reasons, really," Gabriel replied, as he maneuvered the cart around. They left the paved parking lot and headed back on the dirt trail towards the gated town of Windy Shot. "One, the horses don't really like me, so Caleb doesn't want me using them, and then there was a little incident. The damage wasn't that bad, but Caleb doesn't want me using the buggies anymore, either."

"I see," Tim replied, feeling a sense of relief that the golf cart could only go a max of about 15 miles per hour.

They'd met Gabriel at the ski lodge in Vermont where they'd been dealing with a Bigfoot problem. Gabriel was an excitable young man in his early twenties that was working for the lodge at the time. He'd been in a variety of different positions there also, Tim recalled, due to his being a tad-bit accident-prone.

"By the way," Gabriel added, "I appreciate you and Scott getting me this gig. It's off the hook, I always wanted to work at one of these resorts."

Gabriel had been a big help to them and in return they'd gotten him a job here at Windy Shot. The golf cart swerved back and forth as the spring breeze kept blowing Gabrielle's red hair around his face and into his eyes.

Tim held on a bit tighter and admired the view as they approached the town. It was nestled in a valley with rocky bluffs extending upward on three sides of it. No matter how often he came here, Tim was still awed by the majestic beauty of that view every single time.

"What exactly do they have you doing, just running the guests from the parking lot into town?"

No vehicles were allowed within the town limits and the lot was a mile away. That was primarily so that it couldn't be seen and affect the nineteenth century atmosphere for the patrons, once they were a part of the town and its activities.

"Leona keeps trying me out at different jobs. So far, it looks like the safest place for me to be is the Mercantile, I help stock the shelves and stuff."

"What do you mean, the safest?"

"Well, I cause the least amount of damage there." Gabriel giggled nervously. "Leona is really patient with me but her husband, Caleb, he's scary, man, and he don't like it when things are out of whack."

"He's not so bad, but I see your point, he can be a little gruff sometimes."

"For sure, a regular curmudgeon."

"What was the second reason you came to get me in this silly thing?"

Gabriel nodded his head as if having some sort of internal conversation and then he floored the gas pedal, which was comical because they only picked up a minimal amount of additional speed.

"Leona wanted me to bring you to her as soon as you showed up. I've been waiting in the parking lot for a couple of hours."

"Is something wrong?"

"I'm not sure, but she was acting a little funny today, not like herself. She usually walks around and is totally in charge of every part of what goes on in town. But today she seems distracted and confused. It's weird. And Caleb is being a dick, oh, sorry, he's a friend, right?"

"Yes, he is. What's he doing?"

"He's just angry and is lashing at everyone. I've been trying to avoid him, so I didn't mind hiding out in the parking lot."

Tim half-suspected that Leona sent Gabriel there on purpose, just to keep him under Caleb's radar.

Caleb was a man who had seen a lot of ugly in his life and when he got in a mood, no one wanted to be too close to him. No one, except Leona, she was the only person who could talk him down when he went to his dark place.

Tim was curious about what was going on, usually the two of them were on an even keel, especially during the week of the Gathering, because it was mainly for fun and catching up with other hunters who could share their stories and understand yours.

He pursed his lips and narrowed his eyes as he tried to figure out what could possibly have happened to affect the two of them to such a degree.

Gabriel slammed on the brakes and waited for one of the other employees to open up the tall iron gates at the entrance to town. A huge wrought iron sign reading WINDY SHOT hung just above it, creaking back and forth in the slight breeze.

There were two side streets that ran off to their right, the first was Chickabiddy Lane and then The Fandango. Straight ahead, and directly in front of them, was the Sheriff's office and, when Gabriel neglected to brake at all, Tim thought they might end up going straight through that building.

Fortunately, at the last minute he made a hard right onto The Fandango and Tim quickly grabbed hold of the side of the cart so that he didn't roll right out of it.

"Hold up, Gabriel," Tim yelled, once he got his balance back. "There she is."

Gabriel brought the cart to an abrupt stop and Leona rushed over to Tim as soon as he extricated his long limbs from it.

"I am so glad to see you, Tim." Her voice was soft and as melodic as always, but there was a tremor to it that Tim had never heard before.

"Me, too," he responded, drawing her into his arms and giving her a warm hug. Leona had always been close to him and his brother, not so much like a mother, more like a really cool aunt, and the death grip that she hugged him with now was unnerving. "What's going on?"

"Gabriel," she called out, "please deliver Tim's things over to the main hotel and have them taken up to his room."

"Yes, Ma'am." Gabriel headed off and Leona watched him fondly. "He's quite a character, thanks for sending him our way."

"I know how you like taking in strays, Leona, and he seemed to fit the mark."

"Yes, he definitely does. Come along, walk with me."

Leona was dressed, as usual, in a long denim skirt with cowboy boots and a flowered shirt that brought out the color in her cornflower blue eyes, her long gray braid once again hung down her back.

Even with the boots on, her head barely made it to Tim's shoulder, and he shortened his stride to keep to her slow, deliberate pace. He kept quiet, waiting for her to share what she needed to, in her own time.

They made their way along the cobblestone street, passing the fronts of buildings from times gone by, most with board and batten siding that gave them a rustic appearance and immediately made you feel like you were in another world.

The sun was bright overhead and there was a nice breeze to keep it from being too hot. Tim would have really appreciated the beauty of the moment, if he wasn't so worried about Leona.

"We got the last of the streets paved with cobblestones, finally. What do you think?"

"Looks good, it'll make a big difference when you get rain, won't it?"

"Hell, yes. That was always the biggest complaint that we got." Her whole face changed as she began to mimic a woman's nasally high-pitched voice, "*I paid a lot of money for this costume and the whole bottom of it is caked in mud and it's ruined, just ruined.*"

"So much for appreciating an authentic experience," she added in her voice.

Tim laughed out loud but stopped abruptly when he looked down into her eyes. They were glazed over with some emotion that he couldn't quite discern.

"What is it, Leona, what's going on? Talk to me."

"Oh, Tim, I'm scared, really, really scared."

Emma and Scott didn't arrive at Windy Shot until late morning the next day, they'd taken a little extra time on their road trip to have a proper reunion after their brief hiatus.

They were taken from the parking lot via the official horse and buggy, driven by one of the other resort employees who was dressed in appropriate period attire. The only feature that detracted from it was the small name tag pinned to the lapel of his leather vest.

Malcolm loaded their bags onto the boot of the buggy and jumped up to begin their short jaunt to town. He was an enthusiastic young man, with curly blonde hair and light blue eyes.

The buggy's canvas top was down, giving them a great view and Emma was enchanted as they approached Windy Shot's tall iron gates. Malcolm handled the pair of horses well, even when a breeze came up and he spent more time attempting to keep his cowboy hat on his head than he did trying to control them.

"Oh, Scott, I love this place." Emma's head swiveled back and forth as she tried to take in the scenery and all the buildings. It was like stepping back in time, the streets were cobblestone, there were wooden sidewalks and the buildings looked like something straight out of a history book.

Little islands of colorful flowers and cacti were placed strategically throughout the town, the colors vibrant under the bright sun.

Immediately to their right was a large schoolhouse and beyond that building, Emma could see a playground for the children. There was a wooden sign indicating the street name, Chickabiddy Lane.

"Malcolm," Emma called out to their young driver, "do you know what Chickabiddy means? I've never heard the word before."

"Of course, Ma'am," Malcolm replied, his chest puffing out in importance. He had recently been promoted to this position and now gave tours of the town, so he knew every detail about every square inch of it.

"Chickabiddy was a term of endearment for children and everything on that road is geared towards the young ones. The kids can experience a school day from back in the eighteen hundreds and there's also a playground for them.

Beyond that is the family hotel which has game rooms and an indoor kiddie pool and lots for the kids to experience and explore to keep them busy. Out beyond that is an Olympic size pool and basketball and tennis courts. We also have a bunch of actors here and they usually try to get the youngsters involved in at least one show a day."

Malcolm passed Chickabiddy Lane and continued with his tour, practicing for when the real customers would arrive.

"To your right is the local bank and telegraph. Rumor has it that Billy the Kid and his gang rode into town one hot summer day in 1880, less than a year from when he was shot dead by Pat Garrett. They went to the bank to make a withdrawal, so to speak, but came away with just twenty dollars. He was so mad that he shot and killed the Sheriff, just out of spite."

"I see," Emma replied, enjoying the story almost as much as the view. "Why do you need a bank here now?"

"For effect, Ma'am," Malcolm replied, as the horses plodded forward. "The front of the building looks like an old-time bank, but inside is mainly just ATM machines."

Straight ahead of them was a large building and the wooden sign overhead read SHERIFF, with an enormous star at either end of the word. The windows were barred and there were wooden chairs sitting on either side of the small porch. One man, with an obligatory tin star pinned to his denim coat, was standing on the porch watching them as they rode by.

"Is the Sheriff one of the actors?" Emma asked.

"No, not really, that's Travis Seavey. He dresses the part, but he's more like a security guy. He works for Leona and Caleb and makes sure everyone behaves themselves while they're here."

The older gentleman tilted his hat towards them, and Scott gave him a brief nod of acknowledgment as their buggy veered sharply to the right down The Fandango.

"Emma, you're going to get whiplash if you don't relax for minute." Scott sounded grumpy but was actually enjoying her response. He was finding that, no matter how many times he had done something in his life, when he experienced it now with Emma, it was brand new again and he was loving this aspect of his life.

They passed a theater on their right and what looked to be a picnic area with tables and some tents scattered around, off to the left. Then the buggy slowed to a halt beside a large, imposing hotel.

Malcolm jumped off the driver's seat, wrapped the reins around the hitching post and ran back to help Emma out of the buggy. Then he grabbed their bags and led them inside the hotel.

Scott and Emma followed him, and Emma was immediately struck by the grandeur of the building.

"Scott," she whispered, "I thought this would be something nineteen century-ish, but slightly ramshackle. I was so wrong, this is absolutely amazing."

He smiled at her wonderment. "It really is. They charge a pretty penny for a stay and you get what you pay for, trust me. This hotel has the all amenities of any first-rate modern hotel, plus the old west atmosphere. Leona and Caleb have really done a fantastic job with this town. We'll go exploring later, so that you can get the whole picture of this place. We are fortunate to be able to come spend time here every year."

Emma's eyes were wide as she tried to take in all the features. They walked into the lobby, a smallish area with a patterned rug and flowered wallpaper, all in deep rich colors. Through an archway, which was almost as high and as wide as the wall itself, Emma could see the Lounge, with a dark burgundy carpet and bold wallpaper with swirls of peacock tails in different shades of blue, green and maroon.

The young woman behind the desk checked Scott in and gave him an old-fashioned key for their room.

"Will you be signing up for one of the teams?" she asked, sliding a chart over towards him. Scott pulled it closer and scanned it quickly.

"What's that? Emma asked, peering around his arm.

"We hold competitions each year and can sign up for one of four teams."

"What do the winners get?"

"Bragging rights."

"That's it?"

"That's it." He turned his attention back to the young woman behind the desk. "We've missed quite a few already, haven't we?"

"They did hold a few this morning." She lowered her gaze from Scott's and her cheeks flushed. Emma could appreciate the poor girl's discomfiture, not only were Scott's chiseled features absurdly handsome but, when he fixed those dark brown eyes on you, it could be a bit overwhelming. And, amazingly enough, he never seemed to notice the affect that he could have on people, women in particular.

"Probably not then, thanks." He gave her a fleeting smile and turned towards Emma.

The girl behind the desk looked around impatiently until she spied Malcolm over in the corner, rapidly finishing up a text and sliding his phone back into his pocket.

"Room 105, Malcolm," she called out, a little louder than she needed to. He ran over to grab their bags and Scott stropped him just before he bent down to pick them up.

"Thanks, pal," Scott said, shaking his hand and leaving a hefty tip in the boy's palm. "Especially for the tour, you did a good job."

"You're welcome, sir, and thank you very much. If you need anything while you're here, just have them page Malcolm for you."

"Will do."

Just before the entranceway to the lounge there was a steep set of stairs heading to the upper floors, which Malcolm took two at a time. Emma started to follow him, but Scott shook his head. "That's for the employees, come with me."

Emma hesitated. "What about our luggage?"

"He has a passkey and it'll be waiting for us when we get to our room."

They headed into the lounge, but stopped abruptly when a tall, slim man came down the stairs and walked towards them.

"Ambrose, how the hell are you?" Scott walked over to greet the man and they gripped hands tightly, each genuinely happy to see the other.

"I'm good, real good, and you?"

"Couldn't be better, Emma, this Ambrose Chipperfield, an old friend. Ambrose, Emma Draper, a new friend."

He extended his hand, but his faded blue eyes looked her over suspiciously. "Ma'am."

"Nice to meet you, Ambrose," Emma responded, but when she reached out to shake his hand, he took it hesitantly and wouldn't look at her, focusing on the wall behind her head. She couldn't help but see how the tips of his ears reddened and was surprised to find that she was making him uncomfortable.

Emma kept the handshake brief, and said, "You two catch up, I'm just going to look around at this beautiful room a little closer."

Once she stepped away, he relaxed and continued his conversation with Scott.

"Is everyone here?"

"Most," Ambrose replied.

"Have you been here long?"

"No, I was just heading over to the saloon. Wanna come with?"

"Maybe in a bit," Scott replied. "Everything quiet here so far?"

"Pretty much, some shit going around about you and your brother that you better be ready for though."

"What kind of shit now?"

"I can give you the skinny on it, but only as much as I know."

"Which is?" Scott ran his hand roughly through his hair, wondering what nonsense was going on now.

"Someone's saying that you and Tim bailed on Joey and because of you, he got killed."

"That's not true," Scott said, feeling his blood pressure rise.

"I knew it was bogus and most of the others do, too, at least the ones that know you well. But, you're gonna to have to stomp on this, before it builds."

"Yeah, thanks, man. Any idea who came up with this to begin with. I think I'd best cut off the head of the snake, if you know what I mean."

"I read you, but I got nothing else."

"Thanks for the head's up. I'll talk to you some more later."

"Catch you on the flip side," Ambrose said, they shook hands once again and he headed over to the saloon, looking forward to the first of many beverages that he would imbibe today.

CHAPTER 3

Scott walked over to Emma, who had been admiring the décor of the Lounge. There was an open staircase made of dark mahogany with black wrought iron rails that twisted up and around, exposing the landing on the floor above.

Pictures hung everywhere, all in varying sizes and shapes, all in heavy ornate frames and all depicting life as it would have been back in the eighteen hundreds.

"Let's stop in the bar for a minute before we go upstairs, okay, Emma?"

"Sure," she replied, dragging her eyes away from the pictures. "Is something wrong?"

"I don't know, exactly, but it sounds like someone has a problem with what happened to our friend, Joey, when Bigfoot attacked him. They're telling people that Tim and I didn't come through for him, and that's why he died."

"That's horrible," Emma exclaimed, as the two of them sat down at the bar.

"Draft is fine," Scott said to the bartender, when he came over to take their orders. "What would you like?"

"I'm fine, thanks."

"Still not feeling well?"

"Just a little off, I'll be alright. Any idea who could be behind it?"

"Not yet, I just got here."

"You're such a smart ass," Emma replied. "Tell me about Ambrose."

"Not much to tell, he's a quiet guy. I think he's a seventies reject, you can tell by the red pants and the long gray hair, right? And when he does talk, he can't help throwing out phrases like, 'I can dig it'."

"I'm serious," he added, seeing the skeptical look on Emma's face.

"The outfit did kind of give him away, but he didn't seem at all comfortable talking in front of me."

"I think you'll find that all the hunters here are a little wary of speaking in front of strangers. People don't understand what we do, or even believe what we tell them in many cases, so don't get insulted if some of these guys don't warm up to you right away."

"I hear that." The voice came from close behind them and both Emma and Scott turned quickly.

"Lisa, how are you?" Scott asked, a little taken aback.

"I'm as good as can be expected. Give me a hug, you're not getting out of it," she added when he hesitated.

Scott rose awkwardly and wrapped his arms lightly around her large frame as Emma looked on in amusement.

Lisa was a big-boned woman, with small dark eyes and short black hair that seemed to fly off in all different directions on her head.

Scott stepped back out of her embrace and hoped that his sigh of relief was not too obvious.

"Lisa, this my friend, Emma Draper. Emma, this is Lisa," Scott hesitated, unable to recall her last name.

"Lonegan," she offered, through thin lips. "Nice to meet you."

She shook Emma's hand vigorously and Emma couldn't help but notice how large her hands were, and that some of the knuckles were oversized, almost as if she'd broken the fingers at some point in the past and never had them set properly.

"I'm surprised to see you here," Scott said.

"I have been a little lost since losing Jason," Lisa replied quietly. "I was spending time with my brother, he's a doctor in Washington and has more money than he knows what to do with, if you know what I mean."

She giggled and looked at Emma to be sure she was sufficiently impressed, but the only thing that Emma noticed was the odd noise Lisa made in her throat as she talked and the way her face was flushing.

Emma's initial impression was that this woman did not seem to be sincere in anything that she was saying. Unfortunately, Emma's face tended to show her thoughts and Lisa's eyes narrowed as they met Emma's. Then she turned back to Scott and continued her story, making that odd throat clearing sound as she did.

"He told me, 'Lisa, you get yourself out there to that Gathering and you spend time with those people that knew and loved Jason as much as you did.' I thought it over and realized that he probably knew best. He's my older brother and always seems to know the right thing for me to do."

Scott and Emma just looked at her, trying to feign interest.

"Good," Scott finally said, "I'm glad you came. I hope we can help ease some of your grief."

"You have always been strong for me, Scott. I'll never forget what you've done."

That odd clicking noise in her throat was even more pronounced when Lisa made that last statement and Emma felt a little shiver go down her spine. She had taken an immediate dislike to the woman but couldn't put her finger on exactly why that was.

"We haven't checked out our room yet so we're going to head upstairs." Scott drained the rest of the beer from his glass and stood up. "It is good to see you again, I'm glad you came, maybe we can talk more later."

"Of course, pleasure to meet you, Emma. I'm sorry that I didn't know Scott had a new girlfriend."

Emma found that to be a curious turn of phrase, but just smiled and said, "I'm glad to meet you, too."

"If you need any pointers on how to get in good with this pack of hunters, you come see me. I just went through that a couple of years ago and it's not an easy task."

"I appreciate that, thank you," Emma said, as Scott took her hand and led her out of the bar and back into the lounge.

They headed up the main staircase which was off to the side of the room. Neither of them spoke until they reached the first landing, Scott stopped to double-check the number on their key and then looked around for the right hallway.

While he was doing that, Emma peered out over the open staircase to look down into the lounge below. It was hard to appreciate the beauty of that room because Lisa was taking her time walking through it towards the front of the hotel. Her presence distracted Emma enough that she barely noticed the huge ornate fireplace, or the colorful, oversized stuffed chairs scattered willy-nilly around the room.

Her attention was completely focused on Lisa when she came to a complete stop, turned and stared hard up at Emma, almost if she had sensed Emma watching her. Lisa lifted her lip in a one-sided grin, more like a sneer than a smile, then nodded her head, turned and started walking again.

Goosebumps rose on Emma's arms as her eyes continued to follow Lisa. Sighing in relief when she saw her exit through the large double doors at the front of the hotel, Emma rubbed some warmth back into her arms and tried to focus once more on the décor.

The opulent chandeliers that hung from the ceiling were very impressive, their small candelabra bulbs gave the impression that candles were being used in them and added to the ambience of the entire room.

"Close your mouth, Emma, you're ogling the place and look like a tourist." Scott had stepped up close behind her and she could feel the heat emanating from his body.

"I am a tourist. What's up with that woman, Lisa, who is she and who is Jason?"

"Jason was a hunter who died a couple of years ago. She was his woman."

"His woman, is that how we are referred to with this group?"

"Sometimes," Scott replied, giving her a twisted grin. "But, no worries, I won't let anyone disrespect you like that."

"What will you have them call me instead?"

His grin widened. "My main squeeze probably wouldn't be appropriate, would it?"

She didn't answer but narrowed her glittering green eyes at him as he hurriedly backed up along the hallway, his hands held up in the air in surrender.

"Why don't you come with me and we'll work on our terminology issues."

"Keep that up and it'll be all we work on," she replied with a laugh, as she quickly headed down the hallway.

"Scott, this is marvelous," Emma said, once she caught up with him and they entered their room. The deep, rich colors of the bold wallpaper along with the over-stuffed chairs and old-fashioned writing desk, which came complete with an oil lamp, made for a perfect old-time atmosphere.

"Bad news, though."

"What?"

"No TV, they won't have any here, not even in their own home." Scott sounded scandalized at the thought.

"You can get by without TV for a couple of days, can't you?"

"I'm not really sure. Whatever will we do with our free time?" Scott asked innocently, running his hand over the heavy quilt on the king-size bed, which took up the majority of the room.

"Oh, I imagine, you'll think of something."

Gifting her with one of his most captivating smiles, he replied, "Yes, I imagine I will."

*   *   *

"Come along, Meg, what's holding you up this time?"

"I had to pee, don't get your shorts in a bunch, asshole."

"Meg, do you kiss your girlfriend with that mouth?"

"Damn right, I do," she replied proudly. She was wearing jeans and stopped to unbutton and roll up the long sleeves of her blouse.

She paused as the rolled-up sleeves began to reveal faint scars along the underside of her arm. Life was better now that she was with Liz and she didn't cut herself as often as she used to. Even when the need did possess her, she rarely made the cuts deep enough to leave serious scars, but sometimes shit happened, and it was with these scars that she was able to trace her past.

Nonetheless, they were her business, no one else's, so she didn't roll the sleeves up any further, even though it had warmed up considerably in the short time they'd been hiking up the trail towards the mine. The sun was now blazing down upon them and Meg could feel the sweat beading under her arms and trickling down between her breasts. She could deal with that, but what she could not tolerate was having to continuously shove her glasses back into place, as they once again slowly slid down her nose.

She pushed them back up on her face irritably and flapped her arms, trying to dry out her armpits a little, scowling as she realized that now she would have to change her entire outfit before the barbeque this afternoon.

'*Which is just as well*,' she commented silently to herself, '*because these glasses are going to be shit-canned as soon as I get back to my room*'.

These particular glasses had a bold purple frame, which matched not only her shirt and high-top sneakers, but also the purple tips of her brown hair. That was her signature, her one concession to vanity, the colors of the important items of her outfits must always match.

It was ironic that she always ended up with more pieces of luggage than her lover, Liz Miller, when they travelled. Liz was proud of her femininity, but usually dressed casually in capris and a tank top. Her short hair was stylish but required very little attention, she packed light, but always looked good.

Meg, on the other hand, was more at home in jeans and a button down long-sleeve blouse. Her brown hair was worn shoulder length, with the tips dyed according to the color of her outfit.

"But, seriously, Meg," Kevin asked, interrupting her thoughts, "what made you go gay? Tell me the truth, was it because of a bad experience with a guy?"

"I can't believe what an asshole you are to even ask that question. You have no knowledge of what is PC and what isn't, do you?"

"Can't say as I even know what the term means."

"Exactly, which is why I forgive you every year for your continuing insensitivity."

Kevin flashed her a brilliant smile and she once again wondered what his game was. He was a handsome man and could have pretty much any woman he wanted. She couldn't help but think he was just trying to add a lesbian conquest to his resume.

If she had any interest in men, she would probably have taken Kevin up on it, he could be very charming when he chose to be. He was fit and trim, his dark brown hair was shaved along the sides and back, while the top was allowed to grow a little longer. Kevin's eyes were a golden brown and he always seemed to be sizing people up, for what purpose, Meg didn't even want to venture a guess.

"Hey, you two coming or not?" Brad Fletcher called from above them.

He was what Meg called 'a wannabe Kevin'. He tagged along with Kevin wherever he went, tried to act like him and to dress like him, but always fell short. He was not as handsome, not as smooth, not as charming, and Meg felt kind of sorry for him.

She knew what it felt like to not fit in but could never understand why Brad didn't try to figure out who he really was, rather than pretend to be something he wasn't. But he was harmless and not her problem, so she tolerated him as best she could.

They were getting close to the top of the hill and the wind shifted just as they arrived on the bluff next to Brad. They had a clear view of the mine entrance from here but, one by one, their heads turned away from it and slightly to the left, then rose up to the wall of rock jutting out well above the mine entrance.

"What is that?" Meg whispered, rubbing away the goosebumps that had risen on her arms despite the heat.

"Don't know, coyote?" Brad responded, his deep voice was low, barely audible.

"It's no coyote, looks like one of the biggest wolves I've ever seen."

The three of them stared straight at it and the creature's burning red eyes were somehow capable of holding all of them captive with its gaze at the same time, and they could not look away.

"I don't feel so good all the sudden," Brad said, as the wind suddenly picked up and swirled a blast of sand into their faces. They all coughed and rubbed their eyes and when they looked back up at the jutting rocks, the creature was gone.

Not one of them could state with any certainty just how long they had stood locked in the creature's gaze. With no further conversation, they turned and made their way back to town as quickly as they could.

* * *

Emma and Scott had stolen some time together under the covers of their huge bed and were not quite ready let go of each other just yet. They snuggled together, their hands continuing to explore while they enjoyed the intimacy and solitude a little longer.

Their peace and quiet was shattered when an incessant pounding began on their door, so loud and forceful that the vibration made it look as if the oil lamp was dancing towards the edge of the desk of its own accord.

"I know you're in there, Scott. Open the goddamn door, right now."

"Knock it off, Timmy. I'm coming," Scott yelled, meeting Emma's eyes, letting her know that this was not the way he had intended to end their delightful afternoon tryst.

She shrugged. "C'est la guerre."

Emma remained burrowed under the heavy comforter, hiding her nakedness while Scott quickly donned some jeans. He yanked the door open just as Tim was getting ready to start pounding again. Tim stumbled across the threshold and had to catch himself before he fell on his face.

"What the hell?" Scott asked.

"Right back at ya. Did you really drive all this way just to find some other place to get naked together?"

"Hold up, Tim. What is your problem? We've been in town about an hour or so. Sorry we didn't check with you about our schedule when we arrived."

"I'm sorry, that was out of line." Tim shook his head and exhaled a deep breath as he walked over to look out the window. "I spent some time with Leona and she needs our help. I don't even know where to start and I've been waiting for you to get here so we could talk it out. If she's right, there isn't much time and I'm feeling frustrated."

"What's going on? Why does she need our help, what about Caleb?" The questions came rushing out of Scott's mouth, his concern evident in the tone of his voice.

Emma sat silently on the bed, the covers pulled up to her chin, watching the two of them, having no idea who they were even talking about.

"Have you ever heard about the Black Dog?"

"The Black Ghost Dog, sure, there are dozens of different stories about it, what it is, where it comes from. Just stories though, there's no proof one way or the other if it's a real entity or just a figment of someone's imagination."

"Well, Leona believes it is real, but Caleb doesn't. And therein lies the rub."

"Did she see it?"

"Yes, and so have a few other people. A couple of guys that work here saw it a week or so ago. They were both involved in freak accidents shortly afterward and now they're both dead. To make matters worse, a few hunters were hiking up by the mine today and they saw it, too. I guess they're starting to feel sick now and Leona's freaking out. I've never seen her scared before and she's so petrified that it's almost paralyzing her."

"Alright, give us ten minutes and we'll meet up with you in the lobby. I guess we need to start with Leona, do you know where she is?"

"She's over in the Town Square, getting things set up for the barbeque. Just come over there when you're ready."

"Okay, see you in a few."

"Hi, Emma, sorry I barged in like that," Tim added belatedly, then turned towards the door.

"No problem, it's good to see you again."

"You, too. Where's Callie?"

"She's still a little banged up and Callie and your mom have developed quite a friendship, so I left her behind this time."

"Probably a good choice, if people are freaking out about black dogs, I don't think this would necessarily be a good place for her right now."

He grabbed the door handle and turned it, then looked over at Scott. "No dawdling, you hear me?"

Ignoring the blistering scowl on Scott's face, he left the room and closed the door securely behind him.

"Caleb and Leona Evans own this town." Scott explained as they were getting ready. "It used to be a real mining town. I'll show you where the mine is, but they don't let people in it anymore, it isn't safe."

"What kind of mine?"

"Silver, I think. If I remember correctly, the mine ran dry back in the 30s or the 40's. Then ten or fifteen years after that, the new highways were put in and they don't come within fifty miles of this place. There was no business, no way to earn a living and the town just died off."

Emma hesitated as she was buttoning her blouse, a faraway look on her face. "Isn't it hard to believe that this town was fully functional, just like it is, back less than a hundred years ago? That just seems so surreal."

"It does, doesn't it?"

"So, how did Leona and, what's her husband's name again?"

"Caleb. How did they end up with it? Well, Leona's dad had some money and bought it, tore down a lot of the old buildings that were in disrepair, fixed up the town and made a resort out of it. When he died, Leona inherited and she and Caleb have made it even bigger and better."

"But, how do you know them, why do they host this hunter's thing?"

"Caleb has been a hunter all his life. He was close friends with my dad and is semi-retired now. Leona pretty much runs this place, so he comes and goes as he's needed. The Gathering was his idea, he thought this would be a great place for all of us to get together once a year, to share information, check up on each other and say good-by when we have to."

"Sounds like you all have a very special relationship. Will it be a problem that I'm here?" she asked, as they headed out the door.

"Not at all, a lot of the guys bring their girlfriends or their wives, although they don't usually bring both at the same time."

Emma looked at him in confusion and then slapped him when he started laughing at the expression on her face.

"Aren't you bringing your pistol? I don't think I've ever seen you without it before."

"That's one of the very few rules here. No guns, at least not out where anyone can see them. Everyone has one and, with the alcohol consumption and the inevitable fights, it's just a safety feature that Caleb insists on."

"Probably a good one," Emma commented drily, noting the big bowie knife that Scott carried in a sheath attached to the waistband of his jeans, which was probably as deadly as any pistol would be, but, apparently, not a safety concern here in Windy Shot.

CHAPTER 4

The Fandango was on one side of their hotel and Chickabiddy Lane ran perpendicular to it along the other side, both of them ended at Diversion Street which ran across the front of the hotel.

Scott and Emma exited through the main doors which took them onto Diversion Street, then they headed west, crossed over The Fandango and arrived at the Town Square which was bustling with activity.

There was a large fire pit in the center of the open area where a side of beef was turning on a spit. The succulent aroma wafted over to them and even Emma could hear Scott's stomach growl in anticipation.

Picnic tables were scattered around and there were some tents set up along the outskirts. There were probably twenty to thirty people milling around, some were sitting or standing in small groups, others were off by themselves or with just one or two other people.

Emma couldn't help feeling a little intimidated, if she hadn't had advance notice of what this gathering was for, she could only have assumed that she was at a Hells' Angel convention. The men, and even some of the women, looked strong and weathered, like they had been around the block and nothing would scare or hurt them ever again.

The majority were either tall, broad and heavily muscled or sinewy and lanky, but no less threatening looking, many with a multitude of tattoos and scars. And Scott was not the only person who came armed with a sizable knife as part of their attire.

As a group, they all seemed wary and vigilant, and Emma could feel the weight of many eyes upon her as they walked towards the others.

Scott felt Emma grab hold of his arm with both hands and looked down at her curiously. "What's wrong?"

"Nothing, I just don't really feel like I fit in here."

Scott looked around and it was as if he was seeing his compatriots for the first time. "They are an imposing group, aren't they? You know that you have nothing to fear here, don't you?"

Emma nodded nervously, continuing to study the other hunters.

Scott took her chin and lifted it with his finger so that he could look straight into her glittering green eyes. His voice was low when he spoke, so that no one could overhear.

"I'm not going to lie and tell you these people are all warm, fuzzy and good-hearted. There are reasons that they all got into this life to begin with, and the things they have seen since doing so would change anyone. But we are a family of sorts and, even if some of us disagree on certain things, there is a respect and loyalty among all of us that will not be breached. You have nothing to worry about."

"I understand and, as long as you stay right by my side, I promise that I will fear no evil," she replied with a wavering smile, trying to appear light-hearted about the situation. But there was no way she was going to relinquish that death grip on his arm and take a chance of being left on her own with these people.

Scott wasn't sure if he was completely comfortable with her response, but he was confident that once she actually got to know some of these folks, she would realize that her anxiety was unfounded.

He looked around briefly, nodding towards some of the others in greeting. Then he spied his brother and smiled to himself when he recognized the woman who was standing at Tim's side, talking up a storm. He peeled Emma's fingers loose from his arm, grasped her hand firmly in his own and pulled her along as he made his way towards his brother.

Tim was facing their way, but the woman that he was speaking with had her back to them. She was wearing a long denim skirt and boots, her gray hair was in a braid that hung halfway down her back.

Scott put his finger to his lips, to ensure that Tim didn't give him away as he slid up behind the woman and wrapped his arms around her, twirling her several times.

She squealed good-naturedly, but when Scott set her down, she pinched his cheek in a none to gentle manner, and admonished him, "How many times do I have to tell you not to do that?"

"Apparently a few more than you already have. How are you, Sweetheart? It's good to see you."

"You too, come here and give me a proper hug."

"I think you best take your hands off my woman, Son."

The voice was deep and the threat sounded real. Emma looked over at the tall, broad man nervously, relaxing only when a smile lit Scott's face and he reached out to grab the other's massive paw in a warm handshake.

"Good to see you, Caleb."

"You, too. Can't believe it's been a year already. Heard you had a little excitement over the winter."

"Yeah, I guess you could say that."

Emma just stood quietly by, hoping Scott would eventually remember that she was there, but it turned out that Leona had to bring his attention back to her.

"Why you pretty, young thing, come here and let me take a look at you. Scott, you certainly can pick them, but you have the worst manners. Introduce this lovely young woman to us properly."

"I'm sorry," he said, extending his hand towards her, "this is Emma Draper, and Emma, these are our hosts, Leona and Caleb Evans."

"Hello, it's so nice to meet you. Thank you for allowing me to come along."

"Maybe you can help make these two behave. If so, it'll be the first time in years, but anything's possible."

Leona was making an attempt to be light-hearted, but there were deep lines around her eyes and Emma wondered if they were due to her age or her worry about the Black Dog.

"That's not fair, Leona," Tim interjected. "We did not start that fight last year, we just finished it."

"Seems that every year someone ends up with a bone to pick with one of you two, so just keep your hands to yourself and your mouths shut this year."

Caleb sniggered. "I don't really see that happening, Dear. Those two just do not know how to pull in their horns, so don't get your hopes up."

"How are the competitions going?" Scott asked, tactfully deciding that a change in topic was in order.

"Pretty good," Caleb responded. "We got the minor stuff out of the way this morning, horseshoes, darts, that kind of nonsense. I'll tell you what though, some of these young folks came to win. Did you sign up?"

"No," Scott replied. "I'm sitting it out this year. I knew we'd be late getting here and, if I can't be in the running to win the whole damn thing, I ain't playing."

"So, it isn't just the youngsters being all competitive then, is it?" Leona asked, lifting her eyebrow at Scott.

He chuckled and then his brow furrowed as he stared towards one of the tents. "Hey, Caleb, who's that guy just coming out of the beer tent? He's almost as tall as Tim and he's wearing a cowboy hat."

"The gray hat?"

"Yeah."

"That's one of our actors, I think. What's his name, Leona?"

She peered across the crowd. "That's Chuck Hensley. He plays one of our gunfighters, why?"

Scott shook his head, his lips pursed. "I don't know, there's just something really familiar about him, but I can't put my finger on it. Why's he here with us?"

"Some of the employees come early, before the season actually begins, to get themselves in character. I imagine he is just enjoying the party."

Emma was only half-listening to their chatter as she looked around at the crowd of people growing within the Town Square. Leather and denim seemed to be the fabric of choice amongst them, along with either cowboy or work boots.

There were all shapes and sizes of men and women and their ages crossed every generation. Just when Emma thought she was might be getting a handle on who these people were, she would notice others who seemed to be of a completely different ilk, people she would never have pegged as hunters, a little like Ambrose, the man she had met in the hotel earlier.

One man in particular caught her attention, she tried not to stare but couldn't drag her eyes away from him. He'd just come out from under the beer tent with a bottle of beer in each hand and managed to down half of one before he even got completely out of its shadow. He was tall and thin, wearing red shorts with a gray hoodie and flip flops, and had thick, riotous hair that could only be compared to a red cloud of cotton candy. After draining the bottle, he wiped his lips and grinned broadly at nothing in particular.

"That's Pinwheel," Scott murmured in her ear.

"Pinwheel, seriously?"

"Yep, that is what he goes by, swear to God. He has a great attitude about life and doesn't let much of anything get him down. You'll like him."

"And he's a hunter?"

"Yes, he is. I've worked with him a couple of times, he's a little too laid back for my taste, but he always gets the job done, eventually."

"I'm finding that, Pinball,"

"Pinwheel."

"Whatever, he and some of the others that I'm starting to notice don't have that same scary exterior that struck me when we first walked over here."

"They're pretty much just people, not necessarily regular people because they do all have their quirks, but most of them have good hearts and you'll find that out once you get to know them better."

Emma squeezed his hand, and they turned their attention back towards Tim, Leona and Caleb.

"What's this I hear about there being some sort of problem that we need to talk about?"

Leona face went pale and Caleb's flushed red in anger.

"There is no problem," he said, his gravelly voice coming from low in his chest. They could still hear him grumbling as he turned and stalked away. "I better go check on the beef, those chuckleheads have no idea what the hell they're doing."

As he approached the spit, his voice rose and he took out his frustration on his employees, berating them severely and then watching in satisfaction when they immediately jumped up and started basting the roast.

Leona's eyes were sad as she watched Caleb walk away. With a heavy sigh, she turned and grabbed Scott's arm, leading him towards the other end of the Town Square, away from the crowd.

"Did I ever tell you about my father?" she asked.

Scott shook his head.

Leona took a deep breath. "He was a big, strong man, a lot like Caleb, now that I think about it. I guess all my daddy issues must have factored into my attraction for Caleb to begin with. Anyway, about ten years ago my dad called me in a panic, said he saw the Black Ghost dog and was worried. I'd never heard of it before and didn't know what he was talking about."

She stopped and the three of them made a little semi-circle around her, straining to hear the words when her voice got smaller.

"Caleb and I checked with his other hunting buddies, but no one thought it was a real thing, just a legitimate urban legend. We came out to Windy Shot to try and talk some sense into my dad, but he was insistent that it was real and that he was in danger. We stayed for a couple of days, trying to reassure him, but when nothing happened, we had to get back to our own lives."

She stopped talking and stared down at the ground, hoping no one noticed the single tear that fell into the soft earth at her feet. Blinking back the rest of them, she lifted her chin and continued.

"It was no more than a couple of hours after we left that I got the call that he was dead. No one could ever explain to me what happened. The official cause of death was organ failure and they just blamed it on his age, which was ridiculous because he was healthier than most men half his age.

It took a long time for me to forgive myself for leaving, but it's been even worse for Caleb, to this day he won't even acknowledge what happened. I think the burden of guilt would be too much for him if he had to admit that the Black Dog did exist and that he didn't step up to help my dad."

There wasn't anything they could say to ease her pain, so Scott just wrapped his arm around her shoulder and gave her a little hug.

Leona smiled up at him. "You are good boys and I know how much Caleb means to you, which is the only reason that I would share that with you. No one else can know, he'll think it's a weakness and God forbid that he actually have to admit that he might not be perfect. Come along."

She and Scott started walking again and Tim and Emma followed along behind them. Their little group meandered down to the far end of the field, near a large wooden bar that was fixed on two beams. There was a small platform underneath it and Emma had no idea what it could be used for.

Leona saw her look of confusion. "It's the hanging bar, Dear."

"The what?"

"It's more formally known as The Gallows, but we usually just call it what it is, the Hanging Bar. It's a piece of the original town that we chose to keep. On the other side of this Town Square is the Courthouse, another original town building. The trial, or at least what they called a fair trial, would have been held there. People would come from all over the countryside and spend the day in town, they would socialize and picnic, right here in the Town Square, just waiting for the big moment."

Her voice was low and measured as she continued.

"The condemned prisoner would be walked across the Square, and all the good citizens would throw their uneaten food or waste at him as he passed them by. He would be led up onto this platform. A stool would be placed under the noose and, when he was properly situated, the stool would be kicked out from under him and he would hang until he died. And that death did not always come quickly or easily."

Emma shivered and moved up closer against Scott's side.

"Leona," Tim said, "that was one cold story, are you alright?"

She looked at each of them in turn, her face devoid of expression. "It's the truth of what happened, why would I tell it any other way?"

"Here, have a seat, Leona." Scott took her arm and helped her over to a nearby bench, catching Tim's eye above her head, seeing the same anxiety on his face that was burning in his own chest.

Her voice had been filled with emotion when she told them about her father, but now she seemed almost robotic and the abruptness of the change in her personality and demeanor was unnerving.

"Leona, tell us about the Black Dog."

"There isn't much more to tell. I assume Tim already gave you most of the details. Two employees saw it a week to two weeks ago, both of them are now dead. I saw it twice, the last time was earlier today." Her voice was still an emotionless monotone.

"Tim said some hunters saw it, too. Is that correct?"

She nodded and looked down at her hands. "Kevin Paxton, Meg Lynch and Brad Fletcher went out hiking earlier today and all three of them saw it."

"Are they okay?"

"I ran into them when they first got back after seeing it and they were complaining of not feeling well, they felt a little off with flu-like symptoms. I'm not sure if they came over to the Town Square yet or not. I haven't noticed them, if they did."

"What exactly did you see, Leona?"

"Just a very large, black dog with glowing red eyes that was staring at me. When I blinked it was gone, and there was no where for it to go. As it was looking at me, I could feel something, I can't find the right words to describe it, but it was as if the creature was sending some sort of telepathic signals to me. And whatever it was trying to say filled me with absolute terror."

Leona shivered suddenly, and Emma saw the goosebumps raise on her arms. She sat down beside her and took the older woman's hands in her own.

"We'll find out what's going on, you don't have to worry. Are you feeling sick, like the other hunters?"

"I'm a little queasy, but mainly I just feel numb."

"Scott and I will go talk to the others and, if there was ever a good time for something like this to happen, it's now, with all these experienced hunters around. Someone will have the answers we need. You stay strong, Leona. You've taken care of us for years, now it's our turn to take care of you."

"Thanks, Tim, I do love you fellas, but I think it might be too late for me."

*　　*　　*

The four of them were each lost in their own thoughts as they made their way back towards the crowd in the center of the Town Square.

"The barbeque is going to start in just a few minutes," Leona said, gathering her wits about her once again and remembering her duties. "Let me get all of that taken care of and once we've eaten and had a few drinks, maybe then we can broach the subject and see what everyone has to say about it."

"Good thinking, Leona, we'll mingle a little in the meantime and see what we can find out. Tim, you want start on that side, I'm pretty sure I saw Theo over by the beer tent."

Tim couldn't stop the smile from spreading across his face. "I didn't think she was going to be here this year."

He turned and made his way through the crowd to search her out.

"And who is Theo?" Emma asked curiously, surprised that she hadn't heard about her before this.

"She's, um, I'm not sure exactly how you would explain her relationship with Tim. They usually hook up during the Gathering and they get along great together, have a lot of fun and then go their separate ways."

"Why?"

"Why what?"

"Do they go their separate ways, why not see each other even when they aren't here?"

"You'd have to ask them that, I have no clue. We do bump into her occasionally at other times and places. They act like long, lost friends, get all buddy-buddy again and then it's over until the next time."

"I just can't understand that."

"You don't have to, it's not your life."

"I know but,"

"Scott Devereaux, you sly son of a gun, who is that beautiful lady hanging on your arm? This time you are going to have to share, my friend."

"You know that ain't happening, Droin. Besides, Wanda would kick your ass six ways to Sunday."

"She wouldn't have to know." He winked at Emma and laughed loudly, causing his graying handlebar mustache to move around on his face like it was a living creature.

He and Scott shook hands and then turned to Emma. "This is my lady, Emma Draper. Emma this old reprobate is Droin Carrion, one of our international representatives."

"That's rich," Droin said, with another laugh. "Sweetheart, that's just a fancy way of saying I'm from Canada. Alberta, Canada, actually. Oh, and here's my beautiful bride now."

He extended his hand out in greeting to his wife as she approached. Wanda Carrion was in her early sixties and was dressed comfortably in an oversized tunic and leggings. The two of them made quite a pair, Droin was as tall and flamboyant as Wanda was petite and conservative. He pulled her up close against his side, ignoring the dubious look that she was giving him.

"What are you playing at, Droin, trying to impress your friends again, are you?" Wanda laughed loudly and honestly. Emma wasn't sure if it was at her own joke or not, but the woman seemed to be a genuinely happy person, someone who made you smile just being around her.

"Of course not." Droin's mustache drooped dramatically, and she squeezed his cheek, then turned towards Scott.

"How are you, Darling, we haven't seen you since last year. You were awful cranky then, if I recall correctly. Was that all because of this pretty thing?"

"I wasn't cranky," he replied, as Emma rolled her eyes and tried hide her smile. "This is Emma Draper, Emma, Wanda Carrion."

Emma reached out to shake the woman's hand, but Wanda was having none of that and pulled her close, into a bear hug that left Emma breathless.

"I'm glad that we've finally had a chance to meet, Tim's told me a lot about you."

"Tim did? When did he do that?" Scott asked in surprise.

"Last year, when you weren't capable of pulling your head out of that keg of beer."

"Hey, Droin, Wanda, glad y'all made it," came a slow southern drawl. They turned as one and Wanda squealed in delight and ran over to give the man one of her special bear hugs. He was slim, probably just a few years older than Scott, and was wearing a baseball cap and windbreaker. He looked less like a hunter than anyone Emma could possibly have imagined.

"Meet our Louisiana representative, Matt Girardin," Scott said with a wide grin, giving the man a hearty handshake once Wanda had released him. "This is Emma Draper."

"Nice to meet ya, Ma'am."

Before Emma could respond, a few more people joined their little crowd. Scott introduced her to everyone as they came over, but Emma was having quite a time trying to remember their names and who they were with.

The group was loud and boisterous, all of them were a little bit bigger than life and all were fighting for a chance to be heard over the others. They obviously hadn't seen each other in quite a while and had a lot that they wanted to share.

Emma tried to join in the conversation, but found she fit in best when she just leaned up against Scott, held tight to his arm and followed his lead. He obviously knew all of these people well and his face was lit up with pleasure as talked with one after the other of them.

It was a side of him that Emma hadn't seen before and made her realize that there was still so much she had to learn about who he was and what his life involved. But, as they continued to share time and experiences, it was easy enough to admit that every day she grew to love him even more than she thought possible.

When Emma was married to Jeremy, especially in the early years, she did love him completely. Looking back, she now realized that, even then, she had never felt the same thrill that she felt now, just to be at Scott's side, to wake up excited about each and every day, simply because he was a part of it.

Emma snuggled up closer against him, appreciating how lucky she was to be able to live her life with such passion and anticipation, never knowing exactly what the day would bring, but having no doubt that it would be something special.

CHAPTER 5

"Hey, gorgeous, where've you been all my life."

"That is so damned cliché that it's not even funny. Get over here and give me a wet one."

Tim never could quite understand the attraction he had for Theodora Duvall, but they'd been going at it hot and heavy for several years now and neither of them seemed to want to stop.

Neither of them wanted this be something exclusive either, which is what always perplexed Tim. Not in a bad way, just in a curious way.

A couple of long steps covered the area between them and they shared a tender embrace and nice, wet kiss, just like she asked for.

Stepping away from Theo and holding her at arms' length, he ran his eyes up and down her figure. "You look good, how've you been?"

"Fine and dandy. How about yourself?"

She had rich, auburn hair and intense blue-green eyes. Theo was not a beautiful woman, she was handsome, striking, but not pretty. She was a natural beauty, tall and muscular, with broad, manly shoulders.

Theo had a pensive, brooding personality and could sometimes be downright rude with her honest assessments of any given situation. But, when she relaxed and let her guard down, Tim enjoyed her great sense of humor and that free spirit of hers that could never be reined in.

She was the only female hunter, that Tim knew of, who hunted alone. It took someone pretty confident in themselves to be able do that, man or woman, and she fit the bill perfectly.

The bell rang loudly just then, dinner was served and people began lining up for the buffet like a bunch of lemmings getting ready to jump over a cliff.

Theo grabbed Tim's arm and walked with him over to the tables that were almost groaning with the weight of all the different kinds of food laid out on them. "Come on, I'm starving. You can talk while we load up. What's been going on?"

"Things have been pretty good, although we did have a rough patch with a Bigfoot over in Vermont a month or so ago."

"Oh, I heard about that." Theo was close to being a chain smoker and, as a result, her voice was always husky and low.

"I don't think I like the way you said that. What did you hear?"

"Only that you and your brother weren't exactly on top of your game and a lot of innocents died." She gave him a sideways glance, then pretended to be occupied with the different array of salads spread out in front of them, finally selecting one that had some veggies mixed in with pasta.

Tim studied Theo for a moment, trying to decide what her play was. Was she trying to stir up trouble, because she did occasionally do that when she was bored or angry, or was she giving him a heads up about what he might expect from some of the others?

"That's half right," Tim finally conceded, grabbing scoopfuls of several different salads and plopping them on his plate.

"It took out more people than I care to think about, but it wasn't because of anything that Scott or I did or didn't do. The thing was smart, too smart, and it was big and strong, not a creature I'd want to go up against ever again. What exactly did you hear and from whom?"

Theo turned to look up at him, her head tilted slightly as she tried to read his body language. She could see the tension in his shoulders and face and decided it would be best to drop the subject, for now anyway. Although she knew that there were other people here that were not going to be so willing to let any part of it drop, not without some pretty harsh words to the Devereaux brothers first.

"I just overheard some people talking, no specific details. I don't even remember who it was." She looked Tim straight in the eye as she lied to him, then turned and walked over to Caleb's station.

"Caleb, that beef smells amazing."

"My very own rub," he replied, with an exaggerated wink in her direction. He threw good, healthy size slices on both of their plates and then they looked around for some place to sit. The picnic tables were filling up fast, but Theo spied two available seats and made a beeline for them.

"Hello, gentlemen, it's been awhile, mind if Tim and I join you?"

"Not at all, good to see you, Theo." She was duly impressed, Snake didn't usually speak full sentences. He was one of the quietest people that she'd ever met, although you couldn't ask for a braver person to be with on a job. He had your back one hundred percent, every single time, but had just never developed very good social skills.

Rumor had it that he'd spent some time in a federal penitentiary and that was where he got most of his tattoos, including the snake that wrapped itself around his neck and, if you caught the angle right, it looked like the damned thing was alive and ready to strike.

"Hey, Snake, Skeezel," Tim said, as situated himself next to Theo.

They both nodded in his direction and turned back to their plates. Tim wasn't offended in the least, neither of them were much for chit-chatting, and actually, the fact that they were here as a part of the Gathering was surprising in itself.

The two of them worked together and had a very tight bond, perhaps because they both found it easier to express themselves by their actions rather than their words.

Skeezel had hunted with Tim's father years ago, but no matter how often Tim and Scott tried to pry information from him, he would never share the story of how Skeezel acquired that brutal looking scar on his face or lost the eye that was now covered with a pirate-like eye patch. He had an intimidating look and every hunter knew that he was no one to be trifled with.

"Sweet tat, Theo. That new?" Snake asked, nodding towards her hand.

"It is, thanks. It's an incredible design, isn't it?" She held her hand out so that everyone could appreciate the intricate spider web that now took up permanent residence between the base of her thumb and index finger. "I had Connie over in Reno do it for me. You ever go to her?"

"No, I got my own guy. He did this." Snake rolled up the sleeve of his shirt to expose a large spider web on his bicep. In the center of it was an angry-looking tarantula with a skull on it's back.

"Very cool," Theo acknowledged, feeling a bit deflated.

Other than a few comments made about the excellent quality of the food, the conversation remained at a minimum after that.

Theo cleaned her plate and wiped her mouth, then she sat back and stretched, feeling full and content. "I think I'm going to go grab a cigarette. I'll hit the beer tent on my way back, can I bring you guys back one?"

"Sure," Tim replied, and Snake and Skeezel just nodded.

*   *   *

"Hey, Liz, Meg, how you guys doing?" Scott asked, as they approached the two women.

"We're good," Meg replied, almost defiantly.

"No, we're really not." Liz corrected, and the wrathful look in Meg's eyes as she turned towards her lover would have made a lesser person wilt under the strength of it.

"Why don't you shut your fucking mouth, you don't speak for me."

"Don't think that you can scare me, Meg, not with your words or your venomous looks. I know you too well, you little she-bitch."

"Ah, the beauty of young lesbian love," Scott drawled. He'd been friends with both of them for years and knew they had a worse potty mouth than most of his male acquaintances.

Meg looked like she was about to retort with another nasty barb but, instead, her face contorted and turned red as she doubled over, coughing so hard that she was afraid she might throw up.

49

Liz rushed over to her side, moved the hair back away from her face and rubbed her back.

"Leave me alone," Meg said, when she could speak again, her voice still dry and raspy from the violent coughing fit. "Just stay the hell away from me."

She turned and ran off towards the hotel. Emma watched Liz, expecting her to follow, and was surprised when she didn't.

"Damn, Scott, I don't know what to do with her."

"What's going on? Leona told us that Meg saw the Black Dog, does that have something to do with all this? I've heard you two go at it before, but this seemed a little more real than it usually does."

"I don't honestly know what the hell's going on. Meg has always been a little rough around the edges, but now she's being an uncontrollable, crazy-ass bitch. As far as the Black Dog thing, I've never even heard of it before, but Meg insists that's what they saw."

"Was she behaving like this before she saw it?"

"No, she was excited to be here, we love coming to the Gathering every year and catching up with everyone. It's where we first met and because of that, it's always a special time for us. Meg just snapped a few hours ago and she's been acting out ever since. I can't be sure, but I think she started cutting herself again. It's hotter than hell out and she won't wear anything but a long sleeve blouse buttoned up tight."

"Damn, I thought she was past that. She saw the Black Dog this morning, right?"

"I guess so, she was off hiking with Thing One and Thing Two. I think Kevin's still trying to get into her pants."

Emma looked back and forth between them, her eyes clouded with confusion, she was completely lost now and had no idea what they were talking about.

"Didn't you and Kevin hook up, back in the day before you, you know?" Scott struggled suddenly, not wanting to offend her, but not sure how to say it.

"Before I figured out who I really was?"

"Yes," he replied in relief.

"I did, but Meg doesn't know that, and don't you dare tell her."

"If I haven't told her by now, why would I ever?"

"I know you wouldn't, Scott, sorry, that was out of line." Liz put her tiny hand on his strong forearm and, even though there were deep worry lines around her eyes, the warmth of her smile confirmed the affection that she felt for him. "You're a good friend, thank you."

"So are you, Liz. Oh, hell," he said, looking over her shoulder and seeing trouble on the horizon. "I better get over there. You let me know if things get any worse or if there's any change at all. We're going to try and find out what we can about this. Don't you worry."

"I won't, and I appreciate anything you guys can do."

*   *   *

"Well, there's the oversized coward himself," came a voice just over Tim's shoulder.

He lowered his fork onto the plate and turned to see who was talking, his eyes widening in surprise when he saw that it was Bobby Montclave.

Tim stood up and extended his hand. "Hey, Bobby, good to see you. I'm really sorry about your dad."

He was more confused than angry when Bobby slapped his hand away. Bobby was shorter than him, but heavier, and he looked disheveled and his eyes were bloodshot. He must have already had quite a bit to drink, so Tim decided to give him a break and not respond in kind.

Other diners in the area stopped what they were doing, Skeezel and Snake put their silverware down on the table and readied themselves. Whether they intended to jump in to break up the fight that they expected to begin any moment, or to join in, Tim couldn't be sure.

Directly behind Bobby were his two buddies, Garrett Williams and Frank Rishel. In all honesty, Tim couldn't always determine which one was which. All three of them were in their early thirties, went heavy on denim and flannel, and their beer guts were getting a little more prominent every year.

"What's the problem, Bobby, you have some kind of a beef with me?"

"Actually, it's more with your brother." His words were slurring just a little.

"What did he do?"

"Got my dad killed, that's what." Bobby's face was getting red, his anger building as he spoke. Tim watched as Bobby clenched and unclenched his fists repeatedly, obviously looking for a fight.

"Scott wasn't even there when Bigfoot got your dad."

"That's the point."

"What are you talking about? You aren't making any sense, Bobby."

"I heard Scott went all soft in the head over some woman, lost his nerve and wasn't there when my dad needed him. He let my dad die."

"That is not true. Your father called me in the middle of the night and I headed out to him as soon as he did. He was already gone by the time I arrived. There was nothing anyone could have done to save him. Scott had nothing to do with it, he wasn't involved at all."

"No, that's not the way it happened, you're making shit up to protect him. And even worse, after you and Scott screwed my dad over, you let this thing follow you to a busy ski resort and let it kill, how many civilians? How many, Tim?"

"Too many, but there was nothing we could do about that, either."

"Bullshit. How many people died there before you two were able to do what had to be done?"

"Do you think you could have done better?"

"I sure as hell couldn't of done worse."

Tim cracked his knuckles and narrowed his eyes as he glanced around, evaluating his odds. If he made a move towards Bobby, then Frank and Garrett would jump right in to help him out. In the condition they were in, he could probably take all three, but looking at the faces of the other hunters watching, he wasn't sure of how much support he would be getting. Or how many might jump in to help Bobby.

Everyone had loved his dad, Joey Montclave, including Tim, and if they thought he and Scott had done wrong by him and caused his death, there could be serious repercussions, deserved or not wouldn't really matter at that point.

Tim's nostrils flared and a vein started pulsing noticeably in his neck as he tried to quickly assess the situation. Whoever had been spreading the lies about what happened with Bigfoot had obviously convinced quite a few people already. Now it was just a question of how many.

Bobby took a couple of steps towards him but stopped abruptly and turned.

"I said, if it isn't Larry, Darryl and Darryl." Scott shouldered his way in between Frank and Garrett and stared straight into Bobby's bloodshot eyes.

"I don't know exactly what's going here," he continued, "but, if you have a beef with me, then talk to me, not my brother. And you might want to try and do it when you're sober, has more effect then."

"Go to hell," Bobby yelled as he took a swing at Scott's head. He was easily able to duck out of the way and landed a solid punch of his own into Bobby's soft gut.

Hearing him start to retch, Scott back-pedaled out of range and waited, along with everyone else, to see if he would lose his dinner or not. It didn't seem like Bobby could even be sure himself, as he struggled to gain control of his body and swallow back the bile rising in his throat when he stood up straight.

"This isn't over," he said, his bravado gone for the moment. He glared at Scott before turning and walking away with as much dignity as he could muster, Garrett and Frank following close behind him.

"Bobby," Scott called after him.

"What?" He stopped but refused to turn around.

"I know how bad it hurts to lose your father. And I am sorry about Joey, we all loved him. I want to talk to you about all of it so, when you sober up, come find me and we will finish this the right way."

"Go to hell," Bobby said once again, as he pushed his way through the crowd.

CHAPTER 6

"Show's over, friends," Scott said, with a wary gaze at the crowd, seeing some unfriendly looks and feeling the tension in the air.

Emma pushed her way through and walked over to his side. She could see how tense Scott was, his body was taut, every muscle primed to go to battle if need be, and his brother stood at his side, just as prepared as Scott, should things turn sideways.

Scott's reassuring words from earlier in the day echoed in Emma's head but, the animosity oozing off some of the people in the crowd was palpable, and she realized that it was not so safe here, after all.

After a few moments, people started going back to their own business and only Scott, Tim and Emma remained standing there, watching to be sure Bobby and his pals were really heading off and not circling around to cause more trouble, and that no one else was going to pick up the gauntlet in their stead.

"What was all that about?" Theo asked, as she walked over and nudged Emma away from Tim's side as she handed him a cold beer.

Emma stumbled a little and Scott reached out to grab her.

"Hey, what the hell, Theo?"

"What?"

"What's with the rough-housing? This is Emma, Emma, this is Theo. Why the hell did you shove her out of the way like that? You that scared that Tim's going to find someone to replace you?"

Adrenaline was still flowing freely and Scott was in no mood for any more nonsense.

"Bugger off, Scott. It was just an accident." After a moment of locking angry eyes with him, Theo turned away. "Sorry, Emma."

The apology was not exactly heartfelt, but Emma had no desire to start making enemies right now, especially with someone that Tim was close to.

Emma and Tim still hadn't quite cemented their own relationship and she knew he didn't always trust her motives as far as his brother was concerned. They were just beginning to get to know and understand each other and now was not the time to alienate him, especially for something this inconsequential.

"It's nice to meet you, Theo, and no worries, I'm fine."

"I should think so, it's not like I knocked you on your ass."

Her comment made Emma start to rethink the taking the high road gig, but, when she saw the muscle in Scott's jaw start to twitch, Emma knew that she needed to keep her head in order to calm him down.

Emma reached out and took Scott's fingers and entwined them with her own, he stared down at their clasped hands and slowly raised his eyes to meet hers. His face softened a bit, his anger faded, and he pulled her up close against his side and took a deep breath.

Tim witnessed the interaction between them and was struck by the fact that Emma could so easily tame the beast that was Scott Devereaux. He had anticipated a potential issue developing here, because he knew Scott would not allow any disrespect to Emma, and Theo would not back down to anyone. It could have gotten uncomfortable, but Emma had managed to find a way to diffuse the situation herself, this time at least.

"So, what was up with Bobby?" Theo asked, totally disregarding the commotion she had just caused. She took the world on like a bull in a china shop and was never overly concerned when she left a little damage behind.

"He seems to think Scott and I contributed to his dad's death. You mentioned something about it earlier. What is the word that's going around about that, there must have been more to it than you told me? You can tell us what you know. I think someone has the facts wrong and we'd better straighten things out with them before it gets spread any further."

"All I know is that most of the people here are blaming Scott for Joey's death."

"But, why, I wasn't even there?"

"Someone has been spewing shit about Joey asking you for help and you refusing him. That's why he was by himself and that's how Bigfoot was able to get the drop on him."

"But, that's not true, not even close" Tim said. "Who's saying it?"

"I don't know who started it," she replied huskily. "I was standing around with a bunch people earlier and that's what was being said. The conversation began with, 'did you hear about', so obviously no one in that little group started it."

"Who would that be?" Scott asked quietly, running his hand through his thick brown hair in frustration.

"Um, let me think, I wasn't really paying attention." She raised her eyes towards the sky, squinting as she tried to remember the scene. "There was Logan, Cassie, Ambrose and, wait, Matt and Nathan were there also, I'm pretty sure."

"Maybe it was Bobby that started it," Tim commented, taking a big swig of beer.

"Why would he? It doesn't make any sense for him to make that up. Unless he just can't accept the fact that his father lost the fight all by himself."

"That could be it," Tim agreed. "He always did have a bit of hero-worship for his dad. He wouldn't want to acknowledge that a creature got the best of Joey."

"I'll have a talk with him when he sobers up and see if I can get to the bottom of it."

"Hello, Scott, how are you?" The voice was soft and sultry and coming from directly behind him. There was no mistaking who it belonged to and Scott steeled himself before he let go of Emma and turned around.

"Hey, Tanya, good to see you."

"Is it?"

"Of course, let me introduce you, Emma, this is Tanya Merrimac, Tanya, Emma Draper."

"Nice to meet you," Emma replied, unable to miss the sudden tension in the air. "Your name is familiar, have we met before?"

"Oh, I think I'd remember that."

"Tanya made that protection necklace for you a few years ago."

"I thought that was for a client of yours."

"It was, she was."

"Well, I certainly wouldn't have expected that you two were an item, especially considering how much fun we had when you came to pick it up." Tanya arched one of her thick black eyebrows at Scott and lifted her chin, almost daring him to contradict her.

Without realizing it, Emma reached subconsciously for the elegant turquoise gemstone that hung around her neck and started rolling it between her fingers. There was a special pentagram etched on it and Scott had given it to her back when they were cleaning the spirits from her home. The necklace was to protect her from demonic possession, and she had never taken it off since that day.

"That seems like a different lifetime ago, Tanya, and there's no need for you to try and stir up trouble, Emma and I weren't together at that time."

The tension in the air was getting thicker and the look Emma caught Tim and Theo sharing confirmed that it wasn't just her imagination.

"Um, hey, Tanya, it's good to see you again. Theo and I are going to head over and chat with the some of the others. See you later, Scott."

"Yeah, okay," Scott replied absently, not sure just how he was going to get himself out of this particular situation unscathed.

"So, Tanya, what are you doing here, you don't usually come to the Gathering."

"Is that why you brought your new friend?"

"No, that had nothing at all to do with it."

Emma watched the two of them curiously, feeling a little constriction in her chest as she realized that they must have shared a significant past together. Tanya was a stunning woman with dark brown hair, dark blue eyes and thick, dark eyebrows that emphasized every expression on her face. She was the embodiment of what one would expect from a free-spirited gypsy.

Tanya was taller than Emma and was wearing an almost see-through, white, open knit sweater. As far as Emma was concerned, Tanya might just as well have been wearing the strapless bra she had on under it all by itself. The skinny jeans and biker boots only added to her mystique and the complete package was beginning to make Emma feel just a wee bit frumpy.

"Would you two like a couple of minutes alone?" Emma asked quietly, surprising Scott.

He scowled when he saw her tugging on her earlobe and knew she was beginning to feel extremely uncomfortable with the current situation. A muscle in his jaw twitched in frustration, there was no reason for her to worry about Tanya and, somehow, he had to find a way to make that clear, without being overly hurtful to Tanya.

"No, why would we?"

"I think maybe you have some unfinished business that you need to talk about." There was no sense pretending she couldn't see what was going on between them.

Tanya was impressed that Emma felt so secure in her relationship with Scott that she was willing to leave him in her hands. Impressed, but also discouraged. Tanya knew Scott saw other women, but he had never brought one of them to the Gathering before.

As she watched the way their eyes met in understanding, Tanya felt like she was intruding on something intimate and deep, something very personal.

Although still not quite able to believe it, Tanya was afraid that this time she may have lost Scott completely, and that did not sit well with her, not at all.

Scott reached out and took Emma's hand in his own and looked down at her tenderly. "Tanya and I, we go back a long way, and we've been very close, but that's been done for awhile. We're just good friends now, aren't we, Tanya?"

He raised his eyes in Tanya's direction and, for the briefest moment, Scott felt a deep sadness, knowing that she would nevermore be a part of his life.

"If you say so," she replied. Tanya's voice was low and even, but her thick dark eyebrows pulled together in frustration and the look on her face belied her words. "I guess I'll see you two around."

Scott watched her walk away and then drew Emma closer to his side.

"You know that I've been with other women, but that doesn't change a damn thing as far as what you and I share right now."

Emma's eyes burned into his. "I know that, but a little forewarning would have been helpful. Will there be others that we might run into here that I should know about?"

"No, she's the only one."

Emma's face was tense as she mulled that over, grateful that she was not going to continuously run into his old lovers over the next few days, but a little concerned that his relationship with Tanya must have been the real thing, not just a fling.

*   *   *

"Is Logan here?" Tim asked, as they walked away, craning his neck to check out the outlying tents.

"He is, but I heard didn't bring his usual supply this year."

"Why not?"

Theo just scowled at Tim and, in her raspy voice she responded, "How the hell would I know?"

"Fine, let's find him and ask."

There were a few tents around the outer edge of the Town Square, most of the tents sold beer and hard liquor, one had soda and lemonade, but there wasn't a whole lot of foot traffic around that one.

"I think that's his across the way."

They inched their way through the crowd until they were outside a rather small camouflaged tent with all of the flaps up. Logan sold quality hunting goods, knives, guns, ammo, clothing, you name it, he had it, and if he didn't, he could find it.

"As I live and breathe, it's the baby Devereaux."

"Wasn't funny last year and it's still not funny this year, Logan. How the hell are you?" Tim said, extending his hand.

Logan gripped it strongly and gave it a vigorous shake before turning to Theo, who gave him a big hug and said, "I thought it was pretty funny."

Tim rolled his eyes and started looking around. "Theo said she didn't think you brought as much stock this year as you usually do, and obviously you didn't. It looks pretty damn sparse in here. What's going on?"

Logan was a big man, broad and muscular. He was wearing a plain white T-shirt and his chest and biceps bulged underneath it. He had thick, dark hair pulled back into a ponytail and his eyes were such a dark brown that they were almost black.

"I'm letting my stock run out."

They both turned to him in surprise, eyes wide, a million questions on the tips of their tongues.

He waved off their comments. "I'm not getting any younger and it's a pain in the ass lugging all this stuff around with me. It used to be fun, heading all over the country, meeting up with you dickheads anywhere you happened to be. Selling some guns, having a few beers, but now things feel different. Everything's a hassle, and since Junior decided this wasn't for him and took off, I'm just not enjoying it as much. Might change, who knows, but that's how it is for now."

"So," Theo asked with a sexy purr, as she ran a finger down his broad chest, "does that mean you plan on having a big old, 'everything must go' sale before you leave?"

"Damn, women," Logan said, brushing her hand away from his torso, "always trying to play me. You'll be paying full price now, little lady."

"Never mind, then," she said with a smile. "I don't need anything, anyway."

"How about you, Tim?"

"I'm good right now, might be in the market for new knife. I'll check in with you again before this is over."

"Good to see you both."

"You, too."

They were immediately waylaid as soon as they stepped out from under the awning of Logan's tent.

"Tim, Theo, how good to see you again."

Tim hesitated, then put a welcoming smile on his face and bent down to give Lisa Lonegan a kiss on the cheek. She apparently didn't feel that was sufficient and reached around his waist, hugging him tight, her ample bosom pressing into his torso, while over her head he could see a devilish smile playing on Theo's lips.

Gently extricating himself, Tim stepped back away from her. "It's good to see you, too, Lisa, I didn't realize that you'd be here."

"Well, I kind of miss all of you and I checked with Leona and she said it would be alright for me to come."

"Of course," Tim replied, "we're your family now, you're always welcome. How've you been holding up?"

She lowered her eyes to the ground. "It's been two years now since I lost my Jason to that filthy Chupacabra. It hasn't been easy with him gone, but I think being around all of you makes him seem alive to me again, that's why I like being here."

Tim didn't know her well, but he knew she had suffered a great loss and understood her need to be here for the Gathering.

"Well, it's good to see you again, we'll talk more later, okay?"

"Thanks, Tim, and it's good to see you, too, Theo."

"I don't think we've ever met before, have we?"

"I'm not sure if we've ever been formally introduced, but I certainly know who you are. One of the bravest, baddest women around, according to Jason. He thought a lot of you."

Theo gave her a genuine smile. "I thought a lot of him, too, and I miss him. We used to hunt together quite a bit."

"I know."

Theo looked at her curiously, not sure what that comment implied, but she decided to give her the benefit of the doubt, for Jason's sake.

"I'll see you both later." As Lisa walked away, they continued to watch her for a few moments.

Lisa was a hard person to get a handle on. She was tall and big-boned, overweight with a shelf of a butt that she carried along behind her. Her small, dark eyes gave the impression of deceit, but her comments were so innocuous that there would be no need for her lie, and she truly did love Jason, so neither of them could really explain why their feelings for her were so ambivalent.

Theo could have easily resented the woman but had realized a long time ago that Lisa had actually helped her out of a personal predicament, without even knowing it. Theo was pretty sure that Jason would never have shared any information about their own hook up several years ago and, with him asking Lisa to marry him out of the blue, it saved Theo from having to find a way to end whatever it was that she shared with Jason.

"Does it bother you to hear about Lisa's relationship with him?" Tim knew all the details and Theo was confident that he would keep her secrets.

"Not really. I still can't wrap my head around why Jason would end up with her, but it made things much easier for me to make a clean getaway without hurting his feelings."

"She must have something going for her, even if we can't see it."

As was her wont, Theo then chose to take the low road. "She seems alright, I'll give you the benefit of the doubt on that, but the hair has to go."

"What do you mean?"

"You can't tell me that you didn't notice. It's so thick and unmanageable, and the bangs are cut at such a sharp, long angle that it makes her face look like something out of a Picasso painting, during his cubism phase, mind you. I swear she didn't even brush it today, it's just all over the place on her head. To steal one of Caleb's classic little sayings, she's ugly as a mud fence."

"And that is somehow a problem for you?"

"Well, yes, it is. You know how much I like order in my life. I can't stand anything in disarray," she replied, moving forward a couple of steps, standing so close to Tim that their bodies were almost touching. She could feel the heat emanating from his as the excitement built in her own.

"You know, it's been awhile since we've played doctor, want to head back over to the hotel and get that out of our system, so we can be more sociable for the rest of the Gathering?"

"It probably would be the right thing to do, wouldn't it?"

"Most definitely."

They meandered through the crowd and stopped a couple of times to say hello to old acquaintances before they were able to make their way across the street and into the backside of the hotel.

CHAPTER 7

"I'm not upset, Scott, really, I'm not."

He grabbed hold of her hand and walked close by her side.

"You'd better not be, there's nothing to be upset about. Come with me, let's take a walk and get away from this crowd, it's starting to make me twitchy."

The Town Square was, ironically, on a plot of ground that was in the shape of large, curvilinear triangle. The small end held the sheriff's office, which they saw when they first arrived. Behind that loomed the large, majestic Courthouse, which also abutted the Town Square on its other side.

Scott and Emma were headed towards the widest end of the Town Square, which held the Hangman's Bar.

"Hold up a second," Scott said, staring back into the crowd. "Do you see that tall guy in the cowboy hat over by the spit for the roast?"

"Yes," Emma responded, he was taller than the others in the crowd around him and was easy to pick out. "Why? Who is he?"

"Chuck something or other, Caleb said he's one of their actors, but I know him. I'm sure of it, I just can't figure out from where."

Scott's eyes were locked on the other man's as they sized each other up across the distance. Chuck sneered at him, raised his bottle of beer in a silent toast, then turned and walked away.

"That was odd," Emma said. "Seems like he knows you, too. And doesn't like you much, either."

"That's the impression I got, as well."

"So, we've only been here a couple of hours so far and there are at least two people who want a piece of you. Should we expect more as the day progresses?"

Scott slowly turned his gaze from Chuck's retreating back to Emma's glittering green eyes. Lowering his head, he caressed her lips with his own and then grabbed her hand.

It bothered him that he couldn't place the cowboy, but he'd be sure to have a conversation with him before the day was done. Scott needed to get a handle on the extent of the threat that the man might pose. In the meantime, there was no need to worry Emma any more than she already was.

"I'm pretty confident that the rest of this crowd should be friendly, but it is the Gathering, so you never know. I still need to get away from them for bit. Let me show you around Windy Shot."

"I'd like that."

"The Town Square is right in the center of town," Scott explained, as they dodged bodies trying to get away from the crowd. "There is one road that goes around the entire area, but different sections of it have different names. The part that we are heading for is called Dead Man's Alley."

"How nice, may I ask why?"

"I'll show you. Trust me, whoever designed this town really thought it out first to make sure the least amount of energy was expended in handling the miscreants."

"What are you talking about?" Emma asked with a giggle.

By then they had arrived back at the hangman's bar and he led her around it, over towards the edge of the road.

"As you can see," explained Scott, the tour guide, releasing her hand and using his own in large, swirling gestures as he pointed out the particular buildings that he was referencing, "down the road to the right is our hotel. Across from that is the saloon and the gambling hall, all the fun places. Hence, that part of the road is called Diversion Street.

Across the street and slightly to our right is another road that heads towards the hills, that is called Bent Elbow Way."

"Bent Elbow?"

"Yes, indeed, in addition to abutting the backside of the saloon, there's also a Cantina and a Brewery down that way, and pretty much nothing else to do but bend your elbow and imbibe heavily."

Scott was encouraged by the amusement that flickered on Emma's face and continued the tour. "Directly across the road in front of us is the doctor's office, which is where Dead Man's Alley officially begins."

They crossed the cobblestone road and stepped up onto the wooden sidewalk in front of the building.

Emma laughed in delight when she saw that the doctor had actually 'hung out his shingle'. There was a piece of signboard next to the door which read 'Quinine Jimmy' and underneath that, 'aka Dr. Jeffrey Higgins'.

"I love this place," Emma said, her glittering green eyes reflecting her happiness. "It's so authentic, I'm really starting to feel like I've gone back in time. But who is Quinine Jimmy?"

"From what I understand, that's what they used to call the doctor on duty at the mining camps which, technically, is what Windy Shot started out as."

They continued down the wooden sidewalk hand in hand, until they reached the next building which had a much bigger sign above the door, this one read 'Undertaker/Cabinet Maker'.

"That's precious," Emma said. "I love that idea."

"This isn't the product of someone's imagination. These are the buildings that were here originally when this was a real town. They've just been upgraded and made functional for the Resort."

"Oh," Emma said, not finding it quite so amusing now. "I guess that makes some kind of gruesome sense. What's next?"

It only took a quick look to see that the next area they were approaching was a very large cemetery filled with ancient looking grave markers.

"So, this was really their cemetery?"

"Yes, it was. There are some neat grave markers and some very sad ones, also. If you get a chance at some point over the next few days, you might want to check them out."

"I'd like that."

"The temperature really drops when evening approaches this time of year. Are you getting cold?" Scott asked, when he saw her shiver.

"I'm okay," she replied, but he wrapped his arm around her and pulled her up close, sharing his warmth with her.

They continued along, their arms wrapped around each other's waist and Emma's head snuggled in the hollow of his shoulder. She stepped away from him when they came to an area with a dozen or so crypts that were positioned in a semi-circle around a several large Rhododendron bushes. The bushes were beautiful and loaded with white and lemon-yellow blooms which gave off just a hint of a clove-like fragrance.

"And what's this?" Emma asked, appreciating the flowers, but a little creeped out by the crypts.

"I can't say for sure," Scott replied, "but I do believe these were for the rich folk and their families."

"And when did you suddenly develop that western twang?"

"Happens every time I come here," he replied with a grin. "Must be something in the air, and it gets worse after I spend time around Caleb, so prepare yourself."

"Does it last long?"

"Comes and goes," he drawled.

"Interesting, but you still haven't told me what you meant about Dead Man's Alley."

Scott stopped to point out the landmarks as he explained. "As you can see, the church is just up ahead. That starts Dead Man's Alley and it ends back at the doctor's office, or vice versa, I guess.

Directly across the road from the church is the Courthouse, where the sentencing would be carried out for the bad guys, then they would take them up to the hanging bar, across the road to the Undertakers and over to the cemetery."

Emma stood quietly at the edge of the cemetery, able to picture in her mind's eye, the convicted man slowly making his way across the Town Square to his death. She shook her head to clear it of that morbid scene as Scott continued.

"Now, for the decent town folk, you have the doctor's office, where the good doc was not always successful in his endeavors. When that happened, he shipped the patient next door to the undertaker, who took them to the church for the funeral and, shortly thereafter, they were buried in one of the crypts, maybe, if they had money, or straight to the graveyard if they didn't. Hence, Dead Man's Alley."

Scott stopped abruptly, and Emma looked up to see what was wrong. He was staring straight into the foothills rising just beyond the town, which began on the back side of the cemetery. He didn't move, wasn't blinking, hardly seemed to even be breathing, and Emma's heart began to pitter-patter nervously.

"Scott," she said quietly, almost as if she was afraid that she might wake him. When he didn't respond, Emma's voice got louder and stronger. "Scott, snap out of it, what's going on? Scott, can you hear me?"

Still he stood trancelike, just staring, and Emma was filled with an unreasonable dread that she couldn't understand or explain. She just knew that Scott was in danger somehow, but it made no sense. Emma looked around to see if there was anyone who could help her, but they were alone on this side of town.

She followed his line of sight and could see nothing up in the hills that would explain what he was staring at so intently. There was nothing there and Emma's agitation was growing. She considered whether or not she should slap him, thinking that might break him loose from the fugue state that he seemed to be in. But, just as suddenly as he went into his trance, he snapped out of it.

"Holy shit," Scott muttered. "Did you see that?"

"No," Emma replied, her voice wavering in relief, "what was it?"

"I saw the Black Dog." His voice was low, almost reverent as he spoke, and Emma couldn't ever recall seeing that particular look in his eyes before.

*   *   *

"Damn it, why now?" Leona realized that she sounded like a bit of a whiner but didn't particularly care.

"You'll be fine in a couple of days, Leona. Don't worry. It's just an infected tooth."

"That's swelled up so bad that I look like a chipmunk, at least half my face does."

Her words were a little slurred because of the swelling and Dr. Higgins was more worried than he let on.

"It's too late to head in tonight, but I would suggest, in the strongest of terms, that you get to town to see your dentist as soon as you can, as in the first thing tomorrow morning. I can give you some anti-biotics for now, but an infection that causes you swell up that bad and that quickly is nothing to mess around with. I am very serious, Leona."

"You know I have a whole passel of hunters here and I need to make sure things go smooth. Having them all together is like sitting on a powder keg and hoping it doesn't explode."

Dr Higgins knew what she was saying but, due to the swelling, it actually sounded more like 'sitting on a power keg an oping it doen't expode'.

"Here, take one of these now and another every eight hours. It's only a small chunk of your day, so get to town tomorrow and get that tooth taken care of. I'll help make sure nothing gets out of hand here."

"Maybe," she replied, grabbing a pill and swallowing down a little water behind it, hastily wiping away the trickle that dribbled out of the bad side of her mouth which wouldn't close completely. "You coming over to the saloon tonight?"

"Wouldn't miss it, I'll bring my bag, there hasn't been a get together yet that hasn't resulted in at least a bloody lip."

*   *   *

A much more relaxed Tim arrived at the gambling hall a couple of hours later. As part of the competition, a Texas Hold 'Em tournament was being held. Usually only the most serious of the gamblers lasted longer than an hour or two, and the losers would make their way over to the saloon next door once they were out.

As was their usual custom, the hunters would meet there and have a few drinks, share a few lies and pretty much just catch up with the others. Some that had started drinking at the barbeque hadn't stopped and were off to Lala land, which was also par for the course.

The tournament was well on its way by the time Tim arrived, so he just checked in to see how the various teams were doing and then headed over to the saloon. He spotted Emma and Scott near the bar and headed their way.

"Beer, please," he called over to the bartender. "Do you guys need anything?"

"I just got a refill and Emma's just a sipper tonight."

"Everything alright?" Tim asked, she did look a little paler than usual.

"My stomach's a little off lately. Nothing to worry about."

"It didn't sound like nothing to worry about this morning when you were losing your breakfast."

"Really, you needed to share that information?"

"Sorry, Honey," he replied, his brown puppy dog eyes begging for forgiveness.

"Don't worry about that, Emma. I can share lots of less than stellar moments in Scott's life, whenever you have an hour or two."

"Such as? Oh hell, never mind. Here comes Lisa, what's her last name?"

"Lonegan, I think." Tim didn't look very excited about her arrival either.

"Who?" Emma asked.

"We met her earlier," Scott replied, just as Lisa was almost about upon them.

Emma spied her approaching and was a bit mystified by her outfit. Lisa was wearing a checkered blouse over a pair of jeans which, for some reason, she decided to roll the legs up to about mid-calf, leaving everyone a view of her boots, which sported a pretty good heel. Unfortunately, Lisa was somewhere in her early to mid -fifties and the look just wasn't becoming for someone her age and size, especially when she stomped around like she wasn't at all used to wearing heels.

"Scott, Tim, good to see you again."

She seemed pleasant enough but there was something in her small, beady eyes that set Emma's teeth on edge.

"Hi, Lisa." Scott went to extend his hand but, as usual, she was having none of that and moved closer, giving him a big hug and a kiss on the cheek.

Scott had to resist the temptation to wipe his cheek off as he turned towards Emma. "You remember Emma?"

"Of course," she replied, with a sweeping glance at Emma. "I'm just glad to see that you have finally decided to get rid of that 'wanna be witch', Tanya, and settle down with a real woman."

Tim covered his mouth, trying to muffle his amusement. Emma wasn't quite sure how to respond, so she just smiled inanely, and Scott chose to ignore the comment altogether and turned towards the bar to pick up his beer.

"I'm sure the guys have warned you about me," Lisa said, barely taking a breath.

"No, not really," Emma replied, and was surprised to see those little eyes narrow even more as Lisa glanced over at Scott. Lisa kept a smile pasted on her face the entire time, but it was impossible to miss the hardness in her eyes and the angry flush of her cheeks.

"Well, I am single now." A strange look came over her face when she spoke those words. "So, all these men have to watch out when I'm around. I have to fight them off back home and here, it's even worse. This place becomes just a big, old orgy after a couple of days, doesn't it, Tim?"

She caught him off guard and he didn't quite know how to respond. "Well, um, not really, Lisa, but, if anyone gives you trouble, let me know. We'll put a stop to it."

"I didn't say I minded it," she replied with a twisted smile. "And now that I'm alone again, it's a welcome change."

Tim looked down into his glass, avoiding any eye contact with her, and Scott continued to keep his back to all of them while he nursed his beer. Lisa seemed to have a way of making any conversation feel awkward and uncomfortable, so Emma tried to change the subject.

"Are you a hunter?"

"Oh, heavens no. My fiancée, Jason Boyer, was a hunter. He was killed two years ago and these people are kind enough to let me continue coming to the Gatherings. I do feel so much closer to my Jason when I'm around his hunter family."

Lisa's cheeks flushed guiltily, which Emma once again found odd, especially considering her comments. Why on earth would she feel guilty about saying that unless it was a complete untruth? And if it was, why was she here?

"I'm sorry to hear about your fiancée, Lisa."

"Thank you, Emma, that's very nice of you to say, especially since you never knew him. Well, I'd better go mingle, I'm sure I'll see you later."

They watched her walk away in stunned silence.

"I really don't know how to take the things that she says," Emma stated, as soon as she was far enough away.

"Don't worry about her," Scott said, finally turning around towards Emma and Tim again. "Lisa's always been a little different and we never could figure out what Jason saw in her to begin with. She certainly isn't the type he used to find interesting. She looks like a freaking troll doll with that hair, and it's not like you can have a scintillating conversation with her."

"I think everyone just feels sorry for her," Tim added. "She has never gotten over what happened to Jason and I don't think she ever will. We all just put up with her because of her loss, but I don't think anyone feels very happy when she heads in their direction."

"How did Jason die?"

"On a hunt."

"Then why on earth would it make her feel better to be around other hunters?"

"No clue, I don't try and understand her. She wasn't here last year and, I've got to be honest, I never expected to see her again after Jason died."

Scott was perusing the crowd in the bar, hoping to catch sight of the unknown cowboy so that he could try and get that situation straightened out. The man would stand out but, so far, he hadn't showed up here.

Then Scott noticed a dapper looking gentleman heading towards the bar and called out to him. "Hey, Nathan, get over here and say hello."

"Scott, Tim, how the hell are you?"

"Doing great, where's Polly?"

"She'll be along momentarily, had to make a pit stop."

There were handshakes and shoulder clasps all around and then Scott turned to Emma.

"Emma, meet Nathan Michaels, a good friend of ours."

"Nice to meet you," she replied. Nathan was an unassuming man, probably in his early fifties. His golf shirt and khakis gave him a completely different look than the other hunters and the dark framed glassed made him look almost professorial. Emma half-expected to see a pen protector in his pocket, but that was not to be.

"Here she is," Nathan said, holding his hand out to a petite woman who was approaching them with a smile blossoming on her face. She was about Nathan's age and had a cloud of black hair that she tried, unsuccessfully, to keep under control with a couple of ornate combs. She was also dressed like she just left an office and Emma found herself intrigued by the two of them.

"Emma, this is my wife, Polly, Polly, this is Scott's new friend."

She gave Scott a sly sideways look and extended her hand to Emma.

"It's very nice to meet you," she said, her voice was soft and sincere, but then she followed it up with a girlish giggle. "I'm so sorry, that was rude. I really am happy to meet you, it's just so unexpected from this fellow."

"Now, Polly," Scott said, taking her into his arms and giving her a kiss on the cheek and a hug that almost lifted her off her feet. "You're going to give Emma a really bad idea of who I am if you keep that up."

"She doesn't know you already?"

"Not like you do," he replied with a grin. "Some things are best left unsaid."

"We'll talk later," Polly said to Emma, with an exaggerated wink.

"My turn," Tim said, actually lifting her up off her feet with his hug.

"And where might your friend be tonight?" Polly asked, once she was released and able to stand on her own two feet again.

"She'll be here, I'm pretty sure of that."

"When are you two going to make it official? Follow your brother's example, even he's grown up enough now to have a real relationship. It's what people do, Honey."

"It's not what I do, but thanks for the advice."

"You are actually just the people we need to see," Scott said. "Let's get you a drink and have a seat, okay? We need to pick your brains."

"Sure," Nathan replied, his curiosity reflected on his face.

*   *   *

"Do you have a fever, Leona? Your face is flushed and blotchy." Caleb put the back of his hand to her forehead. "You're really warm, Hon, why don't you stay here at the house. I can manage over at the saloon."

"Hell's bells, Caleb, you start more fights than any of the others put together."

He drew in a long breath and released it. Leona's eyes were puffy and discolored with fatigue and her voice sounded tired and weak. Her cheek had swollen up even more and now it was beginning to swell on the other side, as well.

Caleb closed his eyes and pinched the bridge of his nose, trying to relieve some of the anxiety he was feeling about Leona's health issues. He really didn't want her to go over to the saloon tonight, but she was one hard-headed woman and would not be told what to do, not now, not ever.

"Then make me one promise and I won't argue anymore."

"What?" she asked suspiciously.

"You go tonight, but tomorrow morning, first thing, we head out to town, see the dentist and get this taken care of."

"That sounds fair," she murmured, placing her hand affectionately on his arm. Leona spoke slowly, struggling to enunciate her words properly. "I think I'm about done with this, it's beginning to make me feel pretty bad. I will probably just stay for a bit tonight, anyway."

"Good, you let me know as soon as you want to leave, and we'll skedaddle out of there. They can take care of themselves for one night."

Leona took his arm and, leaning heavily against him, they headed out into the cool night air. They lived in the only actual house in town, at the far end of Diversion Street. It was a cute little place and just big enough for the two of them, it was one of the original houses in the town which they had upgraded over the years. It was their refuge, from the craziness of the resort and his even crazier hunting adventures. But tonight, even their cozy little home did not feel like the safe haven that it normally did.

CHAPTER 8

"So, what's up?" Nathan asked, once they were all settled comfortably around a table.

"What do you know about the Black Ghost Dog?"

Nathan's eyes wandered towards the ceiling as he concentrated and tried to recall anything and everything he knew about the Black Dog.

"There is quite a bit of lore about it, and a lot of variant thoughts and ideas of what it is, where it comes from and what controls it."

"What do you mean, what controls it?" Theo asked, she had caught up with them just as they were searching out a table.

"Again, there is no definitive information about it, that I'm aware of, anyway. Some people think it's a hellhound, here as an omen of death; other's think that it can be conjured by a sorcerer or a witch who controls it and forces it to do whatever they ask it to."

"Others think it's a shapeshifter," Polly added, lightly rubbing the end of her nose with her index finger as she spoke.

"What's a shapeshifter?" Emma asked, ignoring the looks they gave her, particularly Theo, who scowled as if Emma were completely ignorant and was wasting their valuable time by not being able to keep up.

Scott glared at Theo for a moment and then came to Emma's rescue. "It's a creature that can change into other animals, or even people. I've heard that the stories about werewolves originally started because of shapeshifters."

"So, these creatures that you hunt, you don't always even know if they are real or just urban legends or something from someone's imagination?"

"That's correct," Tim added. "Which is why Nathan and Polly are so important to us."

"Oh, Tim, flattery will get you everywhere," Polly said, with a giggle and an affectionate pat on his arm. Tonight, she was wearing a blazer and black dress pants, along with two colorful butterfly combs that were doing their best to hold her thick, curly hair back into some semblance of order.

"I mean it, they are the keepers of the information, so to speak. They look for anomalies and let whoever's in the area know about it, so it can be checked out. Depending on what is found, the information then goes back to the Michaels and they keep it all in one place for us to refer back to, to help us understand the creatures, to help us learn how to kill them and how to best keep ourselves alive. They are our information highway."

"That is so sweet, Tim, and well said," Polly replied, then turned to Emma. "Nathan and I both worked at the NSA and knowledge is our life. We thrive on learning about things that no one else knows and then sharing that information. It's quite challenging, but we do love it. And these characters are just the best people to be working with."

"But, getting back to the original question," Nathan said, pushing his glasses further up his nose, "we don't have any definitive information about the Black Dog, why do you ask?"

"Apparently, Leona has seen it, as well as a couple of their employees, who are now dead. And there are two or three hunters who have seen it since they've been here."

"Four," Emma stated firmly.

"Who's the fourth?" Tim asked.

Emma didn't reply, just stared into Scott's eyes as he squirmed uncomfortably.

"Me, a little earlier today."

"Why the hell didn't you tell me?"

"I just did."

As if on cue, Leona and Caleb walked over to their table. Every single one of their faces registered shock when they saw Leona's condition.

"Are you alright, Leona, what's going on?" Polly's voice was firm and authoritative now, no longer playful and girlish. Emma got the impression that she was everyone's go-to person when there was a problem.

"I'm fine." The swelling was getting even worse and her words were slurred, she was suddenly feeling exhausted and wished she hadn't come over to the saloon, after all.

"Here, sit down." Tim stood up and offered his seat to her. Leona practically fell down onto it and Caleb hovered close by her side to ensure she remained upright.

"Caleb, I know this is a sore subject with you, but we were just talking about the Black Dog, so if you don't want to be involved in that particular conversation, you may want to find some other people to chat with."

Caleb's steely gray eyes were firmly planted on Scott's face and his jaw was set. He refused to believe the Black Dog nonsense, but he also knew that he had never seen a bad tooth, or any type of infection, take hold as intensely as was happening to his beloved wife right now.

He had lived his life having to accept realities that no one else even considered and, if it was the Black Dog that was responsible for Leona's condition, Caleb knew that no dentist was going to be able to fix her.

He pulled over another chair and sat down close to Leona's side. "Well, let's just see how the cat jumps, shall we?"

Leona hadn't let the fear overwhelm her until that very moment, because if Caleb believed it was possible, then she was probably in very bad trouble.

"So, Leona, when exactly did you see the dog?"

"It was last week, no, two nights ago, no, Caleb?" Her eyes were filled with unshed tears as she looked at her husband for help, her fear and confusion were beginning to overwhelm her.

Leona's face was now even more flushed, and the patches of discolored skin seemed to be growing larger on her throat and the lower part of her face.

"It was two nights ago, Honey. Two nights." Caleb's jaw tensed as he gazed at her flushed face. He took hold of her hand and held it with both of his own, trying to reassure her, and himself.

"Yes, that's what it was."

Tim and Scott glanced at each other in concern and managed to silently convey their agreement that they needed to stop the questions for now. Leona was in no condition to provide them with any further information.

"Now, Tanya," Bobby Montclave said, looking her up and down, appreciating the slim, firm figure and the tight jeans that she was wearing, "you aren't just using me to get Scott jealous, are you?"

"Would you care if I was?"

"Not really, as long as you aren't just jerking me around."

Bobby was staring greedily at what the peach colored bra barely covered under her gauzy, see-through top, and he was beginning to think he may have a chance of actually getting his hands on her. The thought of finally touching what she barely bothered to hide had him pretty well worked up.

"Just shut up and buy me a drink and let's see what happens."

Tanya had seen the cozy little table full of people in the back corner as soon as she stepped into the bar. Those people were Tanya's friends. She didn't always come to the Gatherings, they weren't really her thing, but when she did, those were the people that she usually spent time with.

Her thick eyebrows pulled together in frustration as she saw that Emma was practically sitting on Scott's lap right in the middle of them all, taking Tanya's place as a part of their group.

She knew that if she tried to join them, it would make everyone uncomfortable and uneasy. Tanya didn't generally give a damn about what affect her presence had on people, but this involved Scott. And she was not ready to burn her bridges with him just yet.

As angry as she was that he brought another woman with him, she was honest enough to admit that he had never made her any kind of promise or indicated they would ever have a future together.

That was just something that she had always counted on, always thought would happen eventually. Tanya felt a squeeze around her heart as she watched Scott slide his arm around Emma's shoulder and pull her in even closer against his side.

Then her jealousy began to turn to anger and she could feel the heat of it rising in her body as it started to verge on hatred. She was the one that Scott had always turned to. She was the one that knew him better than anyone else ever would. She would be here for him next year, and the year after that, long after this little tramp was just a faint memory for both of them.

Tanya graciously accepted the beer that Bobby handed to her and, although she continued to smile coquettishly at him as he regaled her with stories that she only half-heard, Tanya made sure that she was angled in such a manner that she was able see the table with her old friends over in the corner.

Tanya didn't know Bobby very well but, he wasn't unattractive and, if he kept his talking to a minimum, she thought they might just be able to help each other through the night.

*   *   *

A group of hunters strolled in just then, loud and boisterous as they made their way over to the bar.

"The tourney must be over," Caleb muttered.

"Who's the big winner?" Pinwheel yelled out, his bare legs wrapped around a barstool, his toes curled into his flip-flops, trying to hold them onto his feet.

"You're looking at him," Kevin Paxton responded. "Texas Hold 'Em champ two years straight. You better all start practicing, man, this is getting embarrassing."

Kevin's cocky words were not reflected in his demeanor or his facial features. He looked pale and sickly, even his thick, brown hair seemed dull and lifeless. He flashed a half-hearted smile at the crowd as congratulations were yelled out to him, then turned and leaned heavily against the bar.

"Tell me more about Pinwheel," Emma said to Scott. "I don't think I've ever known anyone quite so unusual as he seems to be."

"Unusual is probably the best adjective to describe him. Same as everyone else here, he doesn't readily share much personal information, so I don't know all that much about him except that he lives and hunts on the East Coast."

"Does anyone know what he does for a day job?" Scott asked, looking around at the others.

No one answered.

Nathan and Polly probably knew more about each and every hunter than anyone else, but one of the reasons that they were so well-liked and trusted was their ability to keep one's confidences to themselves. Therefore, they refused to join in this particular conversation.

"I worked with him once and asked him that very question, but he just smiled and walked away," Theo responded.

"I've heard all kinds of rumors," Tim said.

"Like what?"

"My favorite is that he's a cat burglar, for some reason I can really see him as one of those. My second favorite is that he's a silver spoon baby."

"A what?" Scott asked.

"Born into money, but I have trouble picturing him wandering around the family mansion in his flip-flops."

There were smiles around the table as they all shared that interesting visual. Pinwheel was oblivious to the interest in him at that moment and continued talking fervently with anyone in his vicinity.

"Now that everyone is here, I think that I might step up onstage and see if anyone else has something to input. Sound like a good idea?" Scott asked.

"Definitely," Nathan agreed. "We need to accumulate as much information as possible to come up with an appropriate theory."

Emma watched Nathan and Scott make their way across the barroom towards the stage. The saloon itself could have been in half a dozen old western movies that Emma had seen, all wood floors, walls, tables and chairs. The only noticeable difference between them was the varying degrees of darkness from the type of wood that was used to make them. There were stuffed animal heads hanging on the walls around the large room but no other adornments.

The bar itself was made out of a lighter colored wood and ran almost the entire length of one wall, it had the obligatory alcohol bottles lined up behind the bartender in front of the large mirror. That man had obviously been here for years because he was able to effortlessly slide a drink the length of the bar with a flick of his wrist and have it stop right in front of the customer that it was intended for.

If Emma concentrated hard enough, she could picture John Wayne and Yul Brenner and a dozen or so other western heroes all sitting at the bar, knocking back shots of rotgut whiskey.

Emma eyes continued to roam around the room, stopping suddenly when she spied Tanya sitting at the bar and the amused smile dropped from her lips. Tanya was leaning forward enticingly towards the man that Scott had almost gotten into a fight with earlier that day at the barbeque. Emma wondered if that was some sort of ploy she was using to get back at Scott, or if she was just making the rounds of the men at the Gathering.

Tanya turned towards her just then, as if she'd felt Emma's burning gaze. Their eyes met across the room and the tautness of their features clearly showed just how they felt about each other.

Neither would break their gaze, not until Tanya spotted Scott walking across the room out of the corner of her eye and turned towards him curiously.

Emma watched her nudge the man next her and whisper in his ear. He shrugged and, with narrowed eyes and pursed lips, turned to watch Scott make his way across the bar floor.

There were many tables scattered randomly around the room and a small piano over against the wall with an older, balding man pounding on the keys. He stopped abruptly when Scott touched on him on the shoulder and said something quietly in his ear, then Scott continued on and up the short staircase to the stage, with Nathan right behind him.

The acoustics in the room were not the best and all Emma could hear initially were the murmurs of many different conversations. After a couple of moments, Scott's voice started overpowering the others and brought most of them to silence.

"Hello, everyone," he said again, projecting his deep voice out into the crowd. "I think I know most, if not all of you, but my name is Scott Devereaux and this is my friend, Nathan Michaels. We are looking for a little information and, hopefully, you people can help us out."

"Good to see you, Scott, you too, Nathan," one of the men close to the stage yelled out. "You know that we'll help you if we can, whatever you need."

Scott nodded down at him. "Thanks, Logan, we appreciate it. We're looking for some intel on the Black Ghost Dog. Some hunters here have seen it and we just want to know what we might be dealing with, and if it's anything we should be hunting right now."

The same man answered. "It's demonic, a hellhound, it'll kill anyone that sees it."

"That's bullshit," someone else yelled. "It's just a freaking shapeshifter and yes, we do need to get out there and kill it fast."

"If it's a shape-shifter, it could be anyone in this room right now."

There was an uncomfortable pause as people started looking suspiciously at the others around them.

"Let's not jump the gun just yet," Scott said, not wanting anything crazy to start up. These people could be a little volatile and didn't always think things through before pulling out a weapon and jumping into a situation.

"Has anyone had an actual experience with one or are you all just relying on folklore?"

No one replied. "I'm going to take that as no one here has had any personal experience then."

A man sitting at Logan's table up spoke up. "I wasn't personally involved, but I know someone who ran into a Black Dog situation in Omaha. There were five people that died, all within days of seeing the damn thing. They called it The Harbinger of Death."

"How did they stop it?" Nathan asked.

"They didn't." He shook his head in a dispirited way. "It just disappeared and the deaths stopped."

"Was something controlling it?"

"Don't know, could have been a demon possessing it, could have been some witch or wizard working some nasty hoodoo. We were never able to find out anything for sure. It came and went too fast."

Scott saw the crowd turn towards Tanya now, everyone knew she was a witch and suddenly their unwarranted suspicions were being turned on her. Her dark brows came together as she stared them all down and Scott felt a little better, he was confident she could hold her own with this crowd. At least for right now.

He did frown a little when he saw Bobby place his arm protectively around her shoulder.

Emma saw the look on Scott's face when that happened and misjudged the reason for it. She thought he might be feeling jealous when, in fact, that couldn't be farther from the truth. He was just concerned that Tanya might be getting involved with Bobby for the wrong reasons and would probably regret it.

"Scott," Bobby yelled out. "Did you see this Black Dog? Is that why you're wasting all our time on this nonsense?"

"I did see it today and it might be nonsense, I just don't know."

"Then step down off the stage and let us go back to having some fun. You sure as hell don't rush out to help anyone else, I don't see why we need to stop everything now for you."

"I wouldn't expect you to, Bobby. But there are other people that saw it, as well, and we're just trying to make sure there is nothing to worry about."

"With you trying to fix things, people should damn well be worried, real worried. You get involved and people die, we all know that."

Emma saw the set look on Scott's face and was afraid there was going to be a fight.

Scott thought so, too, for a moment anyway. Then he saw Bobby's pals, Frank and Garret, sidle up near him, obviously hoping he'd start something so that they could finish it. Scott looked out over the crowd and some of them seemed to be anticipating a row. There was almost always a huge brouhaha at some point during the Gathering and everyone seemed to think this was going to be it for this year.

"Scott," Nathan said quietly from his side, "don't do it, not now. One problem at a time, okay?"

"Fine, but I'm afraid this will have to come to a head, and soon."

"I know, but make it happen on your terms, not his."

Scott gave him a slight smile and turned back to the crowd. "If any of you do see it or if you have any other information that you'd like share, please come see Nathan, my brother, Tim, or me. Thank you and enjoy the rest of your evening."

Emma continued to look around the room, mystified and somewhat anxious being in such close quarters with all of these people. Even relaxing with a few cocktails, the majority of them still seemed very alert, watchful, always on guard. It was intimidating, to say the least.

Then Lisa caught her attention, she was standing back by the far wall, excitedly watching the drama unfold. She seemed deflated when Scott did not pick up Bobby's gauntlet and do battle with him.

Lisa's beady eyes narrowed as she looked out over the crowd and her face just oozed hatred. Emma found it unnerving see such animosity from someone who was supposed to be their friend; someone who was here just for their support in her time of grief.

And it was even more unsettling to watch her demeanor change like quicksilver when one of the women walked over to her and shared a few words. Lisa was able to totally change the look on her face, to smile and laugh and act as if she had never felt happier.

Emma watched her for a few minutes more and saw the mask drop immediately from her face as soon as the woman walked away, but only because Lisa didn't realize that she was being observed.

Emma's attention was drawn back to Scott when he and Nathan stepped down from the stage to make their way back to their table in the corner. Scott had no choice but to stop when Bobby moved directly out in front of them.

"Hold on, friend. I think you and I have a little more to straighten out, don't we?"

"Not tonight, we don't."

"Never took you for chicken, but I guess I should have, always too scared to go help a friend who needs you."

"That never happened, Bobby. I don't know where you're getting your info, but that is not what happened with your dad."

Scott barely saw Bobby's fist heading his way and ducked just in time, the punch missing him completely. While bent over he punched Bobby hard in the stomach and stepped back to let one fly right into his jaw when he found his arm grabbed from behind by one of Bobby's pals.

Bobby stood upright and drilled his fist right into Scott's cheek as he was being held immobile, unable to protect himself. The pain was explosive, but Scott gathered his strength and wrenched his arm free. He kicked Bobby in the groin and turned towards Garrett, dropping him with a left cross.

Everyone stood up at that point and it looked like sides were finally being drawn, until all movement immediately ceased when a godawful wailing began to reverberate throughout the room.

Each and every one of them froze in place as they tried to locate the source.

CHAPTER 9

As one they turned towards the back of the room where the horrific noise was originating. Leona was standing and staring at them, most of her face was swelled up by now and discolored blotches covered her neck and the lower part of her face.

She laid her head back and, once again, let loose the most appalling sound. For a moment, everyone just stood and stared at her.

Scott could see Emma, she was standing right next to Leona, her eyes were wide and her mouth slightly agape, she looked absolutely petrified and he pushed his way through the crowd to get to them.

Leona was still wailing, but now Caleb had his arms around her, he was trying to get her to be still, to calm down, but to no avail. It was as if she were in some kind of trance and didn't even know he was there. She completely disregarded him and continued to bellow out those horrendous sounds.

Caleb looked over her head at Scott, who mouthed 'outside' to him. Caleb nodded and picked up Leona like she weighed nothing at all. Scott grabbed Emma's hand and dragged her along beside him as he made a path to the door. Once outside, Leona passed out and laid limp in Caleb's arms.

Tim and Theo came out right behind them.

"Was Doc Higgins in there, do you know?" Caleb asked, trying not to panic.

No one had seen him.

"Let's hope he's still in his office." They hurried down the walk towards the doctor's office and pounded on the locked door, sighing collectively when they saw a light finally go on inside.

Higgins lived in an apartment upstairs above the Infirmary and had just been getting ready to come over and join them. As he hurried to the door, he tucked in his shirt and grabbed a lab coat before opening it wide and allowing them all in.

"What the hell happened?" he asked, as Caleb laid the unconscious Leona down on the examining table. Caleb took a deep calming breath and tried to explain.

"She started this horrible wailing sound, then she passed out in my arms."

"How long ago?"

"About as long as it took us to walk over here from the saloon, just a few minutes."

"Were there any other symptoms since I saw her last? Did she have a fever? Was she showing any signs of confusion?"

"Yes, to both of those questions." Caleb's deep voice cracked with emotion. "What is it, Doc?"

"Give me minute, I'm calling this in and getting the rescue helicopter here to take her to the hospital as quick as they can."

"But, Doc,"

"I'll explain whatever I can, as soon as I get them on their way here, okay?"

While he was gone, Caleb got on his cell phone and called over to maintenance. "Get that van out in front of the Infirmary, as soon as possible."

He waited a second as the person on the other end responded. "I don't give a damn, get the tank filled and get it over here. You have five minutes."

The doctor returned just a few moments later, the Air Evac helicopter should be there shortly, arriving on the landing pad, which was actually just a rarely used portion of the back parking lot.

As Doc Higgins walked into the waiting room, he could see the fear and concern on all of their faces. Leona was dear to one and all, which made this much more difficult.

"Leona developed this fever so quickly that it was positively freaky, I have no other word for it. We assume it's an infected tooth because of the way her cheek swelled up, but neither she, nor I, could figure out which tooth it was, because she didn't have a problem with any of them, which is odd, to say the least.

She wasn't having any problems before today. Since I saw her earlier, Leona has developed a fever slightly above one hundred and two degrees. She has now also developed those patches of discolored skin on her face and neck and, even unconscious, her resting heartbeat is way too high. All of these are symptoms of Sepsis, which is ridiculous because it could never happen that quickly. But, as a precaution, she needs to be in a hospital."

"I'm just an old coot," Caleb said quietly. "Can you explain to me what Sepsis is, and explain so I can understand, no medical mumbo-jumbo?"

Dr. Higgins hesitated a moment, trying to find the best way to explain it. "Sepsis is a life-threatening illness that is caused by a body's response to an infection. It develops when the chemicals that the immune system release into the bloodstream to fight an infection end up causing inflammation throughout the entire body instead."

"It's terminal?" Caleb asked.

"Doesn't have to be. If treated quickly, most cases lead to a full recovery. She'll be fine, Caleb, she is a strong, healthy woman. Do you want to take the chopper with her to the hospital?"

"Of course. Will you stay here, Doc, and keep an eye on the place. Don't let these damn hunters tear it down."

"Sure," he replied, checking his watch. He would rather go to the hospital with Leona, but he knew the doctors there would have her treatment well in hand and he would be able to provide a greater service for his friend, Caleb, by staying here and doing as he asked.

"Can a couple of you guys help me lift her into the back of the van, so we can head over? The chopper should be here in just a few minutes."

Tim, Theo and Caleb all helped put Leona in the van and rode with them over to the helipad.

Scott and Emma watched them go and then solemnly headed back towards the hotel.

They held hands and walked in silence, each consumed by their own thoughts until they got back to the room.

"Scott, what do you make of this? Is it because she saw the Black Dog?"

"I don't know, Emma. If so, we're really screwed, because we have no clue what exactly it is or what's driving it."

Scott laid down on the bed, his head resting against the headboard. Emma got in beside him and he drew her up against his chest, running his fingers through her silky golden hair and kissing the top of her head.

"Don't you worry, you understand? We'll figure it out tomorrow and get it taken care of."

"I know," she replied softly, although she was not at all confident in their ability to fix this particular situation. "Just how do I keep myself from worrying though?"

He continued to stroke her hair as he contemplated her question.

"Faith," was his response. "The same faith that I have always had in us, in our love, in our ability to deal with whatever situation comes our way. There is too much that you and I still have to do together in this life.

I waited for you a long time and I'm not checking out just yet. Not until I've been able to wake up and find you by my side every morning for many, many more years to come. And that is my promise to you."

"I'm going to hold you to that." Emma wrapped her arms around his waist a little tighter and tried to keep the tears from escaping onto his shirt as she fought to find the strength of that faith inside herself.

*   *   *

They met up with Tim and Theo in the hotel restaurant for breakfast the next morning.

"What now?" Tim asked.

"I'm kerfuffled, man, I just don't know."

They stopped talking for a moment when Lisa walked by, her plate filled to the brim with a little bit of everything from the buffet.

"Good morning," she said brightly, "how is everyone this fine day?"

"We're doing alright, thanks," Tim replied, all of them profoundly grateful that they'd taken a small table that morning and no one else could fit at it. "How are you?"

"I'm ready to take on the world." She made that odd noise in the back of her throat again and the hair on Emma's neck stood on end.

"Any word on Leona? That was just awful to see yesterday."

At first no one responded, then Tim finally replied. "She made it to the hospital and they're taking good care of her there. Hopefully, she'll be back before the Gathering is over."

"My, from the way she looked yesterday, I wouldn't get my hopes up about that. Oh, well, I'd better eat while it's still warm. I'm sure I'll be running into all of you again at some point."

Lisa managed to find an empty spot a table with another group over across the room. They looked less than thrilled to have her join them, but Lisa either didn't notice, or didn't care.

"I don't think she really likes anyone here," Emma said.

"That's not true," Scott replied. "It's hard to deal with her sometimes, and she's a little off her rocker, but she considers us her family."

"No, I sincerely do not believe that she likes anyone here. Don't you see the look on her face when she thinks no one is watching her? It's almost like she hates some of you, well, maybe me, too. And her comments are always a little snarky."

"I think your imagination might be a little overactive as far as she's concerned," Scott said. "She's harmless and we put up with her because of Jason. She's just doing the best she can to be our friend and to fit in."

"Is that what you two think about her?"

Tim shrugged.

"I don't know Lisa and haven't spent any time with her, so I couldn't say either way. Given my druthers, I won't be spending any quality time with her, so I don't really care," Theo replied.

Emma was a little frustrated that they couldn't see the same things in Lisa that she did, but they knew this group of people better than she ever would, so she let the subject drop.

Most of Scott's breakfast was still sitting on his plate and he was just moving pieces around, not eating any of it. Tim watched Scott for a moment and an even deeper furrow developed on his brow when he turned his gaze to Emma and realized she was doing the same thing.

"What's up with you two? Are you sick?"

"No, why do you ask?" Emma replied, her face flushing curiously. Then she noticed Scott's plate.

"Scott, what's wrong with you?"

"Nothing is wrong," he responded irritably. "Why do you both keep asking me that? I'm fine, just not hungry, okay?"

"No need to snap, Darling," she replied, and kicked him in the shin.

"Ouch, you didn't have to do that."

"I know, but I feel so much better now, Mr. Crankypants."

"Well, that's what's important, right?"

"Yes, it is," Emma replied. She could see that he was trying not to smile and hoped that she had successfully broken him free of that moody silence he'd been in most of the morning.

She stood up and threw her napkin on the table. "I am going to go explore this town and leave you three to your hunting. Have fun."

She leaned down to give Scott a quick kiss good-bye. In retaliation for the shin kick, he slapped her butt as she walked away, but just got a giggle in return as she made her way out of the dining room.

"Scott, the shooting competition is this morning," Tim said. "I know we have to get more info, but Caleb was on our team and we need a fill in, you game? I think we can afford a few minutes out of the day for that."

Scott hesitated, he wasn't feeling all that well, but he didn't need Tim, or Emma, knowing that. The shoot-off wouldn't take long, so he nodded his assent.

"Sure, we need to talk to Brad and Kevin, anyway. I'm pretty sure they'll be there, they usually are."

"They're entered in it, but not on my team. We should still have a chance to talk them though."

"You in it this year, Theo?"

"Nah, but I'll be kicking some ass this afternoon in the knife-throwing contest."

The three of them were making their way out of the dining room when Polly and Nathan walked in.

After exchanging greetings, Polly touched Scott's arm. "Can I talk to you for a minute?"

"Sure, what's up?"

They stepped a few feet away from the others so they could have some privacy and Polly's face lit up with excitement.

"Emma's lovely, I was so happy to finally meet her."

"Thanks, Polly, I told you she was something different."

"I know, Sweetie, and I'm so happy for you. Now, tell me, did you get it?"

Scott glanced around to be sure no one was within hearing distance.

His eyes sparkled in excitement when he replied, "Yes, I did and you were right, it was the absolute best choice, she's going to love it. You are, by far, the smartest woman I've ever met, I knew you would point me in the right direction."

"Keep me posted, I can't believe you are really going to do this. I'm am so excited for you both," she whispered, then made her way back to her husband's side.

*　　　*　　　*

Emma walked down the sweeping steps at the front of the hotel and headed off to her right, the opposite direction of the Town Square. She hesitated at the first intersecting street, Chickabiddy Lane, and decided to head down that way to see what treasures it held.

Crossing the street to get a closer look at the buildings over there, the first one that she came upon was the Costume Shoppe. Unfortunately, it wasn't open, but through the large store window she could see all types of costumes that people must buy or rent when they stayed here. What fun it would be to come here for a vacation and get into character with the actors and spend some time away from real life.

In this section of the town there were cobblestone walkways that meandered around the buildings. She walked past the Costume Shoppe and could see what looked like someone's home just beyond it, and down to her right there was a large inground pool, currently gated up and unavailable.

On the opposite side of the pool was another road and beyond that an open field. Emma could see a group of people milling around and others looked like they were bringing in loads of firewood and placing them in an area in the center of the field for some reason.

Then she remembered that later today they would have the memorial bonfire for the friends they had lost over the past year and figured that must be the spot where they would hold it, along with the rest of their games and competitions.

Emma didn't feel like being around anyone right then, so she did not head in that direction. She followed the little walkway past the pool and could see tennis and basketball courts down ahead of her.

Emma stopped when she saw the Mercantile. There was something that she had been deliberating on purchasing and she hadn't been able to decide if this was the appropriate time to do so. With the Mercantile looming right in front of her, Emma took it as a sign and decided she was going to do it, to hell with the timing.

Although the outside of Mercantile building was like any other frontier storefront, inside it looked more like a modern-day Walmart. It was much larger than it looked from the outside and walking up and down the aisles, she could find pretty much any thing that she could possibly need.

Emma grabbed a couple of incidentals as she wandered around, building up enough courage to search out the one thing that she had actually come in to the store for.

She peered to her right and to her left, but there was no one else around, so she checked the boxes on the shelf, grabbed the one that she needed and hid it among her other items. Then she hurried towards the checkout.

Turning at the end of the aisle, Emma let loose a scream when she almost ran into a man stocking the endcap.

"Oh, I'm sorry, hey, Emma, is that you?"

Quickly recognizing who it was, Emma put her hand over her heart, hoping it would calm down enough that she would actually be able to speak.

When it did, she closed the distance between them and gave him a big one-handed hug. "Gabriel, it is so good to see you. I completely forgot you were going to work here."

"I am, yup, I am."

He couldn't keep the smile off his face or stop his head from nodding up and down.

"You look great," Emma said, ignoring the blush spreading over his cheeks. "No more beard?"

"No, it wasn't filling in quite the way I wanted it to."

"I see, and what witty saying do you have on your T-shirt today?"

"My mom gave me this one." He puffed out his narrow chest so that she could read it.

"I was addicted to the Hokey Pokey but I turned myself around." Emma laughed out loud. "That's so cute, I really need to meet your mom someday."

"She would like that, I've told her all about you. And Tim and Scott, too," he added quickly.

"That's sweet." Emma's eyes twinkled with genuine affection as she met his. "Do you like working here?"

"So far, I do. I've tried lots of different things and it looks like working here in the Mercantile is the best fit for me, at least according to Caleb. It'll be a lot different when we actually have guests coming. I mean, I know you guys are guests, but I mean, the real ones."

"I understand, this town is just amazing, isn't it?"

"It's pretty neat, I never saw anything like it. I got to check it all out good by trying to work at most of the different places here."

"Do you think you'll stick around after this year?"

"I might," he replied. "If I can get my mom to move out here. Otherwise, I can't leave her all alone back home."

"You are a special man, Gabriel, I hope you know that."

"Thanks," he replied, staring at the ground and blushing to the tips of his ears. "Of course, if I do stay, I want to be one of the actors, maybe even a gunfighter. That would really make me want to stay."

"You put in the time and learn this place inside and out, then I imagine you can have any job here that you want."

"Yeah, maybe," he said, with a hopeful smile.

"Well, I better check out and let you get back to work. Let's catch up later, okay? I'm sure Scott would love to see you."

"Sure, that would be great. Um, Emma?"

"Yes?"

"I heard that something happened to Leona and they flew her out of here. Is she going to be okay? I really like her, she kind of reminds me of my mom."

"I don't for sure, Gabriel, she was pretty sick. But it sounds like they caught it quickly, so I imagine there is a very good chance that she will come out of this fine. You don't worry about it, okay? I will let you know if I hear anything else."

"Thank you, Emma. It's real good to see you again."

She gave him another quick hug. "It's good to see you, too. I'll talk to you later."

Emma headed over to the checkout counter, only one was open at this point, but there were several others that would be available once the regular tourists arrived.

The young girl behind the counter looked to be in her early twenties. Emma set her items on the conveyor and tried not to show how embarrassed she felt.

"Hi, Zoey, is it?" Emma asked, peering at the girl's name tag.

"Yes," she replied, snapping her gum at a steady pace. The girl was quite pretty, she looked a little like Emma's daughter, Shelly, with blue eyes and stylish blonde hair.

Emma could only hope that her daughter wasn't currently dressing the same way. Zoey's skirt was obnoxiously short, and her tight-fitting blouse was unbuttoned just little further down than was necessary. Being as short as she was, pretty much any customer would have no choice but to look down at her bountiful cleavage.

Zoey continued chewing her gum as she rang up the items, stopping just once to look one over a little closer than necessary, raising her pretty eyes up at Emma.

"Is there a problem?" Emma asked, praying the girl didn't yell out for a price check. For some reason, she found that the thought of Gabriel knowing she was buying a pregnancy test to be quite mortifying.

"Nope," the girl replied, ringing up that last item and cashing Emma out.

Emma sighed in relief and hurried outside. There were little buildings placed sporadically around the village for people to use. They were built to look like oversized outhouses and fit in with the motif of the rest of the buildings in town but, on the inside, they were as modern as anything that you could ask for, complete with running water and a flushing toilet.

She hurried inside the door of one marked 'Filly' and, with shaking hands, opened her package. Emma hadn't done this in so long that she almost forgot how and was so flustered that she could barely think straight.

It seemed like forever before she got the results and, after checking it twice, just to be sure she was reading it correctly, Emma wasn't sure if she wanted to laugh or to cry.

CHAPTER 10

"Whereabouts were you when you saw it?" Tim asked. There was an edge to his voice that gave away his impatience.

They'd finally caught up with Kevin and Brad playing Blackjack in the gambling hall across the street from the hotel and had been trying, unsuccessfully, to coax some information out of them.

"I don't know, really, I don't. We'd been hiking for a bit and were looking up at the mine entrance and it was suddenly just there, staring down at the three of us."

"It was standing at the mine?" Scott asked.

"No, up on some rocks above it," Brad answered. He didn't look well, his face was pale and he seemed sluggish. Scott couldn't see his eyes because he never bothered to take off his sunglasses, whether he was inside or out.

"You feeling alright?"

"Just a little off, I think I had too much tequila last night. Hit me," he called out to the dealer, going bust with twenty-three. "Damn it."

"That shit can certainly kick your ass," Scott agreed, relieved that Brad was just hungover and that his condition had nothing to do with the Black Dog, after all.

Scott, himself, still wasn't feeling all that well. He noticed Emma seemed to be a little squeamish, too, and thought maybe they'd eaten something bad before they got here.

He could handle his stomach being off, but the incessant pounding in his head that had begun a short while ago was close to intolerable.

"Listen" Kevin said, turning to look directly at Scott, "I saw the dog, could have been a big wolf for all I know. I feel fine and think all this shit about the Ghost Dog needs to stop."

"Oh, really, why's that?"

"You're scaring people, making them look sideways at the others here, looking for shapeshifters, witches, who knows what else. Things are going to get real ugly if you don't drop it soon."

"What about Leona?"

Kevin gave a half-shrug. "Love Leona, but that's just one bad, freaking thing that happened, nothing sinister."

"I don't agree." Scott began to explain, but Kevin wouldn't give him the chance to do so.

Kevin glanced at his watch, stood up and started gathering his chips. "You ready, Brad? Let's go show these clowns the right way to shoot a rifle."

Brad threw a chip towards the dealer as a tip and gathered up the rest of what he had left.

*　　　*　　　*

Emma continued on her solo tour of the town over by the Mercantile. She passed the school and the playground, and even spent some time on one of the swings as she let her thoughts wander.

She had a lot to think about and to get squared away in her own mind. Emma knew exactly how she felt about Scott and realized that her feelings for him grew stronger every day. There was no doubt in her mind that Scott was the man that she wanted to spend the rest of her life with.

He'd been a little quiet since they'd arrived here, maybe because of the group they were with, maybe because Tanya had showed up unexpectedly, she really didn't know the reason for it.

Emma wasn't jealous, she was confident in how Scott felt about her, but she had to admit that it was disconcerting to actually meet someone, a very beautiful someone at that, who had shared his bed and a significant chunk of his life before her. It was difficult to wrap her head around that.

Emma knew how much Scott cared for her, but she did not come without baggage, and she did come with three children. Not every man would be willing to welcome a complete family into his bachelor life. And now there were other issues to take into account, as well.

Scott did not lead a normal life and they hadn't really had enough time together to figure out what their future looked like. There had been no pressure to do so, until now.

I guess that's become a conversation that we will have to have sooner, rather than later, she said to herself with a smile, running her hand over her stomach and trying to figure out when the right time might be to broach the subject.

*   *   *

A short time later, Emma spotted Tim and Scott over on the rifle range, near where the bonfire would be held. A huge grin lit Scott's face when he saw her approaching. No matter how often he saw her, the warmth that filled his heart each time that he laid his eyes on her never diminished.

Tanya's eyes narrowed as she watched the two of them and she viciously bit down on the inside of her cheek when Scott leaned down and shared a tender, gentle kiss with Emma, then stroked her face, unwilling to break eye contact with her.

Try as she might, Tanya could not recall him ever looking at her that way.

She tore her eyes away from the two of them and focused on Bobby. It was his turn at the target and he was getting himself into position. She tried to hide her revulsion when he looked over, gave her with a slow wink and slid his tongue around his lips.

Turning back to the target, he let off a quick volley of shots. Each contestant used a similar target which was placed the same distance away for all of them. They would use their own weapons, some years it was pistols, but this year they were using rifles.

Logan always supplied the targets and tried to have fun with them. This year, he thought it would be interesting to see how well they could shoot when the target was a T-Rex. Some of the contestants did not find it at all funny, and there was quite a bit of grumbling about it.

Once a competitor finished his turn, Caleb's employees would grab the dinosaur target, mark the name of the contestant and place it in the pile for the judges to review later. Then a new target was put up for the next contestant.

Scott and Tim had already had their turns and there were only a half dozen or so people left to shoot. Emma looked around at the crowd, deliberately letting her eyes slide right past Tanya, who was now standing close beside Bobby.

Scott grabbed Emma's hand and pulled her back away from the crowd. "And where have you been?"

"Shopping," she replied, holding up her little bag of goodies, relieved that one of them was now sitting in a garbage can in the restroom. "I ran into Gabriel at the Mercantile, it was so good to see him again."

"That's right, I forgot he was here. Wonder what kind of mayhem he's been causing."

"From what he told me, a little bit everywhere. What are these?" Emma asked, as they arrived at a very old scoreboard, no modern technology here, just handwritten team names and number placards showing the scores.

"These are the four team names and the current scores."

Emma squinted at the board, not sure she was reading the names right.

"I'm pretty sure I have no idea what those names mean. Other the Jersey Devil, I've never heard of any of them."

"Caleb tries to get creative and he names each team after a creature that we hunt. He uses different ones every year. Sometimes he stumps us, too."

"Tell me what these are."

"The Jersey Devil is like a kangaroo with wings. It's most commonly known for eating people's pets."

Emma grimaced.

"The Micmac Culloo, I've never seen one myself, but I understand they are part bird and part human and they steal children."

"That's horrible," Emma said, her mouth hanging open as she tried to process the fact that such a creature actually existed.

"I know, right? But I'm still not convinced it's a real thing. The Windigo, however, definitely is. It's believed to be a human that became cannibalistic due to starvation, or it possibly got possessed and got Windigo fever. Either way, it is nothing more than a cannibal."

"For real?"

"Yes, but they are mainly found in the Northwest US and in Canada. We don't run into them in our neck of the woods, but Droin can certainly tell you some tales about them."

"I almost hate to ask, but what about the last team, the Globster?"

"Probably the most harmless creature of them all. It's an enormous glob of unidentifiable flesh and bone that washes up on beaches all over the world. Most of the time, it's just a decaying beached whale or shark, but not always."

"If not, then what is it?"

"To be determined," he replied with brief smile. "Sometimes it's a creature that we didn't know about, sometimes just a mermaid or a siren that died."

"I'm not quite that gullible, Scott. I know that some things do not really exist in this world."

"Emma, do you realize who you're talking to? Did you believe in Bigfoot six months ago? Did you believe in ghosts and demons before you bought your house? There is very little that doesn't really exist."

She stared at him wide-eyed.

"Do you remember Ambrose?"

"How could I forget him?"

"Well, he's a Mariner."

"A what?"

"A sailor, he spends the majority of his time out to sea. He has a super expensive yacht and he hunts all kinds of creatures that we know very little about. Oh, hell," Scott suddenly doubled over in pain.

Emma stepped towards him. "Scott, what's wrong?"

He held his hand out to stop her from getting any closer, not yet able to speak due to the horrible, agonizing pain stabbing into his gut.

Taking several deep breaths, he was gradually able to stand upright again. The pain in his stomach was receding but the pounding in his head got exponentially worse. He closed his eyes and rubbed both temples, but nothing would relieve the excruciating pain trying to hammer its way out of his head.

"What happened?"

"I just had a wicked stomach cramp. I still think we got some kind of food poisoning at that damn little diner on our way here." Scott didn't whole-heartedly believe that and didn't see the need to worry Emma with his pounding, never-ending headache either. "How are you feeling, anyway?"

"I'm much better," she replied.

Just then there was a horrific blast from over near the shooting range and screams of fear and pain came rumbling towards them.

Scott grabbed Emma's hand and the two of them hurried back, but they couldn't see anything through the tight circle of people that had formed. Scott was trying to push his way through when Tim managed to push his way out and grabbed his arm.

"Go to Emma, do not let her see this. I'm running over to Doc's office to grab him."

"What happened?"

"Brad's lucky gun blew up in his face. He's gone and its not a pretty sight. Get Emma away before she sees it."

Tim turned and ran towards the doctor's office. Scott found Emma and took her further away from the small group surrounding Brad.

"Scott?"

"Emma, you need to go back to the hotel. From what I understand, something happened with Brad's gun and it exploded."

"Is he going to be okay?"

Scott shook his head and stared at the ground. "No, he's not, he's gone."

Emma's face paled and her knees suddenly felt wobbly, like they were no longer able to support her weight.

"He saw the Black Dog, didn't he?"

"Don't go there, Emma. Stop worrying about that."

"Sure, because this is just another freak accident, right? Just how many freak accidents have to happen before you guys take this seriously?"

Emma's eyes were wide with fear, she knew there was something physically wrong with Scott, but she'd been willing to play along with his food poisoning theory. It was obvious that there was something much worse than that going on, and it had started after he saw that damned Black Dog.

Scott had no response, he wouldn't lie to her, but he wasn't going to add to her fear by sharing his own concerns, which were growing by the minute.

"Go over to the hotel, please." Scott traced his index finger along her jawline, staring into her brilliant green eyes. "I'll catch up with you in a little while, I promise."

Emma nodded her assent and walked away but her mouth was dry, and her heart was pounding rapidly in her chest. She was suddenly very, very frightened.

*   *   *

Doc Higgins arrived at the scene and confirmed that Brad no longer had a pulse. Scott, Tim, Kevin and Pinwheel carried the heavy stretcher back to the doctor's office and Theo followed along, carrying Brad's 'lucky gun'.

Doc Higgins had hurried back ahead of them to call Travis Seavey, the Sheriff of Windy Shot, and let him know what had happened.

"Call the State Troopers, Travis. They are going to want to rule out any foul play, I'm sure. We'll have Brad here at my office."

"Damn, that's a pity," Travis replied. "I'll get on the horn with them right now, might be a bit before they get here. I'll wait at my office and let them through."

"Thanks, Travis."

Hearing voices raised out in the lobby, Doc Higgins headed out that way.

"Listen, Kevin, don't be stupid. You need to calm down."

"Don't fucking tell me what I need to do, Scott." His eyes were watery, his face slack and pale, it wasn't just grief, there was something else wrong with him.

Scott stepped back, both hands raised in surrender. "Fine, what exactly do you plan on doing?"

"Maybe it's the damn Black Dog, maybe it isn't, but I'm heading up to the mine. If it's there, I'm going to kill it and then there won't be any question, one way or the other."

"You don't know what it is or what you might be walking into. Let us figure this out and then we'll all go together."

"You are just getting old and wishy-washy, Scott," he said quietly, checking the chamber of his rifle to make sure it was loaded. He snapped the weapon back together and looked pointedly at the two brothers.

"If this had happened to either of you, the other would be going bat-shit crazy right now trying to get to that thing and destroy it. So, stop trying to make it sound like I'm out of control. Get out of my way and let me take care of this."

He stepped around them and headed out the door and up towards the foothills.

"Should we go with him?" Tim asked.

"No, what's the point? Even if he does see it, it's not going to stand around waiting to get shot by the dipstick. Hell, we don't even know what it is or if a bullet will take it down."

"So, what do we do now?"

"Wasn't Matt in the bar at the hotel when we came through earlier?

"Yeah, I think he was with Ambrose. What time is it, anyway? And, what are they doing at the bar, it's still morning, right?"

Scott looked at him like he'd taken leave of his senses.

"It's the Gathering."

"Of course, what was I thinking?"

"Coming with us, Pinwheel?"

"Sure, why not."

They headed across the street and into the bar, where they pulled up stools alongside the two men who were still wetting their whistle.

"Morning, fellows," Scott said, and then waved away the bartender, feeling his stomach start roiling just at the thought of alcohol.

"So," Matt said, his voice was always quiet, the slight southern drawl barely perceptible, "we heard some commotion, what happened?"

"Brad's gun exploded in his face at the shooting competition. He's dead."

"No shit?"

"No shit," Scott replied.

"You still think this Black Dog is behind what happened to Leona? Think it had something to do with Brad, too?"

"It could be, what happened to her was not normal and, if there is something funky happening, it's going to hit a few more people very soon. We just want to try to get some more info in case that does happen."

"What can we do for ya'll?" Matt drawled, taking a long pull on his beer.

"You're from New Orleans, right?"

"Not exactly, but close by."

"You must have some insight into hoodoo or voodoo and that kind of stuff."

"I know some, but it ain't something you want to know too awful much about or it'll consume you."

"What do you mean?" Tim asked.

"People use it for dark purposes and it eats them from the inside out. They start in on that shit and there's no turning back."

"Could someone here be using it?"

"Could be, sure."

"To me, this whole thing stinks like witch." The sudden scraping of a barstool being dragged across the floor startled all five of them.

"Oh, apologies, Tanya, no offense."

"Really?"

"Well, I wasn't saying it's you," Scott replied quickly. "It's just that it feels like some kind of black magic to me. So, therefore, it couldn't be you, you're a white witch, right?"

"Most days," she replied, one thick dark eyebrow raised over her dark blue eyes, giving her a very mystical and disconcerting look.

She pulled her chair up a little closer to him and sat down. Tanya pulled it so close, in fact, that their legs were touching, so Scott had to adjust his a little to avoid the intimate contact.

"So, why do you think it's a witchy thing?"

"First off, there aren't a lot of other options. I don't think it's a demon, but I could be wrong. I've never run across one before that was clever enough, and mean enough, to come up with what happened to Leona or to Brad. Only a real nasty-ass human could be behind it, as far as I'm concerned."

"Assuming you're right," Tim asked, "how do we figure out who that would be?"

Scott was silent for a moment, trying to collect his thoughts through the interminable pounding in his head.

"I think we need to start looking at the people that have seen it and find out what we have in common. Maybe if we figure out why it's happening, we can figure out who's doing it and how."

"I think you're right, Scott," Pinwheel interjected. He had his black hoodie pulled up over his head, but that orange cloud of hair would not stay hidden and was trying to escape from all angles. To complete the effect, the color of his hair almost matched the orange and pink floral Bermuda shorts that he was wearing.

"I ran into something similar down in the Caymans and it ended up being all witch, all the time."

"How'd you get her?"

"Was a him this time and it took a few of us to bring him down."

Scott was trying to listen to Pinwheel's story, but Tanya had ordered a glass of wine and was rubbing up against him as she reached for it. He had no problem acknowledging what a beautiful woman she was and, getting a nice whiff of her perfume brought back some very fond memories, but he wanted none of that anymore. It was over and done and, somehow, he was going to have to get her to realize that.

"Uh, oh," he heard Tim murmur, and turned to see one very pissed off little blonde walking into the bar.

"Hey, Emma, there you are."

"Yes, here I am." She strode over towards their little group, throwing a vicious look in Tanya's direction. Tanya had never been very popular with other women and the look did not phase her in the least.

"Good to see you again, Emma. You look a little tired, rough night?"

"Well, I'm sure you must remember how Scott can be sometimes, it doesn't matter if you want sleep when he's in the mood for something else. And really, who could say no to him, anyway, am I right?"

Pinwheel choked on his beer and the other men all looked down into their glasses, trying not to laugh. They didn't want to bring Tanya's ire down onto themselves, but they did appreciate what a fun jab it was.

Tanya gave Emma a blistering look and stood up, downing her drink in one gulp.

"If you imbeciles need some real help as far as witchcraft is concerned, you know where to find me."

Tanya stalked off in her skinny jeans and high-heeled biker boots and no one said another word until they were positive that she was out of hearing distance. Then they cackled like a pack of hyenas.

"Emma, what a great shot. Just be ready, she'll be coming at you with both barrels now."

Tim was actually giggling as he spoke, but Emma just stared at him, then at the others laughing in their beer, well, not Scott, he wasn't drinking.

"Why are you acting like such assholes? Weren't you just being friendly with her, having a conversation?"

"Sure, we were, but that doesn't mean we can't have some fun."

"At her expense?"

"This time, yes. But take my word for it, she'll get back at all of us tenfold, after all, I believe it was Alfred Hitchcock that said, 'Revenge is sweet and not at all fattening.'"

Emma was surprised at the words that were coming so eloquently out of Pinwheel's mouth, he looked more like a circus character than a well-read literary fan, but there was obviously more to him than his unusual looks.

"You'll get used to this group, Emma," Scott said, putting his arm around her waist and pulling her over against his side. At first, she resisted, but only half-heartedly. And when he gave her a long, warm kiss, she completely forgot why she was mad in the first place.

"You see, Emma," Matt drawled, "we are kind of like a big, old family. Just because y'all are family doesn't mean you don't ever have issues with each other, and it doesn't mean you can't have a spat or make fun sometimes. It happens to all of us and we deal with it and, eventually, we get our own kind of revenge."

They heard the click-clack of Tanya's heels coming back across the wooden floor at a very quick pace. "Come on outside, all of you, something's happened."

As one they stood and hurried out onto the hotel porch.

"I heard a gunshot and then a scream. Then silence for a moment and I think another scream, but it was muted, as if it was cut off suddenly by something."

"Where?" Tim asked solemnly.

"Up there." Tanya pointed up towards the mine entrance, which they were barely able to see from where they stood.

"Kevin," Scott stated ominously.

Others heard the shots and screams, as well, and word was spreading. People were coming out of the saloon and the gambling hall across the street and several men were running up to their rooms to grab their weapons.

Within minutes, a dozen or so of them headed up into the hills to find out what had happened, Scott and Tim among them.

CHAPTER 11

Emma didn't want to go back to her room so she paced back and forth in front of the hotel. She stopped abruptly when Tanya crossed the street and headed straight towards her.

"Look, I don't want to start anything," she said, giving Emma a sideways glance to try and gauge her reaction.

"What do you want?"

"I thought you would be interested in what's going on with Leona."

"I am, what did you hear?"

"It's not so good, it's definitely Sepsis and they can't find the cause of the infection. They've got her on heavy doses of anti-biotics and pain meds, she's pretty much been out of it most of the day."

Her soft voice wavered, and she used a long, tapered nail to wipe the teardrop that was escaping down her face.

"I didn't realize that you were so close to her." Tanya appeared to be genuinely upset, but Emma was not sure if the sorrow was real, or if she was just putting on an act for some reason.

"We've known each other a long time. I think Leona is something special to all of us, either a big sister, a mother or whatever you need to listen to your troubles or to just hang out with. She knows what we all need. And we are needy, in so many different ways."

Tanya sighed heavily and stared up into the mountains, seeing some figures moving around up there. They were so far away that you couldn't tell who it was or what they were doing.

"How did you get involved with this group?" Emma asked.

"Nathan and Polly got in touch with me about five or six years ago. They needed some help on a case and had heard of me. I practice white magic and try to heal and protect people and things."

"This will sound pretty naïve," Emma said, feeling a little silly, "but what exactly is magic and how do you practice it? How did you learn it to begin with?"

Tanya smiled slightly and drew her thick, dark brows together, trying to find a way to explain. "Magic is an attempt to bend the universe to your will. There are many different forms of it and many different degrees. Some people believe black magic is more powerful than white, but I don't."

"If white magic is to heal and protect, what is black magic used for?"

"Black magic is generally used to bring something to the spell caster, wealth, power or revenge. It's used by people that are angry or in some sort of turmoil."

"The only type of witch I've heard of before is a Wiccan, is that what you are?"

"No, I work alone, Wiccans most always form covens. They are highly religious and their magic is more ceremonial."

"Have you always worked by yourself?"

Another slight smile creased Tanya's face. "No, not always."

"Did you have a coven?"

"Not exactly, I had a family." She laughed at the confused look on Emma's face. "You are such a babe in the woods, aren't you? Believe it or not, like many others, I was born into a witch family. We're called Hereditary Witches and, to answer your earlier question, we are taught witchcraft all our lives. It was handed down to me by my mother and my grandmother. They are both gone now so I work alone."

"What an interesting life you must live."

Again, she raised one eyebrow and it completely changed her expression. "Oh, it has definitely been interesting."

"So, if this is the work of some type of a witch, how would they be doing it?"

"I'm not sure, I've never run into anything as powerful as the spells this person would have to be using."

"Is there a book we can use to try and find out?"

"We all have our own Grimoires, some people fill them with spells learned from others, some have them handed down, some research and try to go back to the ancient times when magic ruled, then they try to bring back some of the dark energy from those times."

"Does that mean that without the person's Grimoire, we can't ever learn what the spell was?"

"That's not necessarily true. I know my Grimoire by heart and I know there is nothing in it remotely like what is going on here. I would have to find another and go through the spells in it and hope I found something similar, something that shows me how to counter the effects of the dark spell."

"When Scott and Tim were helping with the haunting at my house, we found a big, old grimoire that the Grand Wizard who originally lived in my house had. It was filled with horrible spells, would something like that help?"

'Again with the eyebrows,' Emma thought, watching as this time they were lifted high and widened Tanya's eyes, giving her a look of excited expectation

"That might be just what we need. Where is it now?"

"I don't know," Emma said.

Just as quickly, her eyebrows dropped down and formed a thick line of disapproval over her dark blue eyes. "Damn, no idea where?"

"Tim and Scott may have kept it, we can check with them when they get back. And look, some of them are heading down now."

"It looks they're carrying something," Tanya said somberly.

"Like another person?" Emma asked, her own voice wavering just a bit when Tanya nodded her head.

"What's going on, girls?" came a deep, rough voice from close behind Emma and Tanya.

A truly angelic smile lit Tanya's face and Emma was struck, again, by how beautiful she was. When she went over and hugged Caleb, Emma almost started to like her, and began to think that there might be more to her than just the way she looked.

The affection between the two of them was not sexual in the least, Caleb hugged her close with a loving, fatherly look on his face.

"How is she, Caleb?" Tanya asked. "Doc gave me the basics after he checked in with the hospital, but I want to hear it from you."

She stepped back out of his arms, but held tight to one of his hands, drawing comfort from him.

"I don't know, Tanya, I really don't know. I feel terrible leaving her, but I needed to get back here to find out what's going on."

"Is she getting any better?"

"No, doesn't seem to be. She's in and out of consciousness, her fever keeps spiking and they can't keep it down or get rid of it. I don't think they know what the hell the problem is and it's making me crazy, and it's literally killing my Leona."

His steely gray eyes narrowed in anger and Emma was just grateful that anger wasn't directed at her.

"I couldn't bear looking at her like that anymore and thought I could help more here, so I pulled foot out of there. What is going on here? No one seems to be about."

"Hang onto your hat, big fella," Tanya said, her face filled with sadness. "Brad died this morning, his gun blew up in his face. I'm kind of surprised that the State Police aren't here yet, but they should be soon."

"Damn," Caleb said quietly, pinching the bridge of his nose.

"Kevin took off into the hills trying to kill that stupid black dog. There were gunshots and screaming and then some of the guys went up to see what happened. It looks like they are on their way back now. And they are carrying something big."

Caleb's gray eyes squinted up into the hills and then looked directly into Tanya's eyes, almost as if they were communicating telepathically.

"Is everyone agreeing then that this Black Dog thing is real?" He still hadn't taken his eyes off Tanya's.

"I don't know, there's been more talk and I think some are starting to lean that way, even Kevin. He thought it was all bullshit until Brad died. I know that I'm pretty sure about it, myself."

"You think it started this nonsense with my Leona?"

"Most likely."

"Anyone having similar problems?"

"Not like that, no."

The group of men had entered the town limits by then and Emma, Tanya and Caleb crossed the street and headed down Bent Elbow Way to meet them.

Several of them were carrying Kevin's body. Caleb and Scott's eyes met, and Scott shook his head and lowered his eyes.

"We're taking him over to the Doc's office. We'll all meet up in the hotel bar after that and we can tell you what little we know. Is Leona okay?"

"Not really, talk to you in a few."

*   *   *

The crowd was very somber when they finally all got back together a short time later. No one spoke until most of them had some type of alcohol in their hands.

Scott abstained, his head was pounding so badly that he thought that must be what was making him feel so sick to his stomach.

Emma stood close beside him, she couldn't help but notice how pale he was and how prominent the dark circles under his eyes were now. Scott could see that she was worried and wished he could reassure her, but he wasn't sure just how to do that.

"Someone better tell me what the hell happened." Caleb's booming voice echoed throughout the bar.

Travis Seavey was standing right beside him, almost as tall, but no where near as broad as Caleb, he was still an imposing man, even in his old west garb with a fake sheriff's star pinned to his vest.

Travis was a retired police detective and had worked for the resort for the past three years, mainly breaking up fights and escorting belligerent drunks back to their hotel room. Other than the two employee's fatal accidents a couple of weeks before, the events of today were worst of the incidents that had occurred at Windy Shot since he'd been employed here.

"He was gone when we got there." Nathan stepped closer to Caleb, took a long pull on his beer and then continued.

"We don't know what exactly happened with Kevin. I don't know if he ran into the damn dog or something else. Looks like he ended up flipping over the ledge of an outcropping and he fell, probably six or eight feet, to the rock ledge below. I think he broke his neck, it would have been over quickly, he didn't suffer."

"That damn fool, he always had to go running into a situation before everybody else, before he even knew what the hell he was up against."

"Tanya heard a gunshot, so he must have shot at something, I'm assuming it was the dog."

"Explain to me what happened with Brad."

"He was on his second shot in the competition when his rifle exploded in his face. Killed him instantly."

"Then it wasn't his lucky gun."

"Yeah, it was," Ambrose added. "I saw it. He never uses anything else."

"That makes no sense," Caleb said, his rough voice sounding even angrier now for some reason. "Brad kept that thing so clean that you could eat off it. There is no way something jammed in it and made that happen."

"The fact is," Nathan said quietly, "that the gun did explode, for one reason or another, maybe a bad casing or maybe he got dirt or clay in it somehow. We don't know why, but it did happen."

"He was nursing a serious hangover," Scott added. "Maybe he got sloppy."

"Where's the gun now?" Travis asked, knowing the real police were going to want it to examine.

"Over at the Doc's office with Kevin and Brad."

"What now?" Ambrose asked, finishing his first beer and waving the bartender over for another.

"I called the State Troopers. They said it would be awhile. I guess since the boys are already dead, they aren't putting a big rush on this. I imagine they'll be here shortly with the coroner though, so I'll go back up front and watch for them," Travis said.

"What about the rest of the competitions for today?" Theo asked.

Caleb's silver eyes narrowed. "The way things are going, we can't afford to lose any more people and I think we throw in the towel on them. And we definitely need to forgo the knife competition this year."

There were murmurs of agreement throughout the room.

"We got the bonfire later today, let's go ahead and say our good-byes at that, then we can all hash this out and see what we come up with. Somebody better figure what's happening pretty fast, I think my wife's life depends on it."

Tim clasped him on the shoulder. "We'll take of care of it, Caleb. There are enough of us here to figure this out and to fix it."

*   *   *

For those few who still hadn't heard the news, it was disquieting to see the coroner's van and police cars prowling along the cobblestone streets of Windy Shot.

While the coroner quickly examined the bodies and loaded them into his van, the Troopers interviewed anyone with knowledge of the incidents involving Kevin Paxton and Brad Fletcher.

All of the stories were the same and the condition of the bodies confirmed those stories, so they were on their way in much less time than they had anticipated.

Emma wasn't present at either incident, so she wandered around the Square for a bit and then headed over to the Hunter's field where the bonfire would be held. As she approached, she saw Wanda Carrion standing completely still and staring up into the hills. Emma tapped her on the shoulder and Wanda stifled a scream as she turned around.

"Are you alright? I'm so sorry, I didn't mean to startle you."

"I'm fine, just fine," she said breathlessly, but she was gripping her hands together so tightly that her knuckles were white and her eyes were wide as saucers, with deep lines of anxiety etched around them.

"Hi, Wanda," Scott said, walking towards the two women. She flinched and gave him the barest of smiles, turning her gaze to the ground as she walked away from them.

Scott had a look of utter disbelief on his face as he watched her leave.

"What's up with her?" he asked quietly. "I've never seen her act like that before."

"I don't know, I just came over and that's how she was, the slightest little thing seems to be scaring her."

Scott ran his fingers through his thick, dark hair, rubbed his temples briefly, trying to ease his throbbing head, then grabbed Emma's hand and led her back towards the others.

The Hunters were all grouped together at the empty field where the wood for the bonfire had been laid out.

"I'm going to make this brief," Caleb said, his loud voice booming over the crowd. "We all knew and loved Joey, he is already missed and we will never be able to replace him in our hearts. His passing was not the fault of any person, it happened, and it will most likely happen to all of us in a similar fashion, at some point."

He paused for a moment. "Bobby, we understand your grief, but you need to let your vengeance go, it's misguided, and if you'd just think things through, you'd realize that."

"Go to hell," Bobby yelled back at him. "I know what I know, and I'll make sure the situation is handled."

Caleb shook his head in disappointment and continued. "We lost two young men today and I can't emphasize enough how deeply that cuts me, as I'm sure it does you. Those two were unique and irreplaceable. In honor of their memory, I am ending the games. We would usually finish up tomorrow and then have the awards luncheon. With everything that has happened, this Gathering is officially over with after tonight's ceremony.

You are free to stay the night or head home, whatever you prefer. Please be sure to stop over and say goodbye before you leave. It's been great to see you all again, I'm just sorry we've had so much loss and pain this year. Stay safe, y'all."

He then took a torch and set it ablaze. There were effigies of three men lying on a wooden bed atop the pile of logs, all wrapped in a linen cloth.

"What are those?" Emma asked. "They look like man-size cocoons."

Scott wrapped his arm around her shoulder and Emma snuggled up close to him. "It's a funeral pyre with replicas of the people we lost this year. We can't burn their bodies, so we carry out this ceremony for them."

Emma watched as several hunters threw items onto the burning pyre. Pointing to the people approaching the fire, she asked, "What are they doing?"

"Showing honor to their loved one, pictures, mementos, items to help the dead know they are loved and missed, and to help them move on to their afterlife."

Bobby walked over and stood silently for a moment, then threw a hunting cap into the fire, watching intently as the flames rapidly turned it into ashes.

Then he turned and stared directly at Scott and the hatred in his eyes spoke volumes, even though he never opened his mouth. He spit on the ground, then stalked away, his two minions following right behind him.

Scott saw the look from Bobby but chose to ignore it, he knew that at some point, and soon, he was going to have to have a sit down with that boy and clear the air. But today was not that day.

"Is this some sort of religious ceremony?" Emma asked. "I've never heard of anything like it."

"I think it's more Pagan, maybe even from the Vikings. I'm not sure how we came by it originally, but it's been the way we've said good-bye since I've been involved in hunting."

Scott's voice was low and rough, Emma wasn't sure if he was just feeling emotional or if it was because he still wasn't feeling well. She snuggled up closer against him and could feel the heat emanating off his body.

"Scott, are you alright? You're very warm."

"Yeah, I'm still not quite myself. Hey, Tim, come here," he yelled to his brother as he walked by.

"What's up?"

"I think I might still have a little food poisoning and I'm going to head over to the hotel. Will you watch out for Emma?"

They both looked him quizzically because Scott was never sick. This was unusual and didn't feel right, not at all.

"Sure," Tim answered hesitantly.

"I don't need to be babysat, for God's sake," Emma said, her worry making her a bit irritable. "I'll just come with you."

"No," Scott said, quietly but firmly, "I need you here to stand in for me, be my representative and honor these three men, okay?"

His dark brown eyes burned into hers and Emma's heart skipped a beat in fear, of what she did not know.

"Are you sure?"

"I am, and I'll see you later, you know how much I love you, don't you?"

Goosebumps rose on her arms as a premonition took hold of Emma and she felt like she might never see him again.

"Scott, wait, why did you say that? I really do want to come with you, okay? Please?"

He ran his finger along her jawline, lowered his lips onto hers and gave her a long, sweet kiss.

"I'm fine, I am. I just need to lay down for a little while. Now stay here and don't worry so much. When I see you next, this will be over with and I'll be a new man."

He nodded at Tim, gave Emma one of his special smiles and headed off towards the hotel.

CHAPTER 12

"Why are you acting out like this?" Liz asked, unable to fathom why Meg was continuing to be such a bitch.

"I'm not acting out, I'm being who I am."

"Listen," Liz said, her voice was melodic but firm, her blue eyes piercing as she stared at her lover, "that's not who you are, so knock it off."

"To hell with you," Meg replied, turning her back on Liz. Today she had dyed the tips of her brown hair pink to match her fuschia eyeglasses, blouse and hi-top sneakers. There were multiple tears in the legs of her jeans and she'd paid a pretty penny to get them that way.

"Wait, Meg." Liz followed behind, grabbed her arm and turned her around. They were both tense and, although they cared for each other dearly, neither had the disposition to let anyone disrespect them, they'd each suffered too much of that in their lives already.

"What?" Meg stopped and turned so quickly that Liz almost fell into her.

"What is going on with you? You've never been such a twat nazi before, is it Kevin and Brad?"

"I don't know, that's part of it, of course. I still don't understand what happened with either of them, it makes no sense."

"Death rarely does."

"Knock off the platitudes, I'm not in the mood for them."

"I'm just trying to help."

"Well, it's not working, I need you to get hell away from me, right now."

Meg continued walking towards the bonfire, she didn't even understand what she was feeling, and she had no desire to have anyone else, not even Liz, try to dissect it. She knew it wasn't just Brad and Kevin's death, there was something else eating at her and she couldn't put her finger on it.

The Black Dog kept flashing in her mind, like a shot from a movie on a permanent loop, and she was starting to worry that maybe her friends didn't die because of any stupid accidents, maybe it was because they saw that Black Hellhound. And she saw it too, so maybe she was next.

Meg clenched her jaws together and strode towards the fire, pushing people out of her way. She moved in so close to the fire that she could feel the heat of the flames over her entire body.

Earlier, before the Sheriff arrived, Meg had snuck into the Doc's office where they were keeping the bodies and pinched a couple of her friends' personal effects. She wanted them to throw onto the fire in order to show Brad and Kevin how much they meant to her.

In one hand, Meg held Brad's stupid sunglasses, the ones that he felt he had to wear constantly, even inside where they weren't needed, and which always made him seem a little idiotic; and in the other, she held Kevin's comb. He never went anywhere without that comb in his pocket, he had beautiful brown hair and was constantly grooming it.

Meg stood silently, thinking of her friends and remembering some of the good times they had together. It was easy to become mesmerized by the flames and she didn't realize that the fire was growing or that the heat was intensifying.

She leaned forward even closer to the flames and with both arms extended out in front of her went to toss the items into the fire. As she did, she slipped, although there was nothing on the ground in front of her, and she fell face first into the fire, her screams barely audible over the crackling of the flames.

Fortunately, the other hunters standing near her reacted quickly and pulled her out, some of them sustaining burns of their own while doing so.

Meg's face and throat were already blistering, and both of her hands and arms had been badly burned, as well. Liz rushed to her side, tears streaming down her face when she saw what had happened.

"Quickly," Dr. Higgins said, elbowing his way through to them, "bring her to my office, be gentle with her. Any of you others that were burned, you need to come with us also and let me take care of your injuries."

"Caleb," he turned and yelled to his friend, "get that Medi-evac chopper back out here Stat."

They hurried off towards his office, leaving the rest of the group standing around in stunned silence.

It was finally hitting home that their fellow hunters were being picked off one by one, but in a series of accidents, not outright attacks, and for that, they had no defense.

*   *   *

Scott crossed the delivery road and wasn't sure if he could make it all the way back to the hotel, after all. He had intended to leave sooner but that ceremony was too important to miss.

He was near the pool and leaned against the chain link fence for moment, his head was pounding out of control and he felt woozy and nauseous. He decided that he would make it, he just had to take his time and maybe make a couple of quick stops along the way. He passed the Mercantile and was able to cross the street.

Scott was sweating profusely by now and bile was rising rapidly. He saw one of the outhouses over near the side of the theater, it looked closer than the back entrance to the hotel, so he decided to head that way first.

If he didn't know better, Scott would have said that he was completely hammered. His head was spinning now, and he wasn't sure he'd even make it to the outhouse before he lost what little he'd eaten so far that day.

Through the noisy buzzing in his head he heard male voices just before he reached the outhouse and was not pleased when he turned and saw Bobby walking towards him. To top it off, Garrett and Frank were on either side of him and their faces looked way to eager for Scott's peace of mind.

He weakly held his hand up, trying to stop them before anything bad happened, but they were having none of that. Scott turned to see if there was anyone else in the vicinity, but all he did was make himself even dizzier.

Bobby was talking to him, Scott could see the sneer on his face as his lips moved, but the words sounded like they were coming down a tunnel at him and he couldn't put them together into a sentence. He was pretty sure he knew the gist of what was being said though and prepared himself, as best as he could, for battle.

It only lasted a few minutes, the three of them circled Scott and took turns punching or kicking at him. Feeling one hundred percent, he might have had a chance against them, but feeling the way he did right then, there was no way. He got in a couple of good shots, but they took him down quickly. When his head hit the ground, everything went black and he never felt the vicious kicks that Bobby felt compelled to finish things off with, even though he knew that Scott was already unconscious.

The three of them laughed and patted each other on the back and headed towards the saloon to celebrate their victory, leaving Scott lying on the ground behind the outhouse.

*   *   *

Those at the fire who did not need medical attention returned to their safe haven, the saloon across the street from the hotel. Emma started heading that way herself but stopped when she saw Gabriel. He was standing alone and looking very worried off to the side of the field, so she decided to check on him instead of going along with the others.

"Are you alright, Gabriel?" she asked, when she got close enough.

"Oh, hi, Emma." Gabriel didn't even flush like he usually did when Emma spoke directly to him. "I, um, I really don't know. I decided to leave the Resort because of that Bigfoot thing and now I come here, and all this bad stuff starts happening and I wonder, is it me? Am I bad luck? That's what my dad used to say, before he took off on my mom and me, anyway."

"Oh, Gabriel, you poor thing." Emma walked over and wrapped her arms around him, giving him a loving hug. With her own children so far away, she felt like he was a step-son of sorts and wished she could make him feel better, about himself and about life in general.

"So, you do think it's me?"

"Of course not, it sounds like your Dad was an asshole. Don't you ever believe you are anything other than a kind, decent man and you are loved by, pretty much anyone that knows you."

Then he did blush and look down at the ground. "Thanks, Emma. But what the heck is happening here?"

She shook her head. "I don't know, but I think there is a person behind it all, someone is deliberately trying to hurt these hunters. It sounds like maybe they are all coming around to that conclusion now so, hopefully, they'll take it seriously and figure out what needs to be done."

The two of them started to walk slowly away from the fire, which was beginning to die down. Caleb had sent a couple of his employees to get buckets of water and put out the rest of it, the way things were going, he wasn't taking any chances of that fire spreading.

They crossed the street and walked along the front of the stately Courthouse building, arriving on the opposite side of the Square from the hotel. Directly across the road was the Church that Emma had seen the day before. On the other side of that cobblestone street was a huge, salt-box shaped barn.

"I haven't been down this way before, what's here?" she asked, pointing towards the barn.

"Come on, I'll show you."

They headed over and Gabriel took her on a tour of the barn and stables. They walked in through the stables, or THE LIVERY, as the sign above the door read.

There were not a lot of animals inside right then, most had been let out back to graze. The two of them stood at the open doorway looking out into the field where the cows and horses mingled with goats, and the chickens and ducks scrambled out from underneath their hooves.

"Just down there," Gabriel pointed down towards the end of the barn, "there is a petting zoo for the guests. I was originally assigned there but, some of the animals don't like me. I don't know why."

He held out both hands in supplication, wishing he could find the answers to these questions, but he could not.

Emma smiled as they left the barn and continued down the street. They hadn't even tried to make the next building fit in to the old-time motif.

It was constructed of metal and was double the size of any other building here in town. A bold sign on the front read "MAINTENANCE – EMPLOYEES ONLY.

"This is where they keep the vehicles and the equipment. No one is allowed who doesn't have a key. Most of the guests don't really come down this way. They don't go any further than the stables. I think they may even put up a rope to keep people from coming this far down during the season."

"What type of vehicles are kept here?"

"There are four-wheelers, a van and a couple of small pickup trucks inside. Employees use them only when they absolutely have to. Caleb and Leona prefer that we walk if possible, to do whatever has to be done. This is mainly for storage and for emergencies."

"What's that building across the street?"

"That's the Boarding House, it's where all the employees stay. We have our own rooms and there's a dining room and a laundry room. Boy, did I have a time figuring those machines out," he added in frustration. "Did you know that you have to be really careful how much soap you use or you'll get bubbles all over the place. That got Sally so mad at me first thing."

"Who's Sally?" Emma asked, trying not to giggle.

"She kind of runs that building." He lowered his voice as if afraid she might hear him. "I think she might have actually been here back when this was a real town and she can be really scary when she's mad."

"Oh, Gabriel, you have no idea how much I've missed you."

He flushed and looked down at the ground in embarrassment. "Thanks, Emma, I miss all you guys, too."

"Oh," Emma said, spotting the cemetery in between the old church and the Boarding House. "I think I might head over and check out some of those grave markers. Scott told me that he thought I'd find them interesting."

Gabriel shivered and look at her curiously. "I'll let you do that yourself, I don't do cemeteries."

"There's nothing to be scared of in there."

"I know, they just creep me out. If I look out my window in the Boarding House that what's I see and, after that first night, now I just keep the curtains closed."

"What happened the first night?"

"It wasn't all the way dark yet, just shadowy, so I'm not for sure what I saw, but it looked like a woman, an old-time woman with a long skirt or dress, and a long overcoat. She was walking in the cemetery and stopped and made some motion with her hand and this big black dog came to her. I think it was black, like I said, it was almost dark. Anyway, made me think of Callie at first, but this thing was much bigger, and Callie is such a gentle creature and this one just wasn't. I got goosebumps looking at the thing, it wasn't right."

"What do you mean?"

"I can't explain it, really, it was just the way it made me feel more than anything else. The lady stood there and the dog and her looked at each other, she might have been talking to it, I don't know. Then it just turned and loped away. She watched it for a minute, then she turned straight towards my window like, somehow, she knew that I watching them. I was so glad I didn't turn the light on yet. I don't know if she saw me or not, but she hurried away."

"When was that?"

"When I first came here, maybe two weeks ago now."

"Did you get a good look at her?"

Gabriel scrunched up his face in concentration. "Dark hair, kind of tall, maybe, but it's hard to say because it was almost dark out."

"Long hair?"

"No, short, kind of sticking up all over."

"Have you seen her since?"

"I don't think so, really freaky hair, I would of remembered her. But I spend most of my days in the Mercantile so unless she went in there, I probably wouldn't see her."

"Keep your eyes open, if you do recognize her here, let me know, okay?"

"Sure, Emma. You take care of yourself."

"I will, thanks." With a quick hug and a peck on the cheek, she left Gabriel and headed over into the cemetery.

"And Gabriel,"

He stopped and turned back towards Emma.

"Don't you give any more thought to what your father said, he didn't know what he was talking about, okay?"

Gabriel nodded at her and flushed a little, then turned and walked away with a silly little smile on his face and a pleasant warmth spreading across his chest.

Emma was pretty sure the woman that Gabriel had described was Lisa Lonegan and debated whether or not she should go wake up Scott and tell him or wait for a little while. Just then, she heard the rescue helicopter arriving for the second time in as many days and decided to wait until they took care of Meg. Most likely all the commotion would wake Scott, anyway, so she would talk to him about this afterwards.

*   *   *

Before checking out the cemetery, Emma made a brief visit into the church. She was not a very religious person but wasn't hesitant to ask for help when the situation called for it.

The church was simple and plain, other than three or four stained glass windows that sent colorful shards of light streaming into the building. Emma made her way down to the front of the church and sat quietly on one of the hard, wooden pews, collecting her thoughts.

Then she got down onto the kneeler in front of the pew and made the sign of the cross. "Please God, take care of all of these people. Help them figure out what is going on and how to stop it. Please save all of the people that are in danger from that black dog.

Please protect us from the evil that seems to be oozing through this town right now and keep Tim and Scott safe. I'm being selfish now, I know that, but I need them, both of them, so please be sure to give them some special attention. Amen."

Feeling a little less heavy-hearted after that, Emma wandered over to the cemetery. It was larger than she had realized and ran back far beyond the crypts, into the rocky ground which was covered with brush, tall grasses and blooming wildflowers.

Some of the headstones were ornate, but so old that you could barely read what was written on them. Someone obviously took great care of the cemetery, the grounds were well tended, and lupines, columbine and other flowers sprung up intermittently in between the grave markers.

Emma noticed that a few of the headstones had cut flowers lying against them and decided to check them out first. The flowers all seemed to be near the plain wooden markers which had hand-written lettering. It didn't take Emma long to realize that these were put there solely for the entertainment of the guests, so she assumed the flowers were placed strategically to draw those particular markers to people's attention.

She couldn't keep the smile off her face as she read the first of these of these epitaphs, 'DEAR DEPARTED BROTHER DAVE, HE CHASED A BEAR INTO A CAVE'.

Following along with the fresh cut flowers she stopped to read the others, trying not to miss out on the real stones while doing so. It felt strange, the real stones showed just how difficult and short people's lives were when this town was new. But, just as sadness began to well up inside her, she would spot another entertaining headstone.

"HERE LIES JAKE, HANGED BY MISTAKE 1892," she read, hoping that it was just a joke. "HE WAS RIGHT, WE WERE WRONG, BUT WE STRUNG HIM UP AND NOW HE'S GONE."

Then she spotted a very large stone off to the side which stood out above all the others. There was a beautiful urn on either side of it, filled to overflowing with small flowering plants that were just beginning to bloom.

The engraving was magnificent, and Emma knelt down in front of it while she read the words out loud. "SAMUEL GUNDERSON, BELOVED HUSBAND AND FATHER, FOUNDER OF WINDY SHOT. MAY HE REST PEACEFULLY AMONGST HIS CREATION FOR ALL ETERNITY."

"Nice to meet you, Mr. Gunderson. I've met your daughter, Leona, and she's phenomenal. It seems to me that she is carrying on your dream quite well and must make you very proud."

A strong breeze blew up out of nowhere suddenly, whipping Emma's hair around her face and catching her by surprise. The wind was carrying strange noises on it and she felt goosebumps rise on her arms for some reason.

She stood up to look around and let out a little scream when she found Polly standing just a couple of feet behind her, staring curiously.

"I'm sorry, Honey, I didn't mean to scare you. Did you come to visit the folks here, too? I see you've already met Mr. Gunderson, I try to drop off some flowers for him each visit."

She gently laid down a bouquet of yellow and white wildflowers in front of the large stone.

"I was just exploring, checking out some of the gravestones, when that wind whipped up and kind of spooked me."

"I didn't even notice it," Polly responded politely.

Emma gave her a puzzled look, but then noticed that Polly was still cradling a bundle of flowers in her arms. "Those are beautiful, who are they for?"

"Come with me, I'll show you." Polly turned and walked towards the crypts, but then swerved a little to make her way around them. Just on the backside of the building was a small structure of stone built into the ground.

"What is that," Emma asked, as she approached.

"It's a headstone, shaped like a dollhouse."

"Oh, how sweet, and how sad."

"Isn't it, though? Polly asked, as she read the epitaph out loud, "SARA MAE GARGAS, BORN 1901 AND DIED 1911. SHE WAS DEEPLY BELOVED BY HER FAMILY AND WILL BE FOREVER MISSED."

They stood staring at the masterfully crafted dollhouse, the front looked like a small house and held the epitaph. Emma walked around to the backside of it and tears filled her eyes as she ran her hands over the smooth stones that had been worked on so lovingly to create individual rooms. Wood had been used to provide the flooring and there were miniature pieces of furniture and dolls inside each of those rooms.

"Surely these haven't been here all this time, have they?"

"No, I think that Caleb and Leona have regular customers that bring items for Sara Mae's dollhouse every year so that she has something new to play with. According to Leona, her spirit is still here. Sometimes they'll find a piece of furniture or a doll half way across the cemetery. Leona insists that it was Sara Mae who did it because she is very picky about what goes into her dollhouse. Other things stay inside it for years and years with no problem. Some think it's just a squirrel or some type of animal messing around with them."

"What do you think?"

Polly ran her hand lovingly over the smooth stone house and gently laid the bouquet down in front of it.

"I'm of two minds about it. On the one hand, I know her ghost could very well be walking amongst these headstones and so I bring her flowers every year. Leona tells me that pink is her favorite color so, this year, I brought some pink dahlias and some pink painted daisies. I had to throw in a few white daisies also, just for the contrast, you understand."

"Of course, they're lovely."

"I know you are kind of new to this paranormal world, but do you know how wondrous Spirits can be? They can do as much good as they can evil."

"I didn't know that, I thought they were always bad. So, you do think that Sara Mae's ghost is here then?"

"Could be, I've had no actual interaction with her myself but, others say they've seen her and heard her singing at night while she's playing with her dolls. Hearing those things make me so very sad."

"It's sweet though, why does it make you sad?"

"She had a family that loved her enough to build this for her. I think she should be with them, not here all alone."

Emma didn't reply for a moment. "I hadn't even thought of it that way. Has anyone tried to help her move on?"

"No, she's a part of the town, and I think they like to be able to claim the place is haunted to bring in more customers."

"It seems almost cruel."

"Please don't think badly of Caleb and Leona. They have good hearts, there just isn't a lot of sympathy among these hunters for ghosts, or any other entities that aren't human. They've had too many battles with them to be able to feel any empathy for their plights."

Polly adjusted the glasses on her face, smiled gently at Emma and started to walk away. "I'm going to go make sure Meg got off alright. It's a terrible thing to suffer burns like that. Enjoy the rest of your explorations, I'm sure I'll see you later."

Emma watched her go with a thoughtful look on her face, then she turned her attention back to poor Sara Mae's dollhouse.

CHAPTER 13

"Have you seen, Scott?" Emma asked, surprised that he was not with the others at the saloon.

"No," Tim said, "weren't you with him?"

"No, I was over in the cemetery and just went up to our room and he wasn't there."

"I've been here ever since Meg got hurt and haven't seen him." Tim set his half-empty glass of beer down on the table and stood, his brows furrowed in concern. "Theo, I'm going to go try and find my brother, I'll catch up with you later."

"Okay, I'll stay here and see if I can learn anything else of substance."

Emma and Tim stepped out into the waning afternoon sunlight.

"Where do we start?" Emma asked.

"I have no idea where he would have gone. Let's see, we were in the burning field. Let's walk around the back and retrace our way to the bonfire."

Once they got to the back of the hotel, it was fairly open, so they could see quite a distance and Scott was nowhere to be found.

The two of them walked back to the where the bonfire had been held anyway and looked around, trying to figure out what direction he might have taken.

"Scott would have had to pass the pool and the Mercantile. I can't think of any reason he would have kept going past the hotel, can you?"

"That would take him to Town Square and over to the Church and graveyard. I was over that way and just came back a little bit ago. He's not there, I would have seen him."

"Okay, then, if he went South, he would have come to the basketball and tennis courts and I can't imagine why he would have done that."

"When he left, he was headed straight towards the hotel, which would have taken him past the Mercantile. Maybe he wanted to get something for his stomach and stopped in there."

"Could be." The two of them went inside and the same gum-chewing young girl was at the counter again. Tim took a quick trip around the store while Emma walked over and stood silently in front of Zoey, until the girl could be bothered enough to look up and give Emma her attention.

"Zoey, we're looking for a friend of ours, actually it's the brother of the man I came in here with. They look similar, brown hair, brown eyes, he had on a dark blue shirt and jeans. Did he come in here today? Maybe a couple of hours ago?"

The girl looked as perplexed as if Emma had just asked her to recite the Constitution of the United States.

"Have you had any customers in here this afternoon?"

"Um, yeah, a few."

"Were any of them men?"

She shrugged her shoulders. "Maybe."

"Don't you pay any attention to your customers?"

"Of course, I do, but I seem to forget everything about anyone twenty-five or over as soon as they walk away. Don't know why, I just do."

"Please think about it, could one of your customers have been his brother?"

"Probably," the girl responded, but Emma didn't necessarily believe her. She seemed to just be trying to appease them.

"It doesn't matter," Tim said, walking up next to Emma and getting the same vibes from the girl. "Even if he was here, he isn't now."

They left Zoey vigorously snapping her gum behind the counter, knowing that she would, apparently, forget all about them immediately.

"There's a restroom on the other side of the building, maybe that's where he was headed to," Emma said, directing Tim around the corner of the building.

"Maybe he came for this, but the hotel is closer, so why, oh hell," Tim stopped talking and ran over to his brother.

Scott was lying on the ground, unconscious. His body was cold and lifeless and, for a brief, horrific moment, Tim thought he might be dead.

But then he was able to detect Scott's shallow breathing and was able to breathe again himself.

Emma stood over his shoulder, trying not to scream or to cry or to completely lose her shit.

"Is he alive?" There was a tremor in her voice and she was afraid that she might actually pass out.

"He is, Emma. Are you okay, can you go get help?"

"I don't know." She was frozen where she stood, not even capable of kneeling down onto the ground next to Scott. She could only stare at his face, hoping and praying that his eyes would open and that he would be alright.

Tim realized that Emma was in shock and took a deep breath, stood up and grabbed her hands. "Emma, sit down here next to Scott."

He helped lower her to the ground and then placed Scott's cold hand into hers. "Stay here, I'm going to run and get help, I'll be right back."

He didn't wait for her answer, just sprinted across Chickabiddy Lane and then headed north past the hotel, hoping Doc was still over at his office.

Emma started to come around as she stared at Scott's face. She took a tissue from her pocket and gently wiped away the blood under his nose, finally registering that his eye was swelled up and there was also a nasty bruise on his jaw.

She took both of his hands in her own, saw the bloody knuckles and knew that, although he must have gotten in a few licks of his own, someone had beaten him. Emma shook her head, forcing the cobwebs out of it and looked around.

Anger began to pulse throughout her body. If she had seen the person responsible right then, Emma knew she would have hurt them as badly as she possibly could.

The door opened easily under Tim's hand and he ran into Doc Higgins' office, startling him awake. The doctor was exhausted by all of the mind-bending diseases, injuries and deaths that had been occurring over the last twenty-four hours and, from the look on Tim's face, it wasn't over yet.

"Doc, it's Scott, he's unconscious, don't know why. We need a stretcher, we need to get him help."

"Grab one out of the of the back room, where is he?"

"Over by the Mercantile," Tim yelled, as he sprinted into the storage area.

"Let's stop by the saloon on the way," Doc said, as the two of them headed out the door, "we can grab a couple more guys to help us out."

Skeezel and Snake offered to help and between the four of them they had Scott back at the Doc's office a short time later. Emma followed, her shock replaced by pure, insane anger.

"Let me examine him first, then we'll talk."

Tim paced around the small waiting area, Emma sat quietly, staring at the pale green wall in front of her, unable to think about anything and just wishing they would call that damn helicopter back quickly.

"Tim," Snake said, "you need anything else from us?"

"No, thanks for your help, though." Tim extended his hand to the both of them in gratitude.

"No worries, let us know if we can do anything more, we'll be over at the saloon."

Word would obviously spread as they ran into the other hunters, but there was nothing to be done about that at this point.

Tim continued to pace around the small room until Doc Higgins returned a little while later, not feeling at all encouraged by the depth of the frustration showing on the good doctor's face.

"I don't know what's wrong," he said, rubbing his eyes. "Scott doesn't have a fever, he was obviously in a fight and did sustain some significant bruising but there are no broken bones, he doesn't have any type of a head injury to explain why he is unconscious. I did a quick ultrasound and can't find anything wrong with his main organs and I checked his blood, that's fine, too. I'm at a loss here."

"Did you call for the helicopter?" Emma asked.

Doc Higgins looked over at Tim.

"Emma," Tim said, "I asked him not to, not until we figure out what's going on."

"What do you mean? He needs to get to a hospital."

"A hospital isn't going to help him. The problem is here, and we have to find it and fix it ourselves."

"I don't know what the hell you're talking about, but I want him in a hospital, as soon as possible. It's not negotiable, Tim."

Doc Higgins just stood back, he'd had this same conversation with other hunters in the past and knew that the hunters would always win. He was willing to wait patiently until Tim brought Emma around to his way of thinking.

"Emma," Tim tried to take her hands in his own, but she pulled away. "Someone here has done this to Scott, the same way they hurt Leona. The doctors at the hospital aren't helping her, they can't because there is nothing wrong other than the spell that was put on her. If Scott's here, then we might be able to get some clues from him, so give me enough time to work this out, alright?"

Emma looked from Doc Higgins to Tim and back. "Do you agree with this?"

"I can't honestly say that being in the hospital will help Scott. I can hook up an intravenous line to him and make sure he gets the nutrients he needs. I will not do this any longer than necessary. I will not allow him to be in any more danger than he already is, and I will ensure that he is taken to the hospital when and if it's the only recourse left."

"I don't understand," Emma said, her angering wavering. "How can you not think it's necessary now?"

"Like I said, I can handle this. I can keep him comfortable and make sure his condition doesn't get any worse."

Doc Higgins did not know Emma well, but he could see that she wasn't yet familiar with the hunters' way of dealing with certain issues. He'd learned the hard way that their privacy was more important than proper healthcare, and that there was generally a good reason for it. He had stopped fighting them about the issue a long time ago.

It was the reason this facility was more like a mini-hospital than a doctor's office. When Caleb's hunter friends needed medical treatment, this is where they came, no matter where they were when the injury occurred, or how serious the injury was.

"What you also need to realize," Tim added, "is that the police have been called out here twice in a very short period of time. Once more and they'll shut this place down, send all of us away and no one will be able to find the answers that we need to save Scott's life. Is that what you want?"

"I just want him to be okay, Goddamn it."

Then she broke down and started sobbing uncontrollably. Tim closed the distance between them and wrapped his long arms around her. He wanted to cry along with her but wouldn't allow himself to do more than get a little teary-eyed.

There was work to be done, and no time to lose if he was ever going to get his brother back.

"Are you going to be alright, Emma?"

"I don't know, I guess so," she replied, wiping her eyes and then blowing her nose in very unladylike manner.

"Go and splash some cold water on your face, I'm going to check on Scott one more time and then I have some things to do. If you need me, call me on my cell, okay?"

Emma nodded silently and went off in search of the ladies' room.

Tim walked into the room where they had taken Scott and stood over his brother. It took a lot for him to step into that room and see Scott lying there so helplessly. He felt as if a part of himself was laying there, also, and a wave of fear and uncertainty washed over him.

Scott and he had their issues and there were times it seemed like they would never even speak to each other again. Both of them were head-strong and never had a problem letting the other know exactly what they thought, but they always managed to get over those troubling times.

Tim knew that they could get past any differences that they had because they understood each other so well. He had no idea how other families interacted, but he and his big brother had been hunting together for close to twenty years and they relied on each other for their very lives. Living like that, spending most of their time together and depending on each other so much, created a bond that he imagined wasn't equaled all that often between other siblings.

It was his job to have Scott's back and he felt like a complete and utter failure right now. He didn't take responsibility for what had happened, but he did accept the fact that it was now his duty to make this right, to save his brother from whatever was killing him.

Tim straightened his shoulders, threw off his mantle of guilt and took a deep breath as he grabbed hold of Scott's limp, lifeless hand.

"This is not how you are going out, Scott. There's too much left for us to do in this life. When you do leave this world, it's going to be in a blaze of bloody glory, not like this, never like this. I hope you can hear me, because I need you to know that I will kick Bobby's ass, along with both his buddies'. I don't know if they just roughed you up or if they are behind all of this, but I'm going to find out and you know that I'll make them pay.

I need you to understand that I won't be back to visit you until you're on your feet again. I think you would feel the same, but I can't see you like this. It's not who you are and it's not acceptable to me. So," his voice cracked with emotion and he stopped to get himself under control, "I'll see you soon, Brother, you just hold on until I can get this handled."

He gently laid Scott's hand back on the bed and never looked back as he walked out of the room.

*   *   *

Tim checked the saloon but couldn't find anyone that he was looking for. He headed back to the hotel and spied Tanya sitting at the bar. She was in the middle of a conversation with Snake and Skeezel and Tim strode up and twirled her around on the barstool.

"Hey, what the hell, Tim?"

"Where's Bobby?"

"How would I know?"

Tim scowled and stared hard into her dark blue eyes.

"I'm not in the mood, Tanya, where is he?"

"Okay, yes, I've spent some time with him, but we're not each other's keeper. I'm done with him and haven't got a clue where he is right now."

"Your taste in men certainly has deteriorated."

"Not really your business, is it? How's Scott, Snake was just telling me about him, what's going on?"

"Don't know for sure, but I think your boyfriend and his buddies got it all started by tuning Scott up a little, you know anything about that?"

The blood drained from her face and she was wide-eyed when she responded. "Tim, I swear I don't know anything about that."

He watched her face for a minute, wanting to believe her but, although she didn't give any indication of deceit, Tim knew he couldn't trust anyone at this point.

"I hope I don't find out anything to the contrary, Tanya."

His voice was calm, but Tanya had to rub the goosebumps away that had risen on her arms in response to his words.

He spotted Matt and Nathan over at a table in the corner and headed over to them.

"How's Scott doing?"

Tim just shrugged his shoulders. "I have no idea, he's just laying there in some sort of a coma. Looks like someone, or several someones, had a fight with him first. I think it was Bobby and his buddies, but I haven't been able to find them. Either of you know where they might be?"

"No, they haven't been in here," Nathan replied, he knew how close the two brothers were and saw the way that Tim's jaw was set. "I think you might want to get some rest tonight, we can help you look for him tomorrow. It's not like there is anywhere for him to hide."

"I'd kind of like to get my hands on him right now, I need a little stress relief."

"We don't need any more dead bodies," Matt said, in his slow drawl. "Y'all might want to take Nathan's advice for tonight."

"Yeah, maybe," Tim replied.

"Polly is still trying to find some intel on what we've got happening here. So far, we have nothing concrete but, it's looking more and more like it's witch-related with some sort of a spell put on the Black Dog."

The three of them turned at the same time and watched Tanya chatting away with Snake and Skeezel at the bar, although they were silent and just seemed to be listening as they continued to sip their beer.

Tanya stopped talking to take a sip of wine and then turned towards their table, as if she sensed them watching her. Tanya lifted one eyebrow, glared at the three of them, swallowed the last of her wine and strode out of the bar after exchanging a couple more words with Snake and Skeezel.

"You know," Matt said quietly, following her out with his eyes, "it would be pretty obvious if it was Tanya behind this, being the only witch here. Makes me feel like it isn't her, and if it isn't her, who is it?"

"I agree," Nathan added, "Not only is it too obvious, but we've known and worked with her for quite awhile and she's never been the least bit spiteful, or malicious, for that matter."

"But she is pretty mad at Scott for bringing Emma here, and she's hooked up with Bobby, who also has a bone to pick with him."

"True," Nathan acknowledged, "but something this big wasn't put together quickly, and she didn't even know Emma would be here until a couple of days ago. Besides, there are others, not just Scott, that were affected, and I know for sure that Tanya is very close to Leona. I'm almost positive that she is not behind this."

"Almost?" Matt asked.

"Never say never, right?"

"Right," Matt responded. "I don't know her as well as ya'll do but, if not her, then who?"

"Didn't Bobby date a Wiccan back a year or so ago?"

"Good Lord," Nathan said with a smile. "That Gothic creature that he dragged around was a witch?"

"I'm pretty sure he said she was a Wiccan," Tim replied thoughtfully. "If he didn't piss her off too badly when they were dating, he could have gotten some tips from her on how to pull this off."

Nathan pushed his glasses up further on his nose and thought that over.

"I wish that we had a better understanding of what we are dealing with and what is involved. I think that would help us narrow down our suspects."

"Well," Tim said, standing up and pushing his chair in, "I think I'll take your advice and get some sleep. But, trust me, I'll find Bobby tomorrow and, one way or the other, I'll find out if he's responsible. If he is, I'll try not to kill him, at least until after he tells us how to stop all this."

CHAPTER 14

Emma spent the night with Scott and could easily imagine that she was in a hospital. The room was sterile and white, so white that it was almost blinding when Doc Higgins would come in during the night to check on Scott.

When the sun finally rose, Emma felt even more tired than she had when it first went down. Her eyes were scratchy and blurred, her thoughts were jumbled, and every muscle in her body ached from trying to sleep on one of the uncomfortable chairs in the rooms.

There was no change in Scott's condition and even Dr. Higgins seemed disheartened.

"I'll keep pumping fluids into him, Emma, and keep him as well as I can. Before you get sick yourself, why don't you run over to the hotel, clean up and get some breakfast. You look a bit peaked."

"I don't know," Emma responded hesitantly. A hot shower and a cup of coffee sounded heavenly, but she didn't want to leave Scott.

She was exhausted, overwhelmed and so very, very scared that she was going to lose him. She needed to stay close to his side so that she could hold tight to her belief that he was going to be alright. Emma was afraid that if she let him out of her sight, that belief might crumble away.

"I don't want to upset you," Doc Higgins said, seeing her reluctance, "but Scott isn't going to just suddenly wake up. I can assure you of that. If there are any changes at all, I will make sure you know immediately. In the meantime, please go take care of yourself."

Emma looked down at Scott's handsome face and could almost convince herself that he was sleeping. But she knew better, and she also knew that, somehow, she had to reach down deep and find some courage to keep going and quit wallowing in her own self-pity. That was the only way she would be able to help figure out how they were going to save him.

She bit back her tears as she ran her finger along Scott's jawline, now covered with a bristly stubble, and then brushed a gentle kiss over his still lips.

"I'll be back in an hour or so," Emma said to Doc Higgins, wiping the tears from her eyes before they could fall as she turned and left the room.

"No rush," he called out, empathizing with her heartache and wishing there was something, anything, that he could do for Scott, and for her.

As Emma was walking through the lounge at the hotel, making her way towards the stairs, she thought she heard Tim's voice in the restaurant and headed in that direction instead.

She filled a cup at the buffet and then walked over to the table that Tim was sharing with Theo. Sitting down heavily, Emma savored her first sip of the strong, rich coffee before she even uttered a word to them.

"No change at all?" Tim asked quietly.

"No," Emma replied, "have you guys been able to find out anything?"

"Not much, we had some ideas thrown out last night but still have nothing solid to go on. Most people are leaning towards a witch attack and that sounds right to me."

"Again, we're blaming the witch? Every time I walk into a room, I'm being maligned." Tanya had been walking behind Tim at the exact moment that he made the comment and stopped short at his words.

"No offense intended, Tanya."

"Seriously? A witch attack isn't supposed to be something that I take offense to? Did you notice that I'm the only witch here? Because some of your pals have, based on the nasty-ass looks I've been getting all morning. I'm going to be glad enough to get the hell out of here, that's for sure."

"You aren't going today, are you?"

"Damn straight I am, I don't need this shit, Tim. You came at me pretty hard last night and it looks like today's just a continuation of that, but now the majority seem to be thinking the same as you."

"Wait, we need to talk to you. Seriously, I had some time to think about it and I don't believe that you had anything to do with this, but if it is a witch, we need some input from you."

"I can't help."

"You don't know that, please, have a seat."

She looked at Theo and Emma hesitantly.

"I have to go up and shower, anyway, here, take my chair." Emma just didn't have the fortitude to buddy up with Tanya right then, not when Scott was in the condition that he was in and Tanya was the only witch in the vicinity.

And Tanya had a bone to pick with Scott, and with her for that matter, so there was no way that Emma could, or would, trust her right now.

*   *   *

"What do you think I can help you with?" Tanya asked, once Emma was gone.

"Any insight you can provide would be helpful."

"Such as?"

"Hello, all, mind if I join you?"

Ambrose pulled over a chair, which made a shrill, screeching sound as it was dragged across the floor. He ignored the commotion he was causing and made himself comfortable, pouring himself a cup of coffee out of the carafe.

He looked like he'd had a rough night and when Tim started to ask him a question, he held his hand up to stop him. "Hold tight a minute, Tim."

Curiosity and amusement flickered across their faces as they watched him withdraw a flask from the pocket of his blazer and pour some amber liquid into his coffee. Replacing the flask and slowly stirring his cup, he gently placed the spoon on the plate, making as little noise as possible.

Holding the cup under his nose, he inhaled deeply, savoring the alcoholic fumes before slowly tipping the cup up and consuming at least half of it before setting it back down with a sigh of contentment. Only then did he finally looked up and focus his bloodshot eyes on Tanya.

His voice was low when he started to speak. "Tanya, my dear, you know I adore you, but I think you might want to head out soon."

"Why?"

He motioned his head in the direction of some of the other tables. "Last night there was a lot of talk about the damned Black Dog and your name came up more than once. I am worried for your safety."

"It's that bad already?" Tim asked.

Ambrose nodded and took another long sip of his coffee.

"With all these strange incidents occurring, people are unnerved and, as always, they need something, or someone to blame. They've decided Tanya is the only witch here so,"

"Ow," Tanya said loudly, as Logan Hughes let his tray hit the back of her head when he made his way past her.

Tanya rubbed the sore spot on her head and turned angry eyes on him. "What was that for?"

"Sorry about that," he said with a snigger, "but you can fix yourself up with some of that white magic, can't you?"

Tanya didn't answer and her eyes blinked rapidly as she gazed around the room. Many of these people she had considered, if not friends, at least friendly acquaintances. Right now, all that she could see was the hostility in their faces and it flustered her.

For the first time, ever, Tanya was afraid of these hunters. She knew what they were capable of and had no intention of underestimating them. The time was right to run away, far away, from all of them.

"Fuck off, Logan," Tim said, surprised and angry, every hunter was high-strung, to say the least, but there had never been any reason for them to fear one another, until now, apparently.

"Nice way to have your brother's back, jumping into bed, so to speak, with the witch that's trying to kill him. I thought you were better than that."

"You don't have any idea what you're talking about, so I'd suggest you back off, right now."

"Sure," he replied with a grin. "See you later, Tanya."

"He was one of the guys with the biggest mouth last night," Ambrose said quietly, after Logan walked to the other side of the room.

"But why?" Tim asked. "I always thought he was pretty level-headed."

"Don't know. I do know he has a great deal of respect for your brother, unfortunately, he can't think his way out of a paper bag and jumped to the most obvious conclusion."

"Which would be me?"

"Yes, that would be you. Are you leaving soon?"

Tanya looked at Tim, she could see the desperation in his eyes and knew she couldn't leave with Scott in the condition that he was in. Regardless of the future of their relationship, she cared too much about Scott to let him die like this, especially if there was something that she could do to prevent it.

"I'm not going anywhere for awhile." She saw relief flood Tim's features and knew she was making the right decision.

"Thank you, Tanya. We'll look after you, I promise. I'm pretty sure that most of these people will be clearing out this morning. Only the ones that have someone they care about involved in this mess should be sticking around, and none of us think you're responsible."

"I appreciate you saying that, Tim."

"Let me walk you over to the infirmary, that may be the safest place for you right now, no one should bother you there. I'll be sure the Doc has a head's up about what's going on, too, so he can keep an eye on you."

"I can take care of myself."

"I know you can, but we don't know who's on what side, so let's just watch out for each other for now, okay?"

"Fine." For all her bravado, Tanya was shaken by the ill feelings directed her way and welcomed Tim's presence by her side when they walked out of the hotel.

*   *   *

Emma felt a great deal better on hour or so later when she made her way back to Doc Higgins office. The hot shower did wonders and the bagel she was nibbling at was just what she needed. She felt stronger and now, just needed to figure out what she could do to help Scott.

Her mood changed drastically, and all her good intentions fled, when she opened the door to Scott's room and found Tanya sitting in a chair by the bed, one of Scott's hands held between both of her own.

"What are you doing here?" There was no mistaking the frostiness of her voice.

Tanya stood up abruptly, almost guiltily, and moved over towards the window, away from Scott's bedside. "Tim sent me over."

"Bullshit, are you here to finish the job?"

The heavy brows came together, this time not looking fierce, just sad, as she turned back to Emma.

"I didn't do this, I would never do this. If you knew me at all, you would know that."

"Then I'll ask again, why are you here?"

"Some of the other hunters think I might be involved. It started getting a little hairy in the dining room after you left, and Tim thought I might be safer over here, away from the others, until they can find the real culprit."

"Why should I believe you? Those other hunters know you and yet, they don't."

"There's nothing that I can say to convince you, same as them. Caleb knows me well, so does Tim, and they do trust me, so maybe you should just talk to them."

"You're right, I don't know you. And I don't even particularly like you. So, there is no way that I am going to go look for Tim and leave you here alone with Scott."

"Well, then, isn't this going to be fun?"

Emma took a seat close to the bed and started sipping on her coffee. Tanya moved Scott's clothes off one of the little folding chairs and sat down, trying unsuccessfully to get comfortable as she rearranged his clothing on her lap.

Even that annoyed Emma, she didn't want Tanya's hands on anything of Scott's.

"Here, I'll take those," she said, as she stood up and moved in that direction. Tanya rose to her feet and the jacket tumbled off her lap and something fell out of the pocket.

"Wow," she said, when she realized that it was a ring box. "Should I assume he intended this to be for you?"

Emma picked up the box and rolled it around her fingers. "Well, it certainly wasn't for you."

She turned the box over in her hands, curiosity getting the best of her. "Should I open it?"

For the first time that day, both women smiled.

"That would be your call, if it was me, I most definitely would be checking it out."

Emma moved it from hand to hand, wanting desperately to see what was inside, but also wanting to respect Scott's privacy and let him handle things the way he wanted to.

But she needed to know what this was, she had major questions of her own that required answers, and this might be one of the pieces that would help Emma complete her own puzzle.

"I'm going to do it," she said, raising her voice.

Tanya's eyebrows were drawn together in confusion, but then the corners of her lips raised in a slight smile when she realized what Emma was doing.

"Scott, you'd better wake up now. If you don't, I am giving you fair warning that I will be looking in the box to see what this is. If you don't want me to do that, you damn well better open your eyes, right now."

She paused a moment. "Okay, here I go."

Emma opened the box and stared mutely at what was inside. Although there was no love lost between them, Tanya couldn't stand the suspense and moved closer to see what the box contained.

Tears filled her eyes when she saw the ring. It was stunning, a large diamond shaped Rose Quartz stone surrounded by small diamonds along the outside edge of it. The band was rose gold and had circular and oblong diamonds spaced alternately around it.

Emma's jaw dropped when she saw the ring and she couldn't drag her eyes away from it.

"It's beautiful," Tanya said sincerely, although there was a catch in her voice when she spoke. "Congratulations."

When Emma could finally speak, she whispered, "Thank you, but I'm not even sure this is an engagement ring. What kind of stone is this anyway? I've never seen anything like it."

Tanya gave her a bittersweet smile. "Trust me when I tell you that this is an engagement ring and Scott did a tremendous job with it."

"Why do you say that?"

"The stone is a Rose Quartz, it's called the Heart Stone and it is the stone of unconditional love. It holds romantic energy and will draw more love into your life, attracting harmonious, long-term relationships. It's actually useful for many other things, as well, like healing old wounds and resentments and it can also provide one with a deep sense of personal fulfillment. It's sort of an all-encompassing stone as far as the heart is concerned."

Tanya spoke robotically, as if she were a professor teaching a lesson, not a woman just discovering that the love she felt for Scott had never been, and would never be, returned. Her heart clenched and she felt sick to her stomach as her world was completely upended by the beautiful ring that Emma held so delicately in her hand.

A tear slid down Tanya's cheek at that point and Emma finally noticed how emotional this was making her.

"I am sorry, Tanya, this was so wrong of me to do with you here. I forgot about you two, for moment, anyway."

Tanya waved her apology off. "I'm just so blown away that this is the same Scott that I was with, I never would have imagined him coming up with this. He obviously put a lot of thought into it."

Her voice was wavering, and she hesitated a moment to collect herself before continuing. "I think you can rest easy and know that whatever you share with Scott, you are the only one who has and, most likely, ever will."

"That's a very kind thing to say."

"I'm not a bad person, Emma and other than the jealousy thing, you have no reason to dislike me."

"I'm not jealous."

Seeing the doubtful look on Tanya's face, she said it again.

"I'm not jealous," but this time she added, "anymore."

"I will accept that as a true statement. I know we'll never be BFFs, but I think a hug might be in order right now, would you mind? It's been quite a difficult morning."

Emma shook her head, tears of her own starting to form for some inexplicable reason, and the two women gave each other a heartfelt hug. It was as if by seeing the ring, they both knew where they stood, and that there was no need for any further battles for Scott's attention or his heart. That war was already won.

CHAPTER 15

Emma's emotions were on such a roller coaster that she wasn't able to sit still. She thought that maybe she could walk it off and left to have some time alone, but nothing seemed to help. To see Scott lying so lifeless and still was devasting. To know that he loved her as much as she loved him made her feel complete, and yet, was destroying her at the same time.

She was filled with love and happiness but wasn't able to embrace those emotions. Emma was afraid to feel those feelings, afraid to accept the happiness because her worry for Scott threatened to overwhelm it. She was torn between her joy and her anguish and, if she allowed the anguish to win, she might break apart into a million pieces.

Emma just wanted Scott back, so until that time came, she thought it best to bury the warmth and love she felt for him, to hide it in a little pocket inside her heart, right next to the fear. For now, she would focus only on her anger, and on finding the person responsible for all of this.

Emma didn't understand much about the paranormal, cryptid creature hunting world. She knew that spells involved strange and sometimes gruesome ingredients, with special words to tie everything together but, other than that, much of what was going on seemed surreal.

It was beyond her understanding how a person, witch or otherwise, could control someone's health, their very fate, with some little stones and seeds and a piece of their DNA, and destroy dozens of lives in the process. It was unfathomable.

As Emma walked, she realized that she was being drawn back to the theatre where they had found Scott. She headed over to the grand old building, hoping there might be something there to help her find the answers that she so desperately needed.

She thought the doors would be locked and was surprised to find that they opened easily. Emma found herself standing in a large entranceway with chandeliers hanging from the ceiling and photos covering the walls, the majority of them were black and white and looked to be of performers from times long past. Further on there were posters and, interspersed with the ones from the last century, were more current ones, singers who came to perform, magicians, comedians, a little bit of everything to keep the resort customers entertained.

There was a deep, thick carpet that ran the length of the room and muffled any sound she might make as she wandered around. At the end were large double doors that were currently standing wide open, allowing Emma to look down the sloping floor, across the wooden chairs situated in row upon row down towards the stage.

More large chandeliers hung in this room and balconies ran along either side on the second floor. Heavy curtains draped over the arched doorways behind each box on the balcony, which would be closed during the performances to block out the light from the hallway beyond them. Emma thought she heard a door closing and turned quickly, but there was nothing there.

'*Just my imagination*,' she thought, taking a deep breath and releasing it slowly.

She wandered around the stage, never having been on one before, and found it to be quite an interesting experience. Backstage there were microphones, large lights, pulleys, ropes and pieces of scenery scattered all over. Emma finished exploring the stage and then took some stairs up to the second floor to check out the boxes on the balcony.

Emma wandered around the first one that she came to and couldn't help sitting down in one of the seats and pretending she was watching some old vaudeville shows from a hundred years ago. A smile lit her face and she forgot for a moment why was she there and the situation that Scott was in.

Another vague sound intruded on her and this time the hair

on the back of her neck rose. Emma felt a little unsettled and decided that she'd had enough of the eerie quietness of the theater. There was obviously nothing here to help her with Scott's problem, so she decided that it was time to leave.

She hurried under the archway and something, or rather someone, reached out and grabbed her arm. Emma never turned around to see who, or what, was hiding behind the thick drapes, she just screamed as she wrenched her arm free and started to run.

There were no lights on in the building and no windows along the dim hallway.

Emma reached the end of the hall and could hear heavy footsteps running behind her. She looked around in a panic, there were no stairs at this end of the hall, she was trapped. Then she spied a small door tucked into far a corner and, thankfully, it opened when she turned the knob.

Emma stepped through and closed the door quietly behind her, stopping suddenly when she realized that she was stepping onto a catwalk which extended over the stage. Not being a theater aficionado, she had no idea what it was used for and didn't particularly care, as long as it took her to safety. What did not thrill her, was the fact that it ran across the entire length of the room that the stage was in and had to be at least thirty or forty feet above the ground.

Hearing the sound of footsteps just outside the door, she grabbed hold of the side railing and started across as quickly as she could manage. Emma almost swallowed her tongue in fear when she reached about halfway and felt the catwalk begin to sway. She almost lost her balance but tightened her grip on the railing, as whoever it was behind her began to rock it back and forth, faster and faster.

She kept trying to step forward, but the damn ramp wouldn't stay still. Then the swaying stopped and there was a jerking on the railing and a sound behind her that couldn't be anything other than someone hitting it with knife. They were trying to loosen it enough that Emma could no longer hold on, causing her to fall to her death and adding a little more drama to the quiet stage below that had seen so much already.

Emma was crying now, scared beyond reason, and then a picture of Scott popped into her mind's eye, still and silent on the infirmary bed, and she knew that she needed to get herself together. This was not going to be the way that the two of them left this world.

She bit her lip hard, drawing blood, she wanted to turn to see who it was that was doing this to her, but knew she had to use every available second to get out of this situation. Emma didn't even bother with the railing this time, her assailant was so busy trying to cut it loose that they couldn't cause the walkway to sway at the same time.

Emma ran as fast as she had ever run before, refusing to look down, focusing only on the other end of the catwalk, knowing she had to get there before he realized what she was doing, or before he could cut the walkway completely loose.

All of the sounds stopped when Emma reached the platform at the other end of the catwalk, except her heavy panting as she struggled to catch her breath. She found a ladder that would take her to the floor below and started down, stopping for just a moment to stare back into the darkness at the other end of the catwalk. It was deep in shadows and she couldn't tell if the person was still there or not.

She hurried down the ladder, falling off it just a few feet from the floor, scrambling back up and running towards the front door like all the demons in hell were after her. Forcing the doors open with a bang against the outside walls, she leaped down off the porch and screamed as loud as she possibly could when she ran straight into Bobby Montclave's arms.

*　　*　　*

Once Tim had gotten Tanya safely to the infirmary, he began his search for Bobby, Garrett and Frank. At the least, he knew they were the ones that had jumped Scott. At the worst, Bobby was also behind these other atrocities.

He found out which rooms were theirs at the hotel and tried them first. Although he banged so hard that he was surprised the doors didn't buckle, no one answered in any of their rooms.

Tim's anger continued to build as he wandered through the town, checking every place that he thought they might be, but the three of them seemed to have disappeared.

He could feel the tension spreading throughout his body and the pulse starting to pound in his neck at the thought of the cowardly way the three of them had attacked his brother.

"Hey, Snake," Tim said, as he walked into the gambling hall.

Snake looked up from his Blackjack cards and nodded towards Tim, the motion making the snake tattoo on his neck writhe like it was alive.

"I'm looking for Bobby, have you seen him?"

"Not here, and this is where I've been since it opened."

"You winning?"

A rare smile started to cross Snake's face. "I'm up."

"Good for you," Tim said, assuming that was a yes. "If you see Bobby or his buddies, let me know, or let them know I'm looking for them, okay?"

"You sure you want to do that?"

"Do what?"

"Take 'em on by yourself."

"It might not come to that. I need to know what they did to Scott and what else they might be up to."

"Again, you sure you want do that alone?"

"You offering something?"

"Might be, if you find 'em, you let me know before you start anything, okay?"

"I'll do that, thanks, Snake."

With another nod he went back to his card game and Tim walked away, trying to figure out where the hell those three could be hiding.

He decided to try the basketball courts back behind the family hotel and headed down Chickabiddy Lane. As he got nearer, he could hear a ball bouncing down on the courts and thought he was finally going to find the bastards.

Tim was just about to cut through the lawn between the hotel and the Mercantile to get to the basketball courts when he heard screaming coming from the theater across the road.

He turned and sprinted to the front of the building and, at long last, found Bobby who, for some reason, had his hands on Emma, and not in a gentle way.

"Let go of her," Tim said, his voice was quiet and calm.

Bobby released Emma and held both hands up in surrender. "Hey, she ran into me, I didn't do anything."

Bobby was not a timid man, but he knew the look in Tim's eyes and was not prepared to go one on one with him. His friends were still over at the basketball court so they wouldn't be of any help, and now was not the time to let this escalate.

Emma ran over and partially hid behind Tim, the screaming had stopped but tears were running unbidden down her face.

"What happened here, Emma?"

"I was inside the theater and he was hiding and tried to grab me. When I ran away," she hiccupped through her tears and then swallowed hard, "he tried to make me fall off the catwalk. He tried to kill me, Tim."

"Hey, I didn't do that, I swear." His eyes were wide with fear and confusion.

"What are you doing here then?"

"We just got done playing, Garrett and Frank are still over at the basketball courts. I was heading back to the hotel to take a shower when she came flying out of there and ran right into me. I'm not lying, I was never inside that building."

Tim just stared at him, which made Bobby even more uncomfortable.

"Listen, let's go find Garrett and Frank, they'll tell you the truth."

"Oh, I'll be asking them, don't worry about that," Tim replied, "but I'd rather do it myself without you putting words in their mouth."

"Listen, Tim,"

"Just shut up, Bobby, I can hardly even look at you. I always liked you and I had so much respect for your dad. To see how you've behaved since he died, I'm embarrassed for him now. I know that you my kicked brother's ass, but only when he already sick and with the help of two other guys, because you're a fucking weasel. You make me sick to my stomach."

"Hey, I didn't start that either." Now Bobby was really scared, he'd heard that Scott went into some kind of a coma after they'd had tuned him up a little, but he didn't realize Tim was aware of what they'd done. He figured it would all be blamed on the Black Dog and whoever was behind that.

"I'm sure you didn't, well, now, you can take your chances with me. All by yourself."

"I'm not doing that."

"You don't have a choice. I wanted to just talk to you, find out why you did that to Scott, why you are causing all this other trouble, but I don't feel like talking anymore. I need to have this out with you, so let's do it."

Bobby relaxed a little when he saw his two friends approaching behind Tim. "Fine, let's go."

The two of them went into full frontal attack. Emma held back her screams as she heard the thuds of their fists while they pummeled each other. When she saw the two others hurrying over to help Bobby, she turned and ran as fast as she could towards the infirmary.

"Tanya, Tanya, are you still here?"

"Yes, what's going on?"

"Bobby and his friends are beating up Tim. We need to get him some help."

The closest building was the gambling hall, so they ran in and found Snake.

"Snake, Bobby and his buddies are beating up Tim, will you help?"

He shook his head slowly and looked with dismay at the cards in his hand.

"Damn," he said, then laid his cards on the table with a heavy sigh, gathered his cash and stuffed it into his pockets.

"I told him to come get me first." He sounded like he was talking about a child that had misbehaved, but he followed Tanya and Emma outside and down towards the theater.

By the time they got there, Garrett and Frank were holding Tim's arms while Bobby pounded on him.

Snake pulled out an enormous Bowie knife and threw it towards the four men. It landed inches from Bobby's feet, who stopped what he was doing to turn and see who had thrown it.

Snake pulled another knife out of its sheath and pointed it at Bobby's face. "You know I won't miss."

Bobby backed away at the same time that Garrett and Frank released Tim's arms. He turned in a fury and threw a punch before they could slither away like the cowards they were. Garrett's nose exploded with a spray of blood and he laid whimpering on the ground.

All the blood had drained from Bobby's face and he cast his eyes about nervously, wondering how he was going to get out of this mess.

Tim took a step towards him, but Snake stepped over and put his hand on Tim's arm to halt him. "Ask him what you need to ask him, then I think we have to get them out of town. We don't want them here anymore."

"We can't let him go, he tried to kill Emma, he might be responsible for what's going on here with the Black Dog."

"Tim, I swear I was not in the theater, I didn't do anything to Emma. And the Black Dog thing, I don't have any idea what that is, I didn't have anything to do with it."

A crowd was gathering by then and Sheriff Seavey pushed his way through. He talked to Emma, talked to Tim and he talked to Snake.

"At the least we can get them on assault for Scott, and for you, Tim," he said quietly. "Emma, you never saw who it was that attacked you, so that'll be harder to prove. I've got cuffs and I'm going to take them to town and have charges filed. They'll want your statements, eventually, but at least we can get them out of here for now, so they don't cause any more trouble."

"What about all this Black Dog stuff?"

"Real police can't help with that. See if you can find anything in their rooms that would help point the finger at them. If not, there's nothing we can do."

Snake helped the Sheriff escort the three men towards his office where he would use his handcuffs and then drive them into town. The three of them went quietly, apparently finding it safer to be under arrest than to stay here with the other hunters.

*   *   *

Tanya and Emma returned to the Infirmary with Tim. Doc Higgins checked him over and couldn't find any broken bones.

"Do you think it was Bobby that tried to kill you, Emma?" Tanya asked, feeling more than a little foolish for having spent any time at all with him.

"I have no idea, whoever it was grabbed my arm, but I never saw them or had any idea of who they might be."

"Why would they do that?"

"I don't know, you were here, right?"

Tanya's mouth opened in surprise. "Are you kidding me?"

"Well, other than you, who else would want me dead?"

"You little bitch, I thought we were past that."

"I'm just kidding, I really don't think it was you. But, seriously, I didn't know I'd made such a bad impression on people here that I needed to die for it."

Tim shook his head. "I can't figure out why someone would go after you, but it has to have something to do with the other things that have been happening."

"Damn, another one's coming."

The three of them ran to the outer lobby as soon as they heard Doc state those words, a little louder than he had intended.

"Sorry about my language, ladies, but it looks like I have another customer coming. I don't know what we're going to do now."

Matt Girardin and Droin Carrion entered the building just then, they were on either side of Droin's wife, helping her walk. Wanda seemed to be semi-conscious, babbling something that no one could understand.

Doc had them take her into his other patient room and made them leave while he examined her.

"What happened?" Emma asked.

"No idea, she started having fits, shaking, babbling, foaming at the mouth, almost like a seizure."

"Did she see the Black Dog?" Tim asked.

"Yes, I guess she saw it a day or two ago, but I didn't know about it until this morning."

"She been acting a little off?" Matt Giradin asked.

"As a matter of fact, she has, afraid of her own freaking shadow, jumping out of her skin at the least little noise, but she's never been that kind of a nervous Nellie."

"Ghost sickness."

"What is that, I've never heard of it?" Droin asked.

"Ghost sickness happens when people fear death. They worry about what's going to happen so much that they bring on the ghost sickness. No rhyme or reason to it, it's different in anyone that catches it."

"Are you saying this condition isn't because of the Black Dog, that she did it to herself because seeing it made her so afraid?"

Matt moved his head back and forth with a frown on his face as he struggled to find the right words.

"Could be the Black Dog caused her to get the sickness, or it could be she got it on her own by seeing the Black Dog, can't say which caused it."

"How do we fix it?" Tim asked.

"Depends."

"On what?" Droin asked, his voice rising, as his frustration at the non-answers started to turn to full-blown anger.

"If the Black Dog did it, we gotta start there and find out who's behind all of this. We gotta stop it dead."

"Agreed, but how?"

The men turned to Tanya. "It's not me, I swear."

"We know," Tim said, "but let's get together one more time, because we need ideas and I'm hoping you have some for us. If it is a witch and these are spells that she's using, maybe you can reverse them or stop them or something."

"I don't know, Tim. This is big-ass magic, black magic, which I never get involved with."

"Come on, let's get out of here, there isn't room enough for all of us and I can't stand feeling so crowded. Droin are you going to stay here?"

"For a bit, just to see what Doc has to say and make sure Wanda is comfortable."

"Emma, you coming?"

She glanced back towards Scott's room, feeling the ring box in her pocket, and said, "Give me a minute."

She ran into the room, slid the box back into his jacket, then looked down at him tenderly before kissing his cheek and whispering in his ear.

"Thank you for the ring, it's magnificent. Wake up soon, we have so many things to talk about and to do in our lives. I love you very much and I need you. Come back to me, Scott."

Emma wiped away an errant tear and, with another quick kiss on his cold lips, she ran out to catch up with the others that were just leaving.

CHAPTER 16

They ran into Caleb outside the Doc's office.

"I just heard about Wanda, what the hell is going on here?" His steely gray eyes were even more intense than usual.

"I don't know, Caleb, but we're running out of time and we need to figure out what we're doing."

"I know, Leona's condition hasn't changed at all and I'm getting very worried about her ever being able to snap out of it."

"What do you mean?" Tanya asked.

"They can't break the fever for very long periods of time, it's going to start having permanent consequences if it keeps up."

Tanya wrapped her arm around his waist and rested her head against his chest. He draped his around her and they both held tight to each other, trying not to cry.

"Let's get busy then," he stated gruffly, unwrapping her arm and stepping back. "Come on over to the house where we can talk."

"I'm going to run to the hotel first and check out Bobby's room, and the other two weasels', as well, just in case. I assume all of you heard about my little set-to with Bobby and his goons?"

Caleb nodded. "I ran into Seavey when he was getting ready to take them to the authorities in town."

"Snake was filling Droin and me in when Wanda had her attack. What do you make of it, Tim?"

"In all honesty, Matt, I don't think Bobby has the smarts or the patience to pull this off, but I'll double-check their rooms to make sure there isn't anything to indicate otherwise."

"I'll come with you."

"Alright, Tim, Matt, we'll catch up with you over at the house."

The rest of them headed down Diversion Street to Caleb and Leona's home. There was no further conversation until they arrived at the house and made themselves comfortable.

Emma and Tanya went directly to the kitchen and once Tim and Matt arrived and they were all settled in, sipping the freshly made coffee, the questions started.

"You boys find anything?"

"Not a thing," Tim replied. "I'm fairly comfortable believing they don't have anything to do with the Black Dog nonsense."

Matt nodded his agreement.

"Tanya, do you believe this could all be done with spell work?" Tim asked.

"Of course, it could, anything can be done with spells. It's just that I'm not familiar with any that powerful."

"I had a package overnighted to me here and I forgot to check on it. I'm going to run over to the hotel and see if it's arrived yet. I have to find Theo, too, and then I'll be back. Let's keep whatever we learn here today between ourselves, alright? I'm not sure who we can trust anymore."

"Sure," Caleb agreed, "we understand. A lot of folks have headed out already, but there are still pockets of them hanging around."

Tim strode out of the house and the four that remained, Caleb, Matt, Emma and Tanya just looked at each other, not quite sure what they should be doing now.

"Tanya," Emma asked hesitantly, trying not to sound insulting with her questions, but curiosity was getting the best of her, "if there was another witch here, would you be able to tell?"

Emma ignored the scathing look she was given and waited for an answer.

"Do you think we're something other than human? That we're wearing masks or something and only we can see each other's true face?" Tanya's voice dripped sarcasm.

Emma chose to ignore it. "Of course not, I just don't know anything about witches and thought I'd ask. I didn't realize there were so many of them in the world."

"Well, there are, all different kinds, male and female. It's a vocation, not a condition. Some people are born into it and have a natural talent, but most have to train for years before being able to do the simplest spells correctly."

"Do you know many others?"

"Of course, I do, why?"

"Would they be able to help, maybe have some black magic up their sleeves, so to speak?" Caleb asked.

"I'm not sure, I could make some calls, but I can't promise anything."

"Don't you have to figure out who's doing it before you can try and fix it?" Emma asked, feeling like they were just talking in circles and getting nowhere fast.

"I think Emma's got the right idea," Matt finally chimed in. "I know a little about hoodoo and it's most always personal, most always 'cause someone got hurt and then got angry. I think we need to split up and travel down both paths, the who and the how to fix it. We need to work faster than we are."

"What do you suggest then?"

"Let's start by trying to figure out who had a bone to pick with the people that saw the dog."

Caleb grabbed a piece of paper and a pen and started listing them one by one. "Leona, Wanda, Brad, Kevin, Meg and Scott."

"What the hell could any of them have in common that would make someone want to hurt them?" Tanya asked.

"Damned if I know," Caleb responded. "Leona doesn't hunt, neither does Wanda. It makes no sense."

"Hi, guys," Emma called out, as Tim, Droin and Theo walked in.

Tim was carrying a large bound book and laid it on the end table next to Caleb's list.

"Oh, my," Tanya said, running her hand gently over the weathered tome, "where did you get this?"

"This Grimoire belonged to a warlock that used to own Emma's old house. He was the person that set the demon free that we had to send back to hell. I've looked through some of it and I think he was into some pretty dark shit, thought maybe you might find something in it that would help."

Tanya couldn't tear her eyes off it, but still seemed afraid to actually open it up. "Why do you carry it around with you?"

"I don't, I had my mom overnight it to us when it started looking like there might be a witch behind this."

"I see, well, if you don't mind, can I take this back to my room and go through it? I need quiet, so I can concentrate."

"Of course, have at it. Let us know as soon as you find something."

She nodded absently and headed for the door. "I will."

After she shut it behind her, Matt felt compelled to ask, "I know we're all friends, but are we one hundred percent sure we can trust that girl? If not, we just gave her the only weapon we might have against her."

"I trust her with my life," Caleb said, his voice rough and deep. "And you can too, I assure you."

"I agree," Tim said. "She's not behind this and might be our only chance of reversing what's happening. What's this list on the table?"

"The people that have seen the Black Dog, we're trying to figure what they could possibly have in common, so we can narrow down who might be after them," Matt responded.

"Leona and Wanda don't fit though, so we can't make any sense out of it. Maybe it doesn't have anything to do with hunting."

"It has to, for all this happen at the Gathering, when so many hunters would be here all together, it just has to."

"You know," Tim said, straining steadfastly at the paper, his brows furrowed as he tried to see the connection, "what if we switch Leona for you, Caleb, and Droin for Wanda. Were all of you on a hunt together at any time?"

"I've never been on a hunt with Meg, barely know her actually. I'm much closer with Liz than I am to her."

"Meg and Liz are lovers, right? How long have they been together?"

"Three, four years, I think."

"Okay, try this for your list: Scott, Kevin, Brad, Liz, Caleb and Droin. Any hunt you can remember with that group?"

"Droin, you and me, we only went on a few hunts together, can you recall one with this group?"

"Just the one, but you were there too, Tim."

Tim looked confused. "When?"

"The night Jason died, the Chupacabra."

"Oh, hell, that's right," Caleb said, his eyes opening wide in remembrance of that evening.

"Who's Jason?" Emma asked.

"One of our friends, you met his girlfriend yesterday, Lisa."

"Could she be the witch? She's very fake and I don't think she really likes anyone here, even though she pretends that she does," Emma added.

The men at looked at each other, their eyes filled with doubt.

"If she is, Jason never told us, or maybe he didn't even know, for that matter," Caleb said.

"You know," Tim said thoughtfully, "I never understood what he saw in her, creeps me out to think of it, but what if she worked some spell on him to begin with?"

"A love spell?" Droin asked, disgust evident in his voice.

"Yeah, if she is a witch and powerful enough to pull this shit off, that would have been a piece of cake for her. Poor Jason."

"We don't know that for sure," Caleb said, still trying to wrap his head around the fact that Lisa could be their foe. "She seems harmless enough, really nothing more than an annoying me monster. I would be mighty surprised if it's her but, how are we going to confirm it one way or the other?"

"Is she still even here?" Theo asked, she'd been quiet for most of the conversation, but had been following it closely, for reasons that none of them needed to know.

"Yes, I saw her in the hotel lobby a little while ago. But, if it is her and she's doing this because Jason died, why not me? Why am I the only one that hasn't seen the damn thing?"

"Well, neither Droin nor I saw it either, maybe she didn't care if it got us or our wives, we would be paying one way or the other. Maybe she flipped a coin between you and Scott, and he lost."

"Let's see what Tanya comes up with and then we'll figure out what we do about Lisa Lonegan." Caleb's voice was low and held a very definite threat in it.

*　　　*　　　*

"Come on, Emma, let's go check on Scott. Do you guys want to meet up later? We can find out what Tanya comes up with then."

"Alright," Caleb said, "let's meet at the bar in the hotel in an hour or so. I'll go pick up Tanya then and, hopefully, she will have found something helpful."

"Theo, you good?"

"Of course, I think I can take care of myself for a little while."

Tim gave her a brief smile and left with Emma. Droin accompanied them so he could check on his own wife and Matt made his way to the hotel. Theo stayed back with Caleb and gave him some support while he let his worry about his wife ooze out.

Tim and Emma did not spend very long at the Infirmary. There was no change in Scott's condition, or Wanda's for that matter, and the doctor looked exhausted and very frustrated.

"I have Wanda heavily sedated, but I don't know what the hell to do for either of them anymore. I am going to have to call back the emergency chopper soon if things don't change. If they both keep deteriorating like this, we're going to lose them."

Emma choked back her tears and asked Tim if she could have a moment alone with Scott.

"Sure." Tim stayed with Doc Higgins and they chatted quietly in his office while Emma made her way to Scott's side.

"Scott," Emma whispered, her lips so close they almost touched his ear, "fight this, I need you, we have something very important that's going to be coming into our lives and we both have to be there for it. Fight this, damn you, some stupid witch put it in you, and you have to hang on until we figure it out and reverse it.

Please, Scott, I need you, we need you, and you just have to stay strong a little bit longer. I do have faith Scott, faith in you and faith in us and I know you'll come back to me."

She grabbed his hand and almost burst into tears when it flopped lifelessly away from her. As Emma stared down into his handsome face, she whispered a prayer of desperation, "Please God, watch over him and bring him back to me in one piece. Please let that be soon, because I can't take this much longer."

After kissing him lightly on the cheek she turned and walked out of the room. Emma could hardly bear to leave him, but she couldn't be of any help here, so she trudged out of the room with her head hanging low.

Droin had just come out of Wanda's room and they gave each other a sad smile and a hug, there were no words to express the depth of their frustrated torment.

The three of them left a few minutes later and headed over to the bar in the hotel. Tim hesitated when he opened the door for Emma and saw Lisa heading in ahead of them.

"Listen, you two," he said, his voice low, "we don't know anything yet, so don't attack her, don't accuse her, don't let on that we suspect her at all. If it is her, that will give it away and everyone will be in even greater danger."

Emma nodded her understanding and walked with the men into the bar.

"What can I get you, Emma?" Tim asked.

"Just a cup of tea, if that's possible."

The bartender nodded and walked around the bar and out to the front desk where he whispered in the receptionist's ear. She called over to the kitchen and when the bartender returned, he let Emma know her tea would be served shortly.

Emma jumped when she heard Lisa's throaty voice right beside her.

"You are in a family way, aren't you?" she asked, sounding surprised.

"What, stop that!" Lisa's hand had made its way to her belly and she started rubbing it in a circle, until Emma swatted it away.

Lisa put both hands up in surrender. "I'm sorry, didn't mean to get personal, is it a big secret or something?"

"What's she talking about, Emma?" Tim asked.

"I don't know how she knows, but I think I might be pregnant. Are you okay?"

Tim's face blanched and he sat down quickly on a nearby barstool.

"Tim what's the matter? You're scaring me."

"Does Scott know?"

"I found out after we got here. Scott got sick before I could tell him anything."

Tim stood back up, closed the ground between them and gave Emma a heartfelt hug. "I'm very happy for you, holy shit, Scott's gonna be out of his head when he finds out."

"If he finds out," Lisa interjected sadly, and Tim deftly moved in between her and Emma. If she was the witch, he couldn't take a chance of her harming Emma or the baby.

Emma narrowed her eyes at the other woman but didn't give Lisa the satisfaction of seeing how much her nasty comment had upset her.

"Oh, he will, I have no doubt of that."

"You don't even know what's wrong with him, do you?"

"He's in good hands."

"So, they got him out in time on that damn chopper, did they? It has been showing up here pretty frequently, hasn't it? Scary times."

"That chopper's been here more than we'd like, of course," Caleb said, as he and Tanya joined the group, "but thank God for it, and for how quickly it can get here to help those that need it."

Some nodded their heads in agreement with Caleb's statement, but none of them corrected Lisa's assumption that Scott had been taken to the hospital in town. It seemed safer to keep her in the dark as much as possible.

"Caleb, I'm glad you're here. I'll probably be heading out first thing in the morning and I wanted to thank you for all the hospitality. You've been a wonderful host, even with all these dismaying events. Especially with what's happening to your own dear wife, I certainly hope she recovers soon, it must be killing you inside."

Their eyes met and there was the oddest tension in the air surrounding them.

Caleb extended his hand towards her. "I certainly hope you'll come back again next year. I think I can promise a calmer and safer Gathering next time."

"Unfortunately, I think my time with all of you is done."

"What do you mean?" Droin asked.

"I've really appreciated everyone being so accepting and tolerant of me, but I can tell that I'm beginning to wear on some people, so this will probably be my last Gathering. I wish you all a long and happy life."

"Thanks, Lisa, we wish the same for you." The dishonest words did not flow as easily from Tim's lips as they did from hers, but he managed to make them sound almost sincere.

They watched her walk out of the bar and head towards the stairs. There were just a few hunters left at the bar, but the group was paranoid about anyone overhearing their conversation. Grabbing their drinks, they moved to a large table in the back, well away from the others.

"What did you make of that, Tim? Droin?"

"Total bullshit, now I do tend to think she's the responsible person. She gave me the willies for some reason."

"Same here," Droin responded, twirling the tips of his handlebar mustache viciously. "And it's quite curious that she doesn't feel the need to come to any more Gatherings, almost like her mission has been accomplished and she's done with us."

"I knew she could talk a donkey's hind leg off, but I just thought it was harmless jabbering. I never would have thought she could be at all devious."

"What are you guys spouting off about?" Theo asked, pulling up a chair next to Tim.

"We just had a kind of bizarre conversation with Lisa. She's leaving tomorrow and won't be back."

"Good riddance," Theo said, "she's a two-faced bitch."

"I know, right? I kept trying to tell Scott and Tim that, but they didn't believe me."

"She tells those god-awful stories about herself and her family and thinks they are so entertaining. I thought she was just boring but harmless. Until now, anyway."

Chapter 17

"Please, tell me everything about what happened with Jason," Emma asked. "Maybe it will help us figure some things out."

"I remember that it all started the last night of the Gathering," Tim began. "It was two years ago, right?"

At the nods of consent, he continued. "We were sitting around talking about what we'd been running into recently, where we heading to when we left, that kind of stuff. Then Jason mentioned a friend of his down along the Mexican border that was having some kind of problem."

"That's right," Caleb interjected, "it was Jason that brought it up. Supposedly, something was killing their animals, it started with chickens and goats and then moved on to bigger animals, and by then a young child had also gone missing."

"Yes, and we all threw out ideas and came to the conclusion it was probably a Chupacabra."

"I'm sorry, but I have no idea what that is," Emma said, genuinely confused.

"It's an ugly, little bastard," Caleb replied, his gray eyes looked as though they had hardened into slabs of concrete.

"That it is," Tim agreed. "It's about the size of a small bear but much thinner. It has no hair, but a mouthful of razor-sharp teeth and two extended canines. It has three sharp claws on its front and back feet and can shred its victim if it chooses. It seems to prefer to just subdue them and use those canine teeth to make puncture wounds, then it drains the victim dry of blood."

"That's disgusting," Emma said, her stomach roiling at the thought of it. "But, what exactly are they?"

"No one is sure," Caleb replied, his voice lower and more gravelly than normal.

"Some people think they got left behind by aliens because they have a large oval head and big buggy eyes." He laughed harshly. "And, of course, there are the conspiracy theories about the government finding these alien creatures and cross-breeding them with our animals. We only hear of them rarely, so the word is that those are the ones that have escaped the government facilities."

"Others think they are just dogs or coyotes with a severe case of the mange, even though that doesn't explain why they suck the blood out of their kills. Anyway, we know better," Tim added.

"How?"

"Because Scott and I killed it and cut its freaking head off."

"Oh," Emma said, not sure what an appropriate response would be to that particular comment.

Theo was getting restless, she stood up and walked over to stare out the window. "Who went and why wasn't I invited?"

"I'm pretty sure you were having a baby right about then, weren't you?"

"Damn, that's right, how'd I forget that?"

Emma wasn't sure she heard right and couldn't take her eyes off Theo, unable to picture her pregnant or as a mother.

"As far as who was there, it was me and Scott, Caleb and Liz, Kevin, Brad and Jason."

"Don't forget Droin, remember he'd never been on a hunt that far south and thought it would be an interesting change."

"That's right, I was with Jason when it happened."

"Yes, I almost forgot that. We all paired up that night," Tim explained to the two women, "and headed to different areas on the outskirts of town that hadn't been attacked yet. If anyone noticed anything, they were supposed to let the rest of us know."

"Jason shot us a group text, the creature was hitting a farm on the south side of the town," Caleb continued, his voice beginning to sound angry. "I responded that we all needed to meet up and go out there together, but that damned Kevin had to be a hero, and texted back something stupid, like 'see you there, losers'. He always had to try and be the biggest toad in the puddle and we had no choice but to all jump in our vehicles and head over their PDQ."

"Liz jumped in the truck with me and we lit out. Kevin got there first, the creature was in one of the fields, hitting on some cattle. Kevin drove straight out into the field after it, hit a rock or something and came to a dead stop."

"Brad was in the bed of the truck and could see it in the moonlight, so he tried shooting it with his 'lucky rifle'. Another damn fool," Caleb mumbled.

"I take it he missed?"

"There was no way in hell he was going to hit that thing. It runs on two legs, and its fast. Besides that, there was panicky cattle milling all around blocking his view. It was stupid and it just scared the thing away," Tim added.

"We arrived at the farm just a few minutes after Droin and Jason," Caleb said, picking up the story again. "They were over at the barn already and yelled to us they were going in to check it out. We didn't know what the deal was with Brad and Kevin at that point, but we heard the gun shots and figured it was coming our way."

"Liz lit a torch and was standing between the house and that field, trying to keep it from getting at the farmer's family. Every animal is scared of fire, but this one wasn't."

"I was at the truck, loading a couple of firearms when she yelled to me. By the time I got over there, the thing was running straight towards her. I shot at it twice, but by then it was too close to her and I couldn't take a chance. Liz threw the torch at the thing and it veered away, heading straight towards the barn. She screamed to the guys inside that it was coming."

"We heard her yell." It was Droin's turn to tell the tale now and he spoke quietly as the memories returned. "I was climbing up to the hay mow, to get a better vantage point, when it ran into the barn.

The damn thing was fast, faster than we had anticipated, and it was on Jason in seconds, he didn't even have time to raise his rifle, let alone get a shot off. I was halfway up the ladder and couldn't use my gun. The bastard wasn't wasting any time sucking Jason's blood, it was just tearing that poor boy to shreds. Those screams will echo in my head till the day I die."

He stopped talking and stared down at the table, trying to get the sights and sounds of those memories out of his mind.

Tim clasped him on the shoulder and handed him a beer. "I'll finish it."

Droin nodded his thanks and walked away to a chair in the far corner, where he could be alone with his thoughts.

"Scott and I had been at a place outside the opposite part of town and we got there just as it was attacking Jason. We came in through the other end of the barn and couldn't shoot it because it was right on Jason. I grabbed a two by four and smashed it against the creature's body until it fell off of him.

"Scott shot at it until his clip was empty, then he cut its damn head off, just to be sure it was really dead."

There was complete silence for a few minutes as the five of them dealt with the memories and accompanying emotions that story had stirred up within them.

"So," Emma began, "is Lisa is punishing all of you that were there because you didn't save Jason?"

"Looks like it and she's punishing us by making us lose someone we love, so we can feel the same pain that she did."

"I think," Theo added, sitting back down at the table, "that she is also making a statement about how they let Jason down, with the manner in which she is hurting them."

"What do you mean?" Caleb asked.

"The most obvious is Liz using the fire to deter the creature, which didn't work, and the woman she loves inexplicably falls into a raging fire and has burns over a large part of her body."

"Kevin was being impetuous," Caleb added, nodding in agreement with her theory, "and didn't wait for the rest of us that night. He died being impetuous and rushing up into the mountains by himself."

"And Brad couldn't hit it with his lucky rifle, and that same 'lucky rifle' exploded and killed him," Tim added.

"What about Wanda?"

Emma was thinking out loud and didn't see the anger building on Droin's face when she spoke.

"Droin was heading up into the hay mow to get a better angle. Could Lisa think that he was afraid and that's why he didn't stay down on the main floor with Jason?"

"I wasn't afraid," Droin stated indignantly. "One of us had to go up, one had to stay down."

"I didn't mean that I thought you were afraid, but I'm wondering if that could be Lisa's take on it. I only bring it up because she gave Wanda the ghost sickness, which revolves around fear, right?" Emma asked, turning towards Theo.

"Yes, it does, and I suppose that could be her way of interpreting what went on."

"It makes sense, but what about my Leona? How can an infected tooth be equated with any of this?"

"It's not just an infected tooth, Caleb," Theo replied gently. "It's sepsis, and it's a slow death if it isn't treated properly."

"Which hers is," she added quickly, when he turned angry eyes upon her.

"But, again, how does that fit?"

"Maybe you were a little slow getting over to the creature?"

"It couldn't be helped, I needed more weapons."

"We know that," Theo assured him. "Remember, we're just trying to figure out what Lisa is thinking and how she might interpret what happened. She's warped, so don't get all pissed off at me about it."

"Right," he replied, turning away and grabbing his bottle of beer, downing it in one swig.

"Which leaves us with Scott," Tim said. "We were the last ones there because we were so far away. Putting him in a coma like she did, all I can think is he was 'sleeping on the job', or something to that effect."

"Most likely it is something along those lines."

"But," Tim asked the question they were all thinking, "why not me? Why every other person that was there that night, but not me?"

"And why not me, instead of Scott?" Emma asked.

"That's probably the easier question," Theo replied. "No one knew about you or that you would be here. If Lisa was preparing things in advance, which I believe she had to have done, she couldn't have anything for you."

"That still doesn't explain me," Tim said. "Brad and Kevin didn't have a significant other and they had to pay the price themselves. So why not me?"

"Have you had any contact directly with Lisa?"

"Plenty, big hugs every time I see her," he replied, distaste at the thought of it evident on his face.

Theo was frowning in concentration as she stared hard at Tim. "Can we go to your room?"

"Right now?" Tim asked.

She sighed in exasperation. "Not for that, I think she may have planted a mojo bag, probably one for everyone she put spells on."

"What's a mojo bag?" Emma asked.

"Hex bag, gris gris bag, conjure bag, there many different names for them, they contain a bunch of different items, depending on the purpose of the bag and the spells they're used for. If she planted the mojo bags that would explain how the particular types of incidents are occurring."

"So, if there is one in Tim's room, then why didn't it affect him?" Caleb asked doubtfully.

Tim smiled and shrugged. "I haven't been in my room since the first day, I've been staying with a friend."

"You, dog," Droin said, a leering grin appearing on his face, the tips of his mustache almost vibrating. "I guess that would explain it, let's go take a look."

Caleb chose to wait back at the bar for them. As they wandered out into the Lobby, Emma remembered the two employees that died before any of them arrived and asked Tim and Theo about that.

"I really don't know, they weren't hunters and had nothing to do with the Chupacabra hunt."

"Could she have been practicing?" Emma asked.

"Could be, she may have just managed to harness the Black Dog's power and wanted to be sure she could control it before going after her real targets."

"Or they could have been honest to goodness accidents, but I don't put much faith in coincidences," Tim replied, as they headed over to the stairs.

"Let's grab Tanya first. These things belong in her world and I'd feel better if she was with us. She'll know best what we should do with them if we do find them."

Once Tanya joined their little group, it didn't take long for them to find the mojo bag which was hidden under Tim's mattress.

Tanya grabbed it, rolled it in both hands and stuck it in her pocket.

"Can it still hurt Tim?" Emma asked nervously.

"No," she replied, "once someone else, other than the conjurer, touches the mojo bag, it negates the spell."

"So, if we find Scott's, he'll wake up?"

"Not necessarily," Tanya replied cautiously. "It stops the spell, but it doesn't reverse what has already taken place. We definitely have to find all six of the others to stop anything more from happening. Then we have to figure out what we do next to reverse the spells."

Emma felt deflated, her hopes had swelled at the thought of being able to help Scott, but now she felt as bitterly disappointed as the look on Tim's face showed that he was.

*   *   *

They left as a group and headed to Emma and Scott's room. It took a few minutes, but they found the mojo bag in a pocket of his essentials kit.

Caleb had a pass key that he provided to them and it was fairly simple to find the bags in Brad and Shawn's rooms. Both were just placed between the mattress and box springs, the same way that Tim's had been.

Liz was at the hospital with Meg and it was a little more difficult to find the one for Meg because they didn't know which items belonged to Meg and which ones to Liz. If they weren't sure, how would Lisa have known?

"The glasses," Droin said. "Meg wore different colored glasses with each of her outfits, find them and you'll find Meg's other stuff."

They felt awkward going through the women's items, but finally Theo held up the little bag in triumph. It had been slid into the back of a small upper drawer that was filled with multi-colored glasses and jewelry.

Droin preferred to go through his wife's things by himself and they agreed to meet up back at Caleb's house. That was another difficult hex bag to find, because Lisa would have had to make sure Caleb wasn't affected by it. They eventually found it nestled in a drawer of Leona's desk where she did the bookwork for the park.

Droin arrived a few minutes later and tossed a hex bag at Tanya. She made sure to take each of the bags and roll them slowly between both of her hands.

"Hopefully, whatever damage is being done will stop now," Tanya said. "But the spells have to be reversed before we can get our loved ones back safely."

"How do we do that?" Emma asked.

"First off, that's one hell of a Grimoire you guys have. I found a really powerful reversal spell that might work and I also think I found the spell she might have been using, or least something similar, to get control of that Black Dog. It called for a specific ceremony to be done and some despicable items to be used. I believe as long as those items remain within the circle where she did the spell, the dog is under her control. I'm not sure how that affects anything, but I'd rather not try the reversal spell until we are certain the Black Dog won't interfere, or I could end up making things worse."

"How do we find out where that was?"

Tanya shrugged. "I don't know."

"We are definitely going to have to stop her from leaving tomorrow."

"Are there actual cells in that jail?" Tim asked.

"None that lock, they're just for show."

"So, what do we do with her?"

"Well, she can't leave until I make the arrangements to get her back to the parking area and her car, so I think we're okay for tonight. Why don't we all get some rest, you in particular, Emma," he said with a weary smile, "and meet up again first thing in the morning and we'll confront Lisa."

"Sounds like a plan," Tim said, as Droin left hurriedly to return to the infirmary and check on Wanda.

CHAPTER 18

Emma stepped outside and saw Theo standing off to the side of the house, pulling out a pack of cigarettes and her lighter.

She dropped the lighter and swore. Emma stared curiously at the tramp stamp displayed on her lower back when she bent over to pick it up.

"You like?" Theo asked, as she stood up and realized what Emma had been looking at. Flicking open her lighter, she watched the tobacco flame to life and inhaled deeply.

"What is it? A dinosaur?"

"A Velociraptor carrying an M16. Trust me, it puts the whole world in perspective for some people."

"I see," Emma replied, although she really didn't.

"So, what's up? Other than the obvious?"

"I was just curious about something."

"What?"

"Do you really have a baby?"

"You ask that like you can't quite believe it's possible. But, yes, I do. Why?"

"Well, I, it's just,"

"For God's sake, spit it out. You don't think someone like me is fit to be a mother, is that it?" Both her tone and her eyes hardened as she stared down at Emma. She was a very confident woman in all aspects of her life, except this one where she was most vulnerable and, therefore, the most dangerous.

"No, that's not it," Emma replied, her own voice hardening in frustration. Theo could be overbearing and intimidating, but Emma was sick of being talked to and treated like a child.

"I really don't need your attitude and I don't need you putting words in my mouth. I was simply curious about how you keep hunting when you have a child at home. It must be difficult."

Theo's face softened momentarily as she thought about her daughter and realized that Emma was not questioning her ability to be a mother.

"I don't hunt as much as I used to, but I'm not going to give it up completely. I have family and I have babysitters that can watch Christa for me when I have to go out of town, but I do miss her like crazy when we're apart."

"Why do you keep hunting then?"

"I had a baby, I didn't die for cripe's sake. Why would I give up what I love, what gives my life meaning, just because I had a kid? It would only make me resent her. Wait a minute, you have kids, don't you?"

"Yes," Emma replied proudly, "a girl and two boys."

"You didn't stop living when you had them, did you?"

"I kind of did, that's why I was curious about how you do it. How do you support yourself, anyway? If you don't mind my asking."

"I'm a hairdresser. I rent out space with some other women and can make my own schedule. What did you do before you had kids?"

"I was an Interior Decorator."

"That's sounds scintillating," Theo said, obviously not impressed.

"It's what I liked to do, sorry if it doesn't meet your standards."

"You must not have liked it all that much, if you gave it up just because you had kids."

"I did, though, I loved it. My husband thought it would be best for our children if I stayed home with them. I think it was more of a status thing for him."

"And you didn't mind giving up your own dreams to make him happy?"

"Not in the beginning. When the kids were young, I was so busy with them that I didn't have time to think about it. As they got older, I started realizing that I had no life of my own, that everything revolved around my children and my husband."

"And how did that end up working out for you?" Theo asked, with a sly smile. She took one last drag of the cigarette and flicked the butt off into the cobblestone street.

Emma ignored her question and returned with another one of her own. "But what you do is dangerous, doesn't that make you think twice before going out on a job?"

"Do you hear about many policewomen or firewomen who quit their jobs because they have kids? How about female soldiers? I don't think so. We do what we have to do, if we didn't have the cojones to do the job to begin with, we wouldn't have signed up.

And we sure as hell wouldn't be setting much of an example for our daughters if we gave up helping others and doing what we love because we're mommies now, and suddenly it's too scary."

Emma narrowed her eyes and bit the inside of her lip. She wasn't sure if she was annoyed by the condescension in Theo's voice, or the fact that Theo actually made a very good argument.

"Is Tim the father?" Emma received a scathing look from Theo but didn't care, her curiosity was killing her on that particular issue.

"That's really none of your business, but no, he's not and yes, he knows he's not. And we are all good with the whole situation. Here he comes now, I'll catch you later."

Theo hurried over to Tim, who had just exited Caleb's house, and the two of them headed off towards the hotel.

Emma watched them go and turned to find Tanya at her elbow, catching her by surprise.

Tanya drew in a deep breath and released it slowly.

"Would you mind walking with me for a few minutes, since we have some time alone."

At first Emma was a little suspicious, but tried to reconcile the fact that Scott, Tim and Caleb all trusted this woman, so she was going to have to, as well.

"Okay, but why?"

They turned the opposite way from the hotel and walked towards the water tower at the end of the street.

"I wanted to congratulate you," Tanya said hesitantly.

"For what?"

"The baby." Tanya had a hard time getting the words out of her mouth. First the ring, now this, Tanya felt like she was in a heavyweight boxing match and the hits just kept on coming.

"Word gets around fast in our little world," she added, in response to the look Emma threw at her.

"Well, I'm not positive about it yet, but it wouldn't be my first and I am pretty sure."

"Does Scott know?"

"Not yet."

"I just wanted you to know that I have always cared a great deal for him, but I know when the game is up, and I don't want you to worry about me."

Emma smiled to herself. "What makes you think I am worried about you?"

Tanya felt the sting of that insult and stopped to face Emma head on. "Don't be a bitch, I appreciate your trust in me with all that's going on and I want you to know that you can also trust me as far as Scott is concerned."

"Tanya, I respect that, but you and I, we aren't ever going to be best buddies. I just don't see that happening. Right now, we need to work together to help all of these people. Scott and Tim appreciate and respect you, so I will, too. Unless and until you show me a reason why I shouldn't.

I'm glad that we don't have to feel all awkward around each other, but I am not jealous of you, I am not worried about you stealing Scott away from me. He and I have something real, something that can't be broken by the past. So, you have nothing to worry about on that front. And I'm not being a bitch, I'm telling you the way that it is."

Tanya's brows came together in an almost frightening manner, changing the whole look of her face in the evening shadows. They were at the end of the street and made the turn to walk back towards the hotel.

Tanya was trying to decide how she would respond. She was not used to being talked to in that manner and was not happy about what Emma said or the way she said it. Tanya was just preparing to give her a piece of her mind when Emma stopped short and grabbed her arm.

"What?" She asked irritably, yanking her arm out of Emma's grasp.

"Look up there, do you see it?"

Emma was pointing up the hillside, towards the mine.

Tanya stared for a moment, then whispered. "I see it. Who do you think it is?"

"I have no idea," Emma replied, watching the lantern bob along up the hill.

"Should we go check it out?"

"I'm not sure if that's a good idea. I suppose we could go get Tim to come along."

"Do you think you could find that same spot tomorrow in the daylight?"

Emma looked around getting her bearings. "Yes, I think so, why?"

"Why don't we keep this to ourselves and get up super early, daybreak early, and sneak up there to see what we find."

"Without telling anyone else?"

"For now, if we find something, we'll share it with the others. Sorry, I just get tired of the 'menfolk' always coming to our rescue. I'd like to be the one who solves this particular mystery. What do you say?"

Emma looked at her curiously and decided to go along with it, partially because she would like to be the hero that saved Scott's life and, also because she really didn't want to go trekking up that mountain in the dark, even if Tim was with them.

"I'm game," she said, heading back to the hotel. "I'll meet you right at daylight tomorrow. Don't be late, I won't wait around for you."

"The hell with you," Tanya said, but she gave Emma a twisted smile as she spoke, feeling quite excited about their upcoming morning adventure.

*   *   *

Tim was in the process of unbuckling his belt so that he could drop his pants and crawl into Theo's bed, but she put her hand on his arm to halt his movements.

"What's the matter?" he asked, baffled by the expression on her face.

"Sit with me for a minute," she said, lowering herself onto the bed and turning her body towards him, hoping she wasn't going to regret what she was about to do.

Tim sat down beside her and waited patiently, he could see that something important was weighing on her.

"Tim, I really like being fuck-buddies with you, you know that, right?"

He smiled. "Is that what we are?"

"Apparently, since we never see each other for any other reason."

"Theo, I like being with you, we have fun together, we have a few laughs, we understand each other's lifestyle. Is there something wrong with what we share?" He didn't like the direction this little chat was taking.

"Not wrong," she said, searching for the words to explain how she felt. "A couple of things have really hit home with me with all that's happened these past few days. The first is all this talk about Jason."

"I was wondering how you were doing with that."

Theo blew out a long breath. "I did love him, you know, just not in a 'can't live without him' way. I was actually relieved when he hooked up with Lisa."

"He never knew about Christa, did he?"

"No, he didn't. I was still trying to figure out how to handle that particular conversation when he died. Now my baby will never know her father. And he really was a stand-up guy, he would have been a good dad to her."

Tim reached out and took Theo's hand in his. There wasn't much that could be said in response to that. "And what are the other things that are weighing on you?"

"Bottom line is that I never want to show up at the Gathering and find you here with another woman. Not just another woman, but the love of your life, the one you've been holding out for all this time."

"What are you talking about? I don't understand."

"I can't help but look at Tanya and see myself, maybe next year, maybe the year after that, but it will happen, it's inevitable. When it does, when you finally do find the right woman and I have to watch you with her, I'm going to feel lost and deserted, just like Tanya does right now."

"Well, that's not fair," Tim replied. "Not for Scott or for me, he never made Tanya any promises and I've never made any to you, or you to me. We have a good time together, are you saying that you want something more than that?"

"I know you've never lied to me or promised anything other than what we have, and don't get me wrong, I think I carry love for you in my heart, but I don't love you so much that I want a future with you, at least I don't think so."

Tim shook his head in frustration. "I honestly don't know what you are trying to say or what you want."

"I guess, I don't know myself," she said with a little laugh, staring at the floor, unable to meet is eyes.

"I suppose I always thought this would continue indefinitely, just like it is, and that was okay. I do like being with you and when we're here, there's no questions, we're together and we enjoy ourselves."

"Why do you think that's going to end?"

"Because of Scott and Emma."

"But we're not them."

"I know that, but Tanya and Scott were tight, tighter than we are, I think, and they seemed to have a similar arrangement to ours. A casual, yet passionate friendship. I know Tanya pretty well and seeing Scott show up with Emma tore her up. She never expected it, had no warning, and it hit her hard. I think it made her realize how much she cared for Scott."

"But, again, that's their problem. If she cared for Scott, she should have made that clear a long time ago."

"And that's what I'm trying to do right now, before the same thing happens to me. I want to end this between us, hopefully, in a cordial manner, so we can still be friends. But I don't want to be with you ever again. I don't want to give you any more of my heart than you already have."

"Do you want something more formal, more permanent between us, is that what you are saying?"

"No, if there was going to be something real between us, that would have happened a long time ago. Obviously, both of us can easily get by for long periods of time without seeing each other. I think that if we truly loved one another, we wouldn't want those long, lonely stretches in between."

"I suppose that I should count myself lucky, because even Lisa could tell that there was nothing deep between us. If she did, I'd be over in the infirmary with your brother right now."

"What has that got to do with what we do have? Why not just keep doing things the way we have been? I don't get it."

"Use your head, stupid. You will find someone, you are an amazing, kind, strong, handsome guy and she's out there just waiting for you. I don't want to get blind-sided like Tanya did and start having second thoughts about the time we've shared. I'm not your soul-mate, but I know she is out there somewhere, and I just don't want to get hurt when you two finally find each other."

For being such a confident woman, Theo was finding this one of the most difficult conversations she'd ever had and now just wanted it over with.

"If we let it go now, we're on even ground and we're both okay. It might even make us grow up a little and start looking closer for the right person for ourselves. I don't generally bother because I know I can have a little fling with you whenever I want, and not have to put in the requisite emotions or the damn social skills that I would need to use if I was trying to develop an actual relationship.

I think I owe that to my daughter. I need to grow up, be a little less selfish and put her future first. She's still a baby but, if I play my cards right, maybe I can provide her with a daddy, after all."

Tim wrapped his arm around Theo and pulled her up against his body. He liked the feel of her, he liked her honesty and he liked spending time with her, but he also knew that she was right.

Theo was not the woman he was going to share the rest of his life with. Seeing how happy Scott and Emma were together, it sometimes made him a little wistful, like he was missing out on something important. When those thoughts washed over him, Theo never came to mind, so he did understand exactly what she was saying, as much as he pretended that he didn't.

Tim kissed the top of her head and stood up. "Theo, you're a great woman and you will always be in my heart. I will still be there for you if you ever need me, but I understand and will respect your decision."

She stood up next to him, shaking her head in wonder and trying to control the tremor in her lips as she tried not to cry.

"Go now," she whispered, afraid the tears were going to start running down her cheeks, and she would die if Tim saw her cry.

"I'll see you tomorrow." Tim turned and left the room, never hearing the sound of Theo's heart breaking as the door closed tightly behind him.

CHAPTER 19

"Didn't you have any slightly more practical boots than those?" Emma asked irritably. Dawn was just breaking, her coffee hadn't kicked in yet and climbing up these hills was not exactly a fun way to start the day.

"What's wrong with my boots?" Tanya asked.

"Who goes climbing wearing boots with a heel?"

"I do," Tanya replied, feeling a bit surly herself. "What do you care?"

"Well, if you trip and break your neck, I'll have to carry you back. We should have had Tim come with us anyway, since we don't know where we're going or what we're doing."

Tanya stopped and placed her hands on her hips. "Listen, Emma, stop with the whining and stop worrying about me and my attire. Look down at the water tower and you'll see that we are exactly where that lantern was last night."

"Can I ask you a question?"

"About what?" Tanya's tone was still not very hospitable.

Emma stopped and turned towards her, both of them taking a moment to catch their breath.

"Do you ever do anything with ghosts?"

"I'm not sure I understand what you're asking." Tanya said, somewhat confused by the sudden turn in the conversation.

"Have you ever assisted in releasing a ghost, helping them move on?"

"I've done it before, but not very often. Why? Did you meet Sara Mae?" Tanya actually smiled at the thought of the young wraith.

"No, but I did see her spectacular grave marker and, ever since then, I keep thinking about her and wondering why she is still here."

They started walking slowly up the hill again. "I have seen Sara Mae, and she's a sweet, happy little thing."

"So, why is she still here?"

188

"I have no idea, hadn't ever thought about it. It is weird that Caleb lets her stay, he's not particularly fond of spirits, but I think Leona has a bond with her."

"What kind of a bond?"

"Leona spent a lot of time here when she was young, she and Sara Mae used to play together, and I think Leona still visits with her."

Tanya burst out laughing and had to stop walking again. "Oh, my God," she said, "the look on your face is priceless. Have you no clue what goes on in the spirit world or about their interactions with our world?"

"I know very little, actually, and I'm not afraid to admit that. Seriously though, would you help her? Can you find out why Sara Mae is here and help her move on and be with her family?"

Tanya's deep blue eyes met Emma's, which were glittering with unshed tears.

"Why does it mean so much to you?"

"Every child belongs with its family, particularly when they shared so much love, and her family had so little time with her to begin with."

"Maybe."

"Maybe? Come on, if you can do this, promise me that you will. Please."

Tanya didn't answer for a moment as she contemplated how angry Leona would be with her, but then she realized that one day Leona would be gone, as well, and poor little Sara Mae would be left to wander all alone in this cemetery for eternity. Putting it into perspective that way, it didn't matter one whit whether or not Leona got angry at her. Tanya decided that she would do right by Sara Mae, if she was able.

"Fine, I promise that I will, if I can."

"Thank you," Emma replied, and the two of them continued up the steep incline in silence for a few minutes.

"Holy cow, check that out," Tanya said, pointing to a large sign off to the left which read 'DANGER AHEAD' and just below that 'WARNING: ABANDONED AND INACTIVE MINES ARE DEATH TRAPS'.

Emma shuddered. "I hope we aren't supposed to take that as some sort of an omen about what we're walking into."

"Don't be such a sissy. We just have to go up a little higher and I think we'll find what we're looking for."

"Which is what?"

"The sacred space where the original ritual was held. We need to find that and then we can try the reversal spell."

"How will we know when we find it?" Emma asked, her breathing becoming more forced as they continued upward on the steep, rocky trail.

"We'll know, trust me, it will literally be a circle and there will be...."

Tanya's words were cut off when she bumped into Emma, who stopped directly in front of her.

"What the hell?" Tanya asked.

Emma raised her hand, trying to quiet Tanya. At the same time, Tanya could hear a low growl and peered over Emma's shoulder. Directly in front of them was the Black Dog. It was hideous, huge, covered in thick, wiry, black hair, and its head was massive with eyes that seemed to glow a dark reddish color, and which were focused directly on them.

The growl continued to rumble deep in its chest as it took a step forward. Both women stumbled backwards, neither of them taking their eyes off the creature. Now Tanya did regret wearing the boots she had on, as her heel caught a stone and she almost took a tumble.

Regaining her balance, Tanya grabbed Emma's arm and they both turned away from the dog.

"Walk slowly," Emma said. "Whatever you do, do not run."

They could hear its massive paws hitting the ground close behind them, but they continued to make their way down the trail, ignoring their hearts pounding painfully in their chests, trying desperately to not let their fear overwhelm them.

After a few minutes, Emma could no longer hear the low growl or the clatter of small stones being strewn underneath those great paws and she chanced a brief look over her shoulder.

It was no longer following them, but was sitting up above, watching as they made their way down. Never blinking, just staring at the two women, its muscles primed, ready to leap in their direction at any second, if need be.

"You can speed up a little now, Tanya," Emma said, exhaling a deep breath that she hadn't even realized she was holding. "It isn't coming any more, let's get out of here as fast as we can."

The women managed to make it back to town a little bit later and they hurried straight to the hotel to find Tim.

"Isn't he staying with Theo?" Tanya asked, as Emma started up the stairs and down the hall towards his room.

"That's right, where is that?"

"Next floor up, she's just a couple of doors down from me."

It was still quite early, and they had to bang on the door for several minutes before Theo opened it.

"What do you want this freaking early?" She turned around and placed the pistol back on the night stand now that she knew they were not a threat.

"We're sorry, actually we were looking for Tim, did he leave already."

Theo had a strange look on her face when she replied. "He's not here, check his own room or maybe he's already downstairs, he's an early riser."

Emma and Tanya looked at each other, wondering what was going on with these two.

"It's none of your business," Theo stated drily, seeing the curiosity on their faces. "What do you need him for? Did something else happen?"

"Not really," Emma said, "we just wanted to run something by him."

She didn't want to share information with anyone that she didn't have to, feeling suspicious of everyone right now, except, surprisingly enough, Tanya.

"Right," Tanya said, "sorry we woke you, we'll try and track him down. Thanks."

*　　　*　　　*

"But, how will we keep her here?" Tim asked, shoveling a forkful of omelet into his mouth.

"I have cuffs, we could lock her up in one of the rooms with those and see what we can get out of her," Caleb responded.

"Do you think she'll talk? If not, we need to know where she's from and hightail it out of here and check where she might have done these stupid spells. It's like finding a needle in a haystack."

Tim tossed his fork on the plate, unable to finish his meal, feeling frustrated and dispirited.

"Caleb, we are going to have to force her talk, are you up for that? I know I'm really not, but I don't know how else we can save Leona and Scott."

"It isn't something I feel comfortable with, but I feel less comfortable losing my wife because of this bitch, so yeah, I'm up for it."

"We may be able to save you the trouble," Emma said, sliding onto a chair next to Tim while Tanya grabbed the one across the table from her.

"What do you mean?" Tim asked, surprised to see the two of them together when they didn't have to be.

Tanya replied, "We know, at least the general vicinity, where the spellwork was done."

"How'd you manage that?" Caleb asked, looking back and forth between the two women.

"We saw someone with a lantern up near the mine entrance last night and went to check it out this morning."

"You saw it?"

"No," Emma replied. "It's being guarded by that damned Black Dog, so we couldn't get to it."

"Did it hurt you?"

"No," Tanya said, "scared the shit out of us, but that was all. I think it has its orders and can't deviate."

"What do you mean?" Tim asked.

"Somehow," Tanya replied, looking around the room, making sure no one was close enough to hear their conversation, "Lisa has been able to control this hellhound. It is a part of her spell and she must have also manipulated it so that it acts as guardian of her place of worship. Which is what we have to get to in order to reverse the spells."

"So, we have to get rid of the beast first?" Caleb asked.

"Yes, we do."

"How do we do that?" Tim asked.

"I stayed up late last night going through the Grimoire and I found a section that could apply. Again, this is not Lisa's Grimoire, so we don't know exactly what type of black magic she is using, and I can't be a hundred percent sure that what I read will work."

Caleb's eyes were a steely gray this morning, focused and angry.

"Tanya, the hospital called and said I could lose Leona today. I'm not letting that happen, I don't care if there's a ten percent chance, let us know what we have to do, and we'll do it."

Droin and Matt came in right then and they quickly brought the two men up to speed.

"I know the ingredients that I have to have for the reversal spell. I can head into town and get them."

"Wouldn't we have what you need at the Mercantile?"

Tanya laughed out loud. "Black Magic, Caleb, doesn't use condiments. I have some of the items, but not all of them and those others have to be purchased from a special kind of store. It's going to take me probably most of the morning to get there, get what I need, and get back."

"What do we do in the meantime?" Caleb asked, feeling frustrated and impotent.

"Your job is to neutralize that hellhound. If I can't get into the mine where she did the ceremony, I can't reverse the spell. You guys have got to figure out how to deal with that creature while I'm gone."

"And what about Lisa?"

"We need to find her and keep her locked up somewhere, at least for now, until we can get this straightened out. We cannot let her leave like she planned on doing," Tim said emphatically.

"Agreed, Tanya, I'll have Gabriel take you over to your vehicle. We'll split up and look for Lisa and then we can work on the dog angle."

*   *   *

Tanya was completely focused on the items that the spell called for on her drive into town. She found a shop that carried all of the unusual items that she would need, the reversal candles, oils, Galangal Root, Frankincense, Sage and Rue.

"What is Rue generally used for?" Tanya asked.

She had never been to this particular shop before but was impressed by the items that it held. The shopkeeper looked like a bona fide gypsy, she wore a floor length skirt with a shawl wrapped around her sloping shoulders and her long gray hair was bound by a colorful scarf.

"You want it for a spell, why you ask me that?"

"It's the first time I've run across it in a spell, that's why." Tanya replied, raising one eyebrow at the older woman.

She shrugged her slight shoulders, and said, "Usually an antidote for poison. I assume these items are all for big time reversal spell, yes?"

"Yes, how did you know?"

The woman looked at her slyly, the lines around her eyes deepening. "When Rue and crabshell powder are used together, no other purpose for it."

"Why the crabshell powder?'

"Crabs walk backwards, it's used to send something back, to reverse. Very potent when used with Rue."

"You know people that have used these ingredients before?"

The woman nodded slowly.

"Will it work on an extremely powerful spell?"

Again, the old woman shrugged her shoulders. "Can't know that."

"Why?"

"Depends on the strength of the first spell. If any element is not considered in the reversal spell, it won't break it. Can't."

Tanya was thinking over the old lady's words as she hurried back to Windy Shot. She was driving a bit over the speed limit but wasn't worried, there were no other vehicles on the road for long stretches at a time.

Tanya was a very self-confident young woman, however, this was the first spell that had ever made her feel inadequate. It was so important, and it had to be done correctly and completely, or she would make everything worse. She would ultimately be responsible for the deaths of people that she cared for very much, and she wouldn't be able to live with herself if that happened.

"Momma, where are you when I need you?" she asked, raising her eyes towards the sky.

She was about to make a plea to both her mother and grandmother to help her do this right when the steering wheel suddenly turned hard to the right and the gas pedal went down to the floor. The Honda Civic sped up at a terrific rate as it veered off the roadway.

Tanya was powerless to turn the wheel, regardless of how hard she struggled to do so. She didn't even bother trying to do anything with the gas pedal, that was now flush with the floor. She bit back a scream when she saw how fast the vehicle was approaching the rocky hillside just ahead.

Scrambling to let loose her safety belt with shaking fingers, she took a deep breath opened her door and threw herself out of the moving vehicle, rolling and rolling, smashing repeatedly against the ground, which was hard and unforgiving.

She stopped rolling about the time that the car slammed into the rocky bluff, crumpling the hood and leaving nothing between the dashboard and the back seat.

Tanya limped over to what was left of the vehicle, she struggled to open the back door, but it was so badly warped that it was immovable. Searching the area around the car, she grabbed a large rock and shattered the window, then gingerly leaned in to grab her purse and the bag of goodies that she had purchased in town, trying to keep the glass cuts to a minimum.

Feeling every bruise on her body, she wandered over to a small shade tree, sat down heavily underneath it and began rifling through her purse.

"Well, fuck me silly," she mumbled, pulling out a tiny little mojo bag that Lisa must have slipped into it. "Guess that'll teach me to carry such a big purse."

Tanya wasn't scared, she knew Lisa had done this and actually felt stronger than she did before it happened. Lisa had shown her hand, she was afraid that her spell could be broken, and that Tanya was capable of breaking it. She looked up into the blue sky again.

"Thanks, Momma, for keeping me alive and for giving me faith in myself again."

Then Tanya dug through her purse a little more and found her cell phone which, fortunately, still had some bars, and called Theo to come get her. She needed to get back to Windy Shot as soon as possible and get working on the reversal spell.

*   *   *

While Tanya was off shopping for her witchery items and the men split up to try and find Lisa, Emma made her way over to the infirmary.

The IV was still hooked up and the little monitor blipped at regular intervals confirming that Scott's heart was still pumping faithfully, but tears filled her eyes when she saw how gaunt and pale Scott's face was.

Doc Higgins came up behind her and placed his hand gently on her shoulder. She turned and gave him a sad smile. He looked almost as bad as Scott, there were dark circles under his eyes and his face was pale and drawn.

"Physician, heal thyself," Emma said. "I think you better start taking better care of yourself. You look awful."

"Thanks," he replied with a harsh laugh. "You know, I worked at an ER in Chicago for several years and that's one of the reasons that I took this gig. It was brutal, gunshot victims, child abuse victims, horrendous car accidents, and there weren't many nights that we made it through without losing at least one person."

He paused for moment, lost in his memories.

"I had to dig deep to not feel responsible for those that we lost, but I felt inept, incapable. It was my job to save people, but there were too many of them and they were too far gone by the time they were brought to us. After awhile, I just couldn't do it anymore, it was destroying me. So, I left."

Emma listened quietly, not sure where this was going, but fairly confident that it was probably leading to something that she wasn't going to want to hear.

"I'd met Caleb while I was working there, you don't even want to know that situation but, anyway, when I found out he owned this place I came and checked it out. They were just getting it up and running and needed some type of medical facility in order to get their license. The timing was perfect, and it was just what I needed, bumps, bruises, scratches, things I could handle. Even when a hunter would get hurt and come to me for help, their wounds were more serious but still treatable. I felt like I was finally doing what I set out to do in the beginning, helping people, doing something good."

"Sounds like it has been a great opportunity for you."

"It was, until now. I can't help them, Emma. We're losing the two that are here, Leona is fading fast at the hospital and Meg's burns, they may heal, but she'll never be the same person again. I feel like I'm back in the trenches and can't do a damn thing for anyone."

Emma placed her hand on his arm. "Caleb told you what we think is happening here, didn't he?"

"A spell, black magic, right?"

"Right, and there is nothing medicine can do to fight that, so you can't beat yourself up. You are keeping these people alive and we are grateful to you for that. I feel more comfortable with Scott here, with you taking care of him, then I would if he was at the most high-tech hospital in the country."

He looked at her in surprise, that was definitely not how she felt when Scott was first brought in.

"I'm learning a lot about this world from my new hunter friends that I never knew existed, and I'm re-learning some fundamental things that I'm still processing and learning how to apply. Some just take me a little longer than others."

"Been there, done that," he replied with a weak smile. "It was a bit traumatic for me when I first started working with these people, but you adjust after awhile."

"That's what I'm finding out. I can tell you that we all have faith in you to do whatever can be done for our loved ones. There is no one else that anyone would trust like they do you."

"That's kind of you to say."

"I mean it and now we need to do what has to be done from the other side to finish this, to take care of what no medicine can. We think we have a plan, of sorts, so you keep your faith, in yourself and in us, and by this time tomorrow, Scott will be back."

"I hope you're right. I know Scott well and it is a pleasure to get to know you, too, and in doing so, it's easy to see why you have come to mean so much to him. You have a great outlook on life, don't ever lose that, Emma, no matter what happens. I'll leave you alone with Scott now. Thanks for listening."

Emma watched him go and said a quick little prayer that what she said was true and that Scott really would be back with her by this time tomorrow. If he wasn't, he may never come back, and she simply would not accept that as a possibility.

"Did you hear that, Scott?" she asked quietly, moving his dark brown hair back off his forehead. "You stay strong and fight this thing. We have a plan and we're going to take care of that bitch who did this to you once and for all. I need you and I can't imagine my life without you. I refuse to let you go.

Our future holds so much wonder and there will be something happening soon that you have never experienced before. We're going to share it together and have the most incredible life. So, hang on, let us do what we have to do and then you'll be back with me again."

She leaned down and ran her hand gently along his cheek and gave him a quick kiss on his forehead. "I'll see you soon."

CHAPTER 20

"What now?" Tim asked.

"I don't know," Caleb replied. He and Tim had taken the buildings on the west side of town and had just met up with Matt and Droin, who'd checked out the ones along the east side.

"She wasn't anywhere obvious," Droin said, "but we didn't check every room in every building."

"We shouldn't have to," Tim said. "Why would she feel like she needs to hide from us?"

"Don't know," Caleb said. "When Gabriel dropped Tanya off in the parking lot, he confirmed Lisa's VW is still there, so she's still in Windy Shot, we just have to find her."

"Could she have gone back up to the mine?"

All four men looked up into the distant hills but saw nothing out of place.

"Maybe, but if she did, we can't go up after her just yet. We need to work out the Black Dog issue first."

"Let's grab Nathan and Polly, they've both been doing everything they can to get some intel on how to kill it."

"Alright, Tanya should be back soon and then we can bang our heads together until some ideas pop out."

*   *   *

Emma felt completely wiped out after having gotten very little sleep, having her wits frightened out of her by that damn demon dog and then the emotional toll of talking to Doc Higgins and seeing Scott's deteriorated condition.

She knew Tanya wouldn't be back for awhile, so she decided to lay down and try to catch a quick nap, if sleep was even possible.

Emma was in a bit of a fog and didn't even realize that she opened the hotel door without having to use her key. Neither did she hear quiet footsteps sneak up behind her before she was hit on the head and sank into a black abyss.

"Oh, you're finally awake," Lisa said with a grin, a short time later. "I was afraid that I might have hit you just a little too hard."

Emma was lying on the bed, her head was pounding brutally and her hands were tied behind her back.

"What do you want, Lisa? Why are you doing this?" Emma asked, as she struggled to sit upright.

Lisa opened her beady little eyes wide and made that awful noise in the back of her throat.

"Doing this?" she asked, gesturing her hands to Emma. "Or doing all this other stuff?"

"What are you talking about?"

"I realize you are a true blonde," Lisa said, "but please don't play stupid with me. I know you and your buddies are close to figuring things out. I'm still pissed that the Sleeping Beauty spell didn't work on Tim, too, and he's out scouring the town for me, as we speak."

"I must have done something wrong with his spell," she added absently, then turned her attention back to Emma. "As luck would have it, I was in here looking for something of yours that I could use to make your own special little hex bag, but you came back before you were supposed to."

"Why are you doing any of this? These people are your friends."

"They are not my friends, they never have been, and they never will be."

"Is it because of what happened to Jason?"

Lisa's beady little eyes got even smaller as she narrowed them in anger. "Don't speak his name, ever."

"It was a creature that killed Jason, not these people."

Lisa took two long strides over to the bed and back-handed Emma so hard that she fell back onto the bed again.

"I said, do not speak his name and I mean it. Don't test me, Emma, you will not like what happens. And it was not a creature that killed him, it was lazy, cowardly sluggards that let my Jason die. And they will all feel the same pain that I did, that I still feel every single day."

"Had I known about you, it would be you in the deep sleep, not Scott." She flashed a manic smile. "Now, that would have been so much more fun to see then you scurrying around like a little lost puppy without him."

"What now?" Emma asked, ignoring her comments, she was not afraid, just angry. Emma had no intention of letting this bitch get away with any of it, she just didn't quite know how she was going to stop it yet.

"Let's go." Lisa grabbed her arm and yanked her up on her feet, almost dislocating Emma's shoulder in the process. Emma bit her lip to keep from crying out, she wouldn't give Lisa the satisfaction of knowing how badly that hurt.

Lisa threw a long cardigan over Emma's shoulders, so no one would see that her hands were tied behind her back, and together they walked out of the hotel. Fortunately, for Lisa, most of the hunters had already left and the place seemed like a ghost town.

"Obviously, I can't gag you, that would be just a bit obvious. Just know that if you say a word that I don't like, to anyone, they will die, you will die, and I will see to it that Scott does not live to see another sunset. Are we understood?"

Emma nodded.

Lisa yanked on her arm again, smiling when she saw Emma wince in pain. "Understood?"

"Yes," Emma said, then clenched her jaw tightly, trying to get her anger under control so that she could think clearly.

Lisa looked around furtively and there did not seem to be anyone about. But, as they crossed the road and headed down Bent Elbow Way, Gabriel came running up behind them.

"Emma, hey, Emma," he called as he approached.

"Oh, shit," Emma murmured. "Hi, Gabriel, what's up?"

His brow was furrowed, and he was glancing back and forth between the two women. "Are you okay?"

"Of course," Emma replied, wondering desperately how she could let him know the danger they were both in and keep Lisa unaware of what she was doing.

"We're just, um, taking a walk, getting some fresh air."

"You seem upset."

"I am, a little, and Lisa's letting me chew her ear off. I'm just very concerned about Scott and I need someone to listen, you understand, right?"

"Sure," he replied, but he still looked confused and could not figure out why Emma would keep her hands behind her back, or why Lisa would be standing up so close beside Emma. Something felt very wrong with the whole situation.

"Well, I'll leave you two alone to talk then," he said quietly, looking hard at Emma and seeing the tears collecting in her eyes. "Have a good walk."

"Thanks, Gabriel, I'll stop by and see you later."

Lisa watched him with narrowed eyes until he turned down the street, heading back towards the Mercantile. When he was gone, she roughly grabbed Emma's upper arm and dragged her along the road. There was very little chance of running into anyone this far towards the outskirts of town, so Lisa felt a little more confident in her plans to finish off Emma.

*　　*　　*

"Do you have everything you need?" Caleb asked Tanya, as Tim followed her in, carrying her bag, filled to the brim with various unidentifiable items. They decided to meet at Caleb and Leona's home because they could speak more freely there and not worry about being overheard.

"I should be good," she said. "Now we just need to know where we go to do this."

"What happened to you?" Caleb asked, when he saw that her clothing was torn and there were scrapes, bruises and cuts all over her face and arms.

She waved away his concern. "I had a little vehicle mishap, nothing for you to worry about."

She knew how protective Caleb could be and didn't need his testosterone interfering with their plans right now, so she downplayed what had happened. Only Theo knew the truth and she had gone back to her room.

Tanya wasn't sure what was going on with her, but knew it had something to do with Tim. Theo had been planning on leaving shortly but agreed to stay and take Tanya back with her when she left.

Theo wanted to make sure everyone would be alright before she left, anyway, so this gave her an excuse to stick around. She just couldn't bring herself to hang out with the bunch of them right now, not when Tim was a part of the group.

She was having a more difficult time dealing with the end of their relationship, if you could call it that, than she had anticipated. The one thing that Theo would never do was to show weakness in front of her fellow hunters, so she stayed put in her hotel room while they figured out how they were going to save the day.

"What exactly will you be doing, Tanya?" Caleb asked.

"Remember, I cannot do anything about the hellhound, but for the spells themselves, I have the hex bags, all of them, and I will 'kill the hand'."

Matt nodded his understanding, but the other men looked confused, so she explained further.

"Magic is a dichotomy; black magic is the malicious, left-hand counterpart of the right-hand, which is benevolent white magic. What I need to do is negate the maliciousness of the black magic, kill the left hand, so to speak, and let the right hand or white magic take over. If I can do that, the peril from those spells will be diminished at the least, and completely reversed if I've done things correctly."

"Reversed doesn't mean like it never happened, does it?" Caleb asked hopefully, worried about permanent damage Leona might have already sustained because of the high fevers.

"We can't do time travel, Caleb," Tanya responded with a sad smile, "although I wish we could. Kevin and Brad will still be dead, Meg will still have scars for the rest of her life. I don't know what damage may have already been done to Scott, Wanda and Leona but, although we can stop anything else from happening and wake them up from their comas or whatever you want to call them, we can't make it like it never happened."

"I understand," Caleb said, gently clasping her shoulder with his massive hand. "You get to work on your spell ingredients while we try to come up with an idea, other than just blowing its head off, for getting rid of that dog."

*   *   *

"What's the matter, Emma, hill too steep for you?"

"It's fine," Emma replied, "just a little difficult to maneuver with my hands tied behind my back."

"That's what I hate about you cute, skinny women, you're always whining about something."

There were several less than flattering comments that came to mind, but Emma kept them to herself, no sense antagonizing Lisa any further than she needed to, at least not yet. Emma realized that Lisa must be taking her to the mine, but she had no idea why.

"Lisa, since everyone knows that you are responsible, how do you think you will ever get away with what you've done already?"

"Maybe you are a little denser than I thought, what do you think they'll do? Call the cops? Yes, this witch put my boyfriend in a coma, she made my friend fall in the fire, even though there are dozens of witnesses and she wasn't anywhere around at the time, and on and on, until all of you are locked up in your little white jackets."

She sounded smug and so sure that she would get away scot-free that Emma made herself a promise that, no matter how long it took, Lisa would get what was coming to her.

"Guess, I'll just have to take care of you myself then," Emma said.

Lisa's squinty eyes narrowed, and she felt the need for a little retaliation before the real drama unfolded at the mine.

"Do you realize that Scott is conscious?"

"What do you mean?"

"It's a type of voodoo curse, kind of a zombie thing that I read about and thought sounded intriguing. I call it my Sleeping Beauty Curse, I modified it a little to make it even more potent. I used Bladderwort, have you ever heard of it?"

"No, what is this, a fucking pop quiz?"

Lisa slapped the back of Emma's head and Emma ground her teeth together to get her anger under control.

"Bladderwort is a carnivorous aquatic plant that I ran across. It captures its prey, little tadpoles, minnows, things like that, and contains the victims until they eventually die of starvation or suffocation and decay into a goo which it then sucks up. That's how your lover's life will end."

"That's disgusting, and what in hell would that association have to do with Scott?"

"The 'association'," Lisa replied, with unnecessary emphasis on the word, "you idiot, is to pay back the coward for being such a sluggard and sleeping on the job instead of stepping up and being there for Jason when he needed him. This way, your lover can actually see and hear and feel everything, but his body is shut down while he listens to the world going on around him."

"He knows everything that's happening?"

"Yes, he does, how fun is that? Too bad they whisked him off to the hospital before I could get to him. I was going to tell him exactly what I'm going to do to you and to his baby and let that stew in his little pea brain until his organs shut down and he really does die."

Emma stumbled and stopped, turning back towards Lisa, so grateful that she didn't know Scott was still in town, but horrified at the entire situation and the evil that resided in this woman.

"What do you plan on doing to my baby?"

"All in good time, my dear."

It had been in this general vicinity that Emma and Tanya had run into the Black Dog earlier. She recognized the spot because there was a profusion of yellow flowers growing off to the side of the trail, they looked like a shorter version of a sunflower with thick, green arrow-shaped leaves.

Emma tilted her head as she stared at them, wondering exactly how hard Lisa had hit her, or if maybe it was just the altitude messing with her memory. The flowers had all been facing towards her and Tanya when they passed by this morning but, now they were turned in the opposite direction.

"You really don't know much about anything, do you?" Lisa asked, seeing Emma's perplexed look as she studied the flowers. "Those are Arrowleaf Balsamroot, they follow the sun and look east in the morning and west towards the end of the day."

Relieved that she wasn't going crazy, at least not yet, after being prodded in the shoulder by Lisa once again, Emma continued up the trail.

"You must have also been the one that spread those lies about what happened with Bigfoot, right? What was the purpose of that? What did you think you would get out it?"

"I have no idea what you're talking about. Bigfoot doesn't exist, do you think I'm stupid or something?"

Emma was confused, it was one of the few times Lisa seemed to be telling the truth. But, if she didn't spread those lies, then who did?

That particular issue became completely moot a few short minutes later. Lisa had been following behind Emma, but now took the lead. They were getting closer to the mine entrance and Lisa knew her demon dog would be appearing soon and that she would need to get it under control quickly, so that it didn't attack Emma, at least not until it was given permission to do so.

Lisa planned on completing the spell that would get rid of Emma's baby and then giving her enough leeway to think she was escaping. Lisa would let her run away in a panic and then set the Demon dog loose to finish her off.

Without a doubt, not one of the deaths that had occurred, or that would still occur, could be attributed to a person and, as much as she'd like to personally dispatch Emma, Lisa needed to keep herself out of any potential, provable, criminal activity.

*   *   *

"I've checked all the lore and the only thing I found was not encouraging," Nathan said, shaking his head in frustration.

"So, share already," Matt said irritably, not feeling comfortable with any of this. Living in Louisiana, he had a morbid respect for all things witchery and knew they were powerful and difficult to defeat. He was not feeling at all confident about what they were doing.

"The only thing that I did find said that you can never truly kill a hellhound, that even if you think you have, it will come back and kill anyone that tried to hurt it."

"Balderdash," Caleb said, his deep voice rough and gravelly, "I don't believe that rubbish at all. We're going to have to get it away from the mine any way that we can."

"I'd like to make a suggestion," Tim said. "We don't honestly know if this is some kind of a demon dog or if it's a Black Ghost dog, so why don't two of us take regular shotguns with silver bullets, don't know if that will make a difference but it can't hurt, and the other two will take shotguns with salt pellets. If it is truly a ghost, we can't kill it, but that will at least give us time to get in there and get Tanya's spell in the works."

"Probably a good idea," Caleb said. "Wouldn't hurt to stop off at the restaurant and grab some salt containers to make a circle around her and her spell stuff to keep them safe."

"If it's a ghost," Droin said.

"Right, still a lot of things up in the air, you guys game for this or do you want to stay back?"

Nathan looked at his wife and shook his head. "Polly and I will stay here and keep trying to find more information."

No one was surprised by that, they were not actual hunters, they were information handlers, and everyone had to play to their strengths in this situation.

"I'm in," Droin said.

Matt hesitated but knew he wouldn't ever be able to look himself in the eye again if he didn't make a stand with his friends.

"I'm in, too. What about Lisa though? We still haven't found her."

Caleb was just about to respond when there was a horrific banging on his front door that wouldn't stop. He walked over and peered out the peephole, then opened the door.

"What the hell is wrong with you, Gabriel?"

"Man, I've been looking for you all over," he said, ignoring Caleb and walking straight to Tim.

"What's the matter?"

"It's Emma," Gabriel said, swallowing hard and trying to catch his breath.

"What about her?" Tim asked, realizing for the first time that no one had stopped by to let her know where they would be meeting. He still wasn't used to having her as a part of their activities and had completely forgotten about her.

"Maybe it's nothing," Gabriel said hesitantly, suddenly wondering if he was making too big of a deal out of what he saw.

"Gabriel, tell me."

"I saw her and that big lady with the man hands heading along Bent Elbow. I don't know why, and Emma seemed scared or upset. I think that lady was the same one that I saw in the cemetery one night with that big dog."

"Damn, Gabriel, why didn't you tell me that before?"

He shuffled his feet and looked down at the floor. "I didn't know it was important. There was one really strange thing with Emma though."

"What?" Tim asked loudly, when nothing further seemed to be forthcoming.

"Oh, um, Emma had both her hands behind her back and that lady was like, hugging up alongside her, it just weird."

"Think she had her hands tied behind her back?" Tim asked.

"Could be, she had a long sweater over her shoulders, and it's way too hot for a sweater today."

"Damn, and you said they were going up Bent Elbow?" Caleb asked.

Gabriel nodded.

"That's the most direct route up towards the mine entrance. I don't think we have any time to waste. Let's get going now. Gabriel, run over to the restaurant or Mercantile, wherever you have to go, and get me a bunch of salt containers, large ones, and meet us at the corner of Bent Elbow, quickly."

"Yessir, Mr. Evans."

As Gabriel was running back towards the door, Tim said, "I've got shotguns in my room, I'll run and grab them and the salt pellets. Meet you at the corner."

The other men went off to collect their own weapons and Caleb helped Tanya carry her bag of goodies and they all met up a few minutes later.

Tim tried to grab the salt containers from Gabriel, but he shook his head. "I don't know what's going on, but I know Emma's in trouble, and I want to help, please."

"Okay, you can come," Tim said, after a brief moment of hesitation, "but stay back behind the rest of us."

CHAPTER 21

Emma first heard the low growls, then smelled something like burning sulfur at the same time that she saw the hellhound. This time it was even closer, its thick fur was black as coal, its eyes burned a dark red and it was staring at both of them, blocking their way.

Lisa started murmuring some sort of a chant, the words made no sense and Emma had no idea what was happening. Whatever Lisa was saying did mean something to the dog and even though the low growls continued, it stepped off to the side and allowed them to pass.

Fury grew within the creature, overriding the shards of pain that came from the words that Lisa uttered, and which bounced around unmercifully inside its skull. The only thing that eased its torment was to do as it was instructed.

The creature would bide its time and follow orders but, given the smallest window of opportunity it would kill the wielder of the pain, and it would be a very slow death.

Being a dog lover, Emma was not generally frightened around them, even big dogs, but she held her breath as she walked by this creature. It was so close that its nose almost brushed her leg and she could imagine the feel of those razor-sharp teeth clamping down on her calf. But that didn't happen, and she breathed out a sigh of relief when she managed to get past it safely.

Just ahead was the entrance to the mine which led back into the mountain itself. It was in the shape of a rectangle, with railroad ties going up each side and one large one across the top to fortify the entrance. Brush was growing up around it and Emma could see a chain link fence lying in weeds off to the side of the entrance.

There a large rusted sign attached to it with a skull and crossbones in the center and all types of warnings on it, Stay Alive! Dangers Await Inside! Stay Out! Between the fencing and the warning, it should have kept everyone out of the mine but, apparently Lisa had no fear.

She shoved Emma inside the mine entrance, causing her to stumble, barely able to catch herself before falling and smashing her face against the hard rock floor.

The entrance was wide and let in some sunshine, but Lisa hurried over to light several lanterns. Emma took a moment to look around and could see a few shafts heading into the mountain, most of them were fortified with railroad ties. One was just rock, with a huge hole in the ground just as that tunnel began. Someone had partially covered it with plywood, but even that did not look at all safe. Danger and Stay Out signs had been placed willy-nilly all around the mine.

The entranceway was fairly good-sized, there were abandoned and rusted out mine trolleys off to the side, one still completely filled with rocks. Tracks led down into the tunnels and there were unlit lightbulbs hanging along a wire from the ceiling, Emma assumed the power must have been shut off years ago.

The Black Dog stood at the entrance staring at them, it's eyes almost glowing in their redness and its chest continuing to rumble in a low growl.

Lisa turned towards the hellhound, her face no longer a mask of fake pleasantness, but twisted with hatred and revenge. She reached up and grabbed the green amulet in her hand and started chanting something, and once again Emma was unable to understand the words that she was speaking.

The dog whined in pain and Emma turned her attention back to the creature and realized that there was also a green amulet on a chain around its neck that matched Lisa's. There seemed to be something alive inside the amulets that swirled like green slime or a green cloud that was captured within it.

It was then that Emma realized the amulet must somehow be the way that Lisa was controlling the creature. Lisa finished her chant, shouting something incomprehensible and the Black Dog barked at her one time, it's glowing eyes burning into her, and then it turned and went back outside.

Lisa was able to hurt the Black Dog with those words and the amulet and make it do whatever she told it to do. Emma also realized that the dog looked at Lisa with pure, unadulterated hatred, and knew that it would kill Lisa in an instant, given an opportunity, and might be Emma's only chance to survive this.

"Guard dog," Lisa said, a manic smile lighting her face. "We can't have any of your friends sneaking up and interrupting us, can we?"

There was a rock ledge that Lisa was using as an altar, it held various candles and incense that she was lighting, making the air come alive with strong, unpleasant scents. There were dozens of small jars lined up, filled with her special ingredients.

A large bowl sat in the middle of everything and Lisa started dropping various herbs into it, murmuring some type of incantation as she did so.

Emma was standing off the side, watching her, wondering how the hell she could get out of here, but Lisa wasn't worried about her escaping, not with the hellhound just outside the door and unstable mineshafts inside.

Emma wandered around, trying to find some sort of escape. Her hands were still tied painfully behind her back, but she ignored that, as she desperately tried to find a way out of this predicament.

"Don't step outside that circle," Lisa said sharply, pulling on a pair of gloves. "You'll be fair game for my hellhound, if you do."

The large circle was made of small black berries, Emma had never seen any like them before.

"What are they?" she asked, trying to distract Lisa from whatever it was that she was doing.

"Belladonna berries, you've heard of belladonna, right, great little herb to use for assassinating someone. Its berries are just as dangerous so don't even touch them. Several of the items that I use are dangerous, thus the gloves," she added with a wicked smile.

"Let me see, what else do I need?" She looked over her treasure trove of spices and suddenly smiled wide. "Oh, this one will work exquisitely."

"I've never done a thing to you, I never even knew you until this week. Why do you want to hurt me?"

"Because they all care about you and I want to hurt each and everyone of them. You are an arrogant little bitch and think you are better than me, so you are the perfect patsy for me to use as my final sacrifice in this game."

"It's not a game, Lisa, it's people's lives that you're destroying."

"You certainly won't have to worry about that much longer, so shut your mouth, I can't even stand the sound of your voice."

"It was you that attacked me in the theater, wasn't it?"

"Of course, I saw an opportunity and took a chance. Thought for sure I had you on that catwalk, but you were lucky that day. I couldn't even finish you off outside because that damned fool, Bobby, was there. I just snuck off to wait for another opportunity and here it finally is."

Lisa came over and pulled out a few of Emma's hairs, wishing she had cried out, but feeling some satisfaction in the grimace of pain on her face.

She took the hairs and threw them in the large bowl with the other ingredients. Then she picked up the last little jar filled with tiny white berries that had black dots on them.

Lisa looked over at Emma, her eyes filled with hatred. "These are called White Baneberry, but they also have another name, Doll's Eyes, can you guess why?"

"Because that's what they look like." Emma couldn't help the condescending tone of her voice but did regret it when Lisa took two large strides forward and backhanded her across the face. This time Emma fell and hit her tailbone on the hard rock ground, it also jarred her shoulders painfully because of the way her hands were tied.

But there was one saving grace to the incident, Emma landed next to an outcropping of rock. The rope around her wrists was already loosening, so Emma stayed where she landed and gently moved her hands up and down against the sharp rock while Lisa went back to her concoction.

Emma could feel the rope giving and knew she would be able to break free of her bindings, she just hoped she could do it in time to prevent whatever spell Lisa was preparing.

"It is called Doll's Eyes," Lisa continued calmly, as if her assault on Emma hadn't happened, "because the way it looks attracts children. It is extremely toxic and when they eat the berries, it kills them. In a very unpleasant manner from what I understand, although I've never tested it like I have some of these others."

She turned and gave Emma a ghoulish smile. Emma immediately stopped moving her arms and sat completely still until Lisa went back to her bowl and started crushing the berries in with the other items.

Once that was done, she started waving her hands over the bowl and chanting quietly. Emma was almost free, but not quite. She needed a few more minutes and had to distract Lisa from continuing with the spell.

"What are you going to do with that? Kill me?"

Lisa sighed heavily, frustrated at the interruption, but more than happy to provide Emma with the gory details.

"Nothing so extreme as that. This spell, once it's done, will kill your baby. I'll let you live, but without Scott and without his child. You can spend the rest of your life thinking about this day when your whole world was destroyed, and each time you do, you'll think of me and maybe, just maybe, you'll realize what an arrogant bitch you are and know that ultimately, this was all your own fault."

Emma started laughing hysterically which made Lisa turn to her with a frown. "You find that funny?"

"You are so deluded," Emma said, once she was able to get herself back under control. "Can you really not see who you are or what you're doing? This has nothing to do with me. You lost the man you love, and you are taking revenge on people that had nothing to do with it. Is hurting other people going to make your life better? It certainly won't bring Jason back. Are you really able to justify what you are doing in your own mind?"

"Yes, I can because if they weren't so weak and cowardly, Jason would still be alive. They started all of this and they have to live with the consequences of their actions, and so do you."

"Aren't you cheapening his memory by creating so much hurt and pain?"

"Not at all. You have no idea the lengths I had to go to just to be a part of Jason's life and, no sooner was he mine than they took him away from me. They must be punished."

"What lengths?" Emma asked. "Did you use a spell to make him want you? Were you that desperate to be loved?"

"What would you know, you skinny, little bitch? You don't know how hard it is to find a man, the right man, and Jason was that man. We were meant for each other, we were soul-mates and I was willing to do whatever I had to so that we could be together forever."

Emma breathed a sigh of relief as she felt the ropes pull apart, freeing her hands.

"That's just a pile of nonsense," Emma said, still not sure of what she was doing, but knowing it had to be done now. She stood up, but continued to hold her hands behind her back, as if they were still tied together.

"Jason never loved you, and either he was trying to escape from you or just wasn't a good enough hunter, but he died on a hunt, that's the bottom line. None of the others could save him because he put himself in such a stupid position that it was impossible for them to do so."

Lisa's pig-like eyes widened in fury and her wild hair seemed to stand on end. Emma felt a wave of fear wash through her and then Lisa rushed her, ready to smack her again.

But this time Emma was ready. Lisa approached, Emma side-stepped and hit her in the back of the head, knocking her out of the circle and into the rock wall.

Instantly the Black Dog was at the entrance of the mine, growling louder, ready to pounce.

Lisa shouted something in that other language and the dog hesitated. Lisa could feel her power over the dog waning and took advantage, hurrying back into the safety of the circle.

Again, she headed straight for Emma, who looked wildly around for any kind of weapon. All that she could grab was the bowl with the herbs and other items in it for the spell, it was a heavy clay bowl and Emma turned it on its side and smashed it against Lisa's head.

It didn't break, but all of the items fell out and Lisa's face went red with a fury that Emma had never witnessed before, cementing her belief that the woman truly was insane. Hopefully, she wasn't so far gone that nothing would be able to stop her.

"Well, now you've done it," Lisa said, through grated teeth. "Looks like I'll have to kill you myself, after all. Two birds, one stone, right?"

She punched Emma in the stomach and Emma doubled over in pain. Taking advantage of the moment, Lisa drew back her hand and slapped Emma hard up against the side of her head.

Emma stumbled backwards, out of the circle and the Black Dog moved quickly in her direction.

Emma saw it coming and chose to take on Lisa rather than the creature. She jumped back inside the circle, Lisa was waiting for her, a heinous smile on her face. Neither of them noticed the dog perk its ears up, growl softly and head back outside the entrance of the mine.

They were just a couple of feet apart, there was no time to think, Emma ran straight at her and, taking advantage of the difference in their heights, she bent forward and buried the top of her head into Lisa's broad stomach. The momentum carried them both up against the rock wall. Lisa had the breath knocked out of her and was, momentarily, at Emma's mercy. Emma knew she had very little time to finish this and, as she straightened up, she saw the amulet swinging back and forth around Lisa's neck.

Emma hesitated, she thought she heard a gunshot, but couldn't be sure. She couldn't rely on anyone else to come to her rescue and knew she had to take care of this herself.

Instinct told her to destroy the amulet, so she ripped it off Lisa's neck and Lisa screamed as if all the demons in hell were after her when Emma smashed the amulet against the hard, rocky ground. The two of them then watched in wonder as the green mist escaped and dispersed around them, the hideous smell of Sulphur engulfing them.

"You bitch," screamed Lisa, "you have no idea what you've done."

She swung hard and hit Emma in the head, knocking her down. Emma's head bounced against the rock floor and she faded into blackness.

*   *   *

Tim led the way up the rocky path towards the mine entrance. They tried to be as quiet as possible but the closer they got, the rougher the ground was, and small pebbles and stones rolled out from underneath their feet making noise that was inevitable.

Tim stopped when they got close to the entrance, the Black Dog was no where to be seen.

"What do you think?" he whispered to the others. "Do we just go for it?"

"Don't think we have any other choice." Caleb tried to keep his voice down, but it wasn't the kind of voice that could speak quietly and boomed a little louder than Tim would have liked.

"Okay, you and Matt go over to that side, oh, shit,"

"What?" Matt whispered.

"There it is." The dog trotted out of the mine and stood just outside, its nose lifted into the air as it tried to pick up the scent of the intruders that it had heard.

"Damn," Caleb said, "well, let's do it. Matt and I to the left, you and Droin to the right. We'll hit it with real bullets and with salt pellets and see what happens. Gabriel, you stay back here with Tanya. We'll let you know when it's safe."

"Is Emma in that mine?" Gabriel asked.

"Most likely, don't worry we'll take care of her."

The dog stood at attention, its front legs braced for action, its glowing red eyes glancing from the right to the left, following the hunters, trying to anticipate their movements.

It had instructions to guard that entrance, so it could not move, could not go forward and attack the men, it was forced to wait for them to come to it. The creature snarled loudly in frustration.

The men had to situate themselves so that their shots would not go directly into the mine because they had no idea how far in Emma might be, and they also had to be careful they didn't shoot each other, so it was a delicate balance getting into the right position before letting off a shot.

Tim was getting settled in when he heard the crack of a gunshot from one of men on the other side and it looked like the dog was hit. Other than seeing the dog move slightly when the bullet hit its shoulder, there was no effect on the creature.

Tim had to assume that was the salt pellet and, therefore, this creature was real, and would require a real bullet. He pulled out his rifle and was aiming at the side of the creature's head when there was a horrific scream from inside the mine.

Everyone froze in place, even the hellhound, but it was the first to move once the scream faded. The green amulet it wore around its neck suddenly burst open, the gold chain that held it fell to the ground and the creature shook its massive head as if it were suddenly free of shackles. A greenish mist rose while the hunters stared, trying to get a handle on what was happening.

The Black Dog hesitated, then turned towards the mine entrance with a deadly growl from deep in its chest. Another shot rang out, careening off a beam right next to its head and the dog stopped and glared its fury at the hunters. Giving up on its revenge, for now, in exchange for its life, the creature turned and disappeared up the hillside.

"We're going after it," Caleb said, as he and Droin headed up right behind it.

"I'm going with them, you alright here?" Matt asked.

"Yes, I'll take care of Lisa."

Tim cautiously approached the mine entrance and stepped inside the dimly lit area, the barrel of his rifle leading the way. Lisa was hiding just to the side of the entrance, she had toyed with the idea of running down one of the shafts, but knew she'd never find her way out again. Her only chance of surviving was to leave the way she came in.

Tim saw Emma lying unconscious on the ground and quickly stepped inside. Lisa heard the gunshots and knew someone would be coming, so she hid herself until Tim stepped all the way into the mine entrance. Then Lisa snuck up behind him, knocking him cold with a large rock.

She slipped outside and looked for any other threats, seeing none, she headed down one of the less obvious trails.

Tanya and Gabriel watched her go from their hiding spot behind some shrubs.

"You go in and do what you have to," Gabriel said. "I'm going to follow her."

Tanya jumped up and grabbed her bag of items and hurried to the mine entrance.

She saw Tim sitting on the hard ground, rubbing the back of his head, his hand coming away slightly bloody.

"Are you alright?"

"I'll be fine, check on Emma, she's out cold."

Emma was just starting to come around when Tanya got to her.

"Emma, holy crap, you look like hell, are you alright?"

"I guess so, my freaking head is pounding out of my skull, but I think I'll survive. Where's Lisa?" she asked, peering around the entranceway.

"She took off, she'll be out of here before we can ever catch up with her."

"We have to stop her, she's insane and isn't going to stop until we are all dead."

"Don't worry, I have everything under control."

She hurried over to the altar and started assembling the tricks of her trade. Tim helped Emma up and kept his arm around her shoulder to steady her while they watched.

It broke Tim's heart to see how battered and bruised Emma's face was, and he knew from the delicate way she was moving that she'd been injured in other parts of her body, as well. He was really going to have a lot of explaining to do when his brother woke up.

"Alright," Tanya said, exhaling a deep breath, "this is Beth Root, which is used to reverse black magic curses, hopefully, it is strong enough for the ones Lisa used. It should be, according to what I've read, but I've never used it before, so let's say a quick prayer, then I'll finish this."

The three of them stood in a semi-circle, each making their own desperate plea to their own god, begging him to let this work so they could get Scott and the others back.

"Stand back, please," Tanya asked, when they were done. She took a long match and lit the ingredients as she started chanting. The chanting continued and her voice grew stronger as she threw the hex bags into the fire, one by one.

When they were all in, her eyes rolled back in her head, she lifted her face to heavens and started shouting the chant. Suddenly, there was a flashfire in the bowl and everything incinerated. Tanya passed out and fell towards the ground.

Tim caught her before she hit, but she didn't come to immediately.

Neither of them knew whether or not what had happened was what was supposed to happen, and they were filled with uncertainty. If the spell didn't work, they would never see Scott again.

Tanya moaned and opened her eyes, smiling up at Tim. "I think we did it."

He helped her up and the three of them kept their arms wrapped around each other as they slowly made their way back to town.

CHAPTER 22

The others hadn't returned yet, so they immediately went over to the Infirmary. Emma was crestfallen to realize that there was no change in Scott's condition, or in Wanda's.

The Doc had lightened up on her sedatives, hoping her condition would be resolved today, but Wanda just laid on her bed, mumbling incoherently and whipping her head from side to side.

"I'm so sorry," Tanya said, tears gathering in her eyes. "I did everything it said. I was sure that it would work."

"We aren't giving up, yet," Tim said, his face drawn and pale, "maybe it just needs more time."

Tanya was heartsick that her spell hadn't worked and needed some time to herself, so she headed outside for a walk to clear her head.

Emma had no words, she was too heart-broken to speak. She let Doc Higgins clean up her cuts and scrapes and then just sat perfectly still on the examination table, staring at the wall.

Tim came in and engulfed her in his long arms, she couldn't hold back her anguish any longer and sobbed out her sorrow against his chest. Tim was glad that she couldn't see his own tears sliding down his cheeks, he felt he had to be strong for her right now but wasn't sure how long he would be able to continue doing that.

After a few minutes, Emma's sobs dissipated and finally stopped. Tim released her and grabbed a box of tissues off the nearby desk.

As Emma blew her nose and got herself back under control, Tim wandered around the room, not sure what to say. He didn't want to make things worse, but he needed her to know she was going to be taken care of, no matter how this shook out with Scott.

He walked over and sat beside her on the examination table. "I am not giving up on Scott yet, Emma, but I want you to know that you, and your baby, are family now, and whatever happens I'll be there for both of you."

Tears slowly continued to slip down Emma's cheeks and her glittering green eyes were glassy and filled with pain. She placed both of her hands over her stomach as if to protect the baby inside.

"Thank you. I feel so empty though, I can't believe we've lost him, it took me too long to get back to Scott and now our baby will never know him, will never know what a brave, wonderful man he was. How am I going to live the rest of my life without him?"

"Emma, don't go there, right now you're overwhelmed. Trust me, I get it. Don't think too far into the future, not just yet. Like I said, I haven't given up on Scott. He's a warrior and he can win this fight. There are things we can still try, it's not a done deal, not even close. I just wanted you to know that I love you like a sister and I'll be there for you, and the baby, in every way that I can."

Emma looked at him tenderly and could see the hurt and pain in his soulful brown eyes. She knew this was as difficult for him as it was for her, and Emma knew she had to stop being an additional burden to him and toughen up. There would be time enough in the future to fall apart, but now was not that time.

"Both you and Scott are amazing, strong, kind and brave, and I hope I can say that about all my own children someday. I think that I have a newfound respect for your Mom and, no matter what happens, I'm going to reach out to her and make sure she knows how much I admire what she's done, and maybe I can learn something from her."

"She's got a pretty good head on her shoulders once you get past her armor. You two have a lot in common and I think you'll manage to make things work out with her."

He gave a sideways glance towards the room where his brother lay unmoving.

"I can't stay here right now, let's head over to the bar."

Emma understood and nodded her agreement.

"Doc, we're going to head over to the bar in the hotel. If you see the others first, let them know where we are, alright?"

"Sure," Doc Higgins replied, watching them leave, wishing he could join them for a nice, stiff drink. After all, there was nothing more he could do for his patients and it was doubtful they would live to see another day.

He wasn't sure how any of them were going to adjust after that happened.

*　　*　　*

While Tim and Emma waited for the others, Emma shared some of the information that she had learned from Lisa.

"She was the one that tried to kill me in the theater."

"But, why?" Tim asked, his brow furrowed in confusion. "You had nothing to do with Jason's death and she barely knew you."

"First and foremost, I am an arrogant bitch. Which may be true, but I think she is just insane and is trying to hurt as many people as she possibly can."

"I'll agree with you on that one. What about Bigfoot, what was her game with that? Was she hoping someone else might kill Scott or me and save her the trouble?"

"I asked Lisa about that and I sincerely don't think she did it. She didn't know what I was talking about and doesn't even believe Bigfoot is real."

"Who then?"

"No idea," Emma said, staring down into her glass of club soda. "I guess in the overall scheme of things, that's the least of our concerns right now."

"True, but I hate unanswered questions."

"Speaking of unanswered questions, what about Leona's father?"

"What about him?"

"Could he really have seen the Black Dog? Obviously, Lisa couldn't have been controlling it back then."

"I don't know the answer to that. Leona swore it was the Black Dog, but it's an odd coincidence that it would have appeared twice in the same place. And I'm not much for coincidences."

"Just one more mystery for another day."

"I guess so, here come the others, maybe they have some good news."

"We never saw hide nor hair of that damned beast again," Caleb said, as they walked over to join Emma and Tim.

"We can only assume that it's gone back to whatever hell it came from to begin with," Matt drawled, taking a beer from the bartender and downing half of it in one pull.

Droin had also made the infirmary his first stop and knew there was no change in the patients.

"When does Tanya plan on doing the spell to make all this shit stop?"

Tim stared down into his own beer, wishing he didn't have to be the one to crush Droin's hopes as badly as his own had been. "She already did it."

"No," he said, the long ends of his mustache quivering as he tried to control his grief. "No, that can't be, she must not of done it right. Can we try it again?"

"I don't know, here comes Tanya now. Let's find out."

She looked embarrassed when they all turned to watch her approach.

"I'm so sorry, everyone. I did it just like the book said, I don't know why it didn't work."

"But, we can try it again, right?"

"I can, but it won't change anything."

"Don't you dare tell me that, Tanya. My wife's crazier than a shit house rat, you need to make this right, and soon."

Caleb moved in between Droin and Tanya, her eyes were wide with fear and Droin's were narrowed in an almost murderous rage.

"Droin, don't get all in a pucker, this ain't Tanya's fault. She did what she could, now we need to find another spell for her to try, that's all, this one didn't work, get it?"

Droin yelled to the bartender for a shot of whiskey and then lifted his gaze to meet Caleb's.

"I get it, but I don't accept it and unless we find one right away, we're going to lose our loved ones. You okay with that?"

"Of course not, you dipstick. We need to just take a breath and then we get back on top of this."

"Hey, where's Gabriel?" Tim asked, suddenly remembering that he'd been with them.

"He followed Lisa down the hill."

"He what?" Tim yelled. "Shit, then where is he? I hope she didn't hurt him."

"I'm okay," Gabriel called out, entering the bar and heading over to their table, "but thanks for caring, man."

"Glad you're alright, kid," Tim said sincerely. "What happened to Lisa, did she get away clean?"

"Nope, that's what's really weird. I'm glad I followed her, otherwise, we'd never know what happened."

"What do you mean?"

"I followed her for awhile and suddenly all these strange things started up."

"Like what?"

"She fell off a cliff, didn't fall too far, but looked like she banged herself up pretty good. I was always above her and could see what was happening. Out of nowhere, she got sunburned, but not like normal, like spontaneous combustion, suddenly any place you saw skin, it bubbled up like she just got burnt.

Then she seemed all scared and kept looking around like something was coming to get her. When she finally spotted me, she pulled out a pistol. I thought I was goner, but it wouldn't fire for her. She screamed then and started running, but then she just fell down in a heap. I waited for a few minutes, but she never moved."

"Is she still up there?"

"No, it took awhile for all these things to happen. When she didn't get up, I ran back to town and saw Malcolm, he and I went back and carried her down the rest of the way. We just got her over to Doc Higgins and he said there's something you guys all need to see and to get your asses over there."

"Sorry, but that's the message, word for word." He looked at Emma apologetically.

She squeezed his hand in gratitude and they all headed back over to the infirmary.

Emma sobbed out loud when she saw Scott sitting up in bed and ran to his side, wrapping her arms around him and burying her head against his chest.

Tanya turned and walked out of the room, relieved that he was alright, heartbroken to have to see the strength of the love that he shared with Emma all over again.

Tim gave Scott a hug of his own, not something they shared often, and left him to talk with Emma.

Droin was in his wife's room, filled with relief that she was now aware and seemed to be fine, the tips of his mustache positively quivered with joy.

Caleb was in Doc Higgin's office, talking to his wife on the phone, unable to believe this was finally over and that she was going to be alright.

"Hold up, Tanya," Tim said, as he saw her push the door open to leave.

She paused and turned back.

"We owe you a huge debt of gratitude. How the hell do we ever thank you?"

"You don't, we're family, right?"

Her voice was so sad. Tim realized why and suddenly he had a much clearer understanding of what Theo had been trying to tell him.

"So, what now?"

"Same old," she said, "guess I get back to some good old-fashioned white magic and clean some of this crap out of my head."

"If there is anything that I can do for you, ever, please let me know."

"I will, thanks."

"Any idea what the delay was in the spell, why it didn't work right away?"

Tanya looked pensive. "I think it was the Law of Return."

"What is that?"

"It's the principle that the force of a spell which fails will then rebound on the head of the sorcerer or witch who first cast it. Think about the things that Gabriel described. She suffered the same things that her victims did, but not to the same extent, all except for Scott's. Now she's in the same sleeping curse that he was, probably that one was the strongest because it was the same curse for both you and your brother and both hex bags were put in the fire.

226

We just had to wait for each of the curses to hit her before they could be lifted from the others that she originally cursed."

"And what about the Black Dog?"

"Not sure about that, you guys told me about the amulet. I think Emma saved the day when she broke it and Lisa lost her hold over the creature. I tend to lean towards it being a hellhound versus any kind of ghost. I think Lisa made a deal and she'll pay for that when she dies.

That's what I have to believe in order to carry on knowing that there are such evil people in the world. That they will have their comeuppance, if not in this world, then in the next."

"My sentiments exactly. Thanks again, Tanya, obviously we never would have gotten through this without you."

"You two have saved my bacon more than once so, maybe, now we're even."

"Maybe." Tim kissed her cheek. "Do you need a ride home?"

"No, Theo is going to take me."

His eyes clouded with sadness for a moment. "I didn't realize she was still here. I thought she left without saying good-bye."

"She probably will, but don't take offense, it has to do with her, not you."

"I understand, really, I do," he added, when she arched her eyebrow at him.

"Good, and Tim?"

"Yes?"

"I do have one more thing to finish before I leave here today. I don't want to see Scott and Emma, right now, and ruin their reunion. Would you let Emma know that I didn't forget my promise and that I will take care of Sara Mae."

"Who's Sara Mae?"

Tanya was surprised that he didn't know, but maybe Leona didn't want the general hunter population to know about Sara Mae, to keep them from taking matters into their own hands.

"She'll know, and please give them both my best, sincerely, okay?"

"I will, you stay safe."

"You, too," Tanya said, as she slowly walked out the door, knowing that she would never see any of these people again. She wouldn't be able to, it would hurt too much.

*   *   *

"I'm going kick Tim's ass."

"Why?" Emma asked, unable to keep the happy grin off her face. Scott was weak, but back to his normal self.

"He let you get all beaten up and that's just not acceptable."

"Tim's been great, there was no way this could have been avoided. Besides, I did a little ass kicking myself."

"Really, tell me all about it."

"I will, but not right now. How are you, really?"

"It was awful, I'm not going to lie. It was like being buried alive. I could feel everything, I could hear, but I couldn't move, couldn't speak. It was horrible."

Emma traced her hand around his face, unable to keep from touching him, her heart swelling with happiness that he was back.

"I know that you and Tanya snooped through my stuff and found my gift for you."

"Yes, we did. It is the most beautiful ring that I've ever seen. Did you want to ask me something?"

"I'm not sure," he responded, watching her face closely.

The smile dropped and she looked at him curiously. "You're not?"

"Do we have something else to discuss first? Because you kept saying we have something serious to talk about. Before I put myself out there, let's have that talk."

They had a bit of a stand-off, neither wanted to start the conversation, but Emma had a sneaking suspicion that he already knew what she wanted to talk about.

"We've never discussed having a little Devereaux," she said, "and, in all honesty, I already have three children and never anticipated having another."

She could see the smile growing on Scott's face and in his eyes, and Emma knew that he already knew what this was about. And it seemed to be meeting with his approval.

"I was scared when I first thought I might be pregnant because we never did talk about it. I didn't want you to feel trapped or have to take on something you didn't want to. Initially, that's what I wanted to talk about."

She hesitated, their eyes completely locked onto one another. "When I saw the ring, I wasn't scared any more. I knew that you wanted to spend your life with me and I'm already bringing three kids into your life, so what's one more, right?"

"I love you, Emma, always have, always will, and I can't even tell you have much it means to me that you are having my baby. Holy shit, that's just unfreakingbelievable."

"Then, there's just one more thing, right?"

"What?"

"I'm going to give you the benefit of the doubt because you've been in a sort of coma for a few days, but do you have something that you would like ask me?"

"This isn't the way I envisioned it happening, but here goes. Emma Draper, love of my life, soon to be mother of my child, would you do me the honor of being my wife?"

*   *   *

Tim stood in the doorway a few minutes later as the two of them shared a deep kiss that he thought might never end. Finally, clearing his throat loudly, he got their attention and Emma stood up and moved away from the bed.

"I assume you shared the good news?" Tim asked, a grin splitting his face.

"That's only part of it." Emma couldn't stop smiling as she held her right hand out in front of him so that he could see the engagement ring dangling from her finger.

"Congrats, Sis," Tim said, giving her a heartfelt hug and a gentle kiss on her bruised cheek. "Welcome to the family."

"Thank you," she whispered, still unable to wipe the grin off her face. "I'll let you have a few minutes, just a few, mind you, and then I'll be back."

"Deal, thanks."

He walked over and clasped his brother on the shoulder and Scott could read the depth of emotion in his eyes and understood that this had been an extremely rough time for him.

"Good to have you back, you had me a little worried."

"Yeah, it wasn't anything I'd ever want to experience again. But, hey, look what I woke up to, can you believe it? I'm going to be a dad to some poor kid."

"Hell, I think you'll do just fine with it. Emma will keep you on track. Mom, too, for that matter."

"I know, I feel pretty damn lucky all the way around, Tim."

"You should, its all working out for you. I'm going to miss you on the road, though."

Scott couldn't ever recall seeing such sadness on Tim's face and he couldn't fathom why.

"What are you talking about?"

"A new wife and kids, you can't keep hunting, you have responsibilities now."

"What else would I do? Hell, yeah, I'm going to keep hunting with you. We're going out in a blaze of bloody glory, remember?

Besides, we had a hunter for a dad and we didn't turn out too bad, well I didn't, anyway. Besides, who would look after you?" He was gratified to see the relief shining in Tim's eyes.

*   *   *

In a room across the hall, Lisa's large body lay as still as death on one of the tables in the Infirmary. Her eyes were closed but she could hear everything; the laughter, the sounds of joyous reunions; and she could feel every blister on her burnt skin and every bruised and broken bone in her body.

And Lisa knew, better than anyone could, that she would suffer this horrific anguish until every organ in her body finally shut down and allowed her to die.

Lisa's lips never moved, and no one would ever be to hear her screams of horror as they echoed over and over inside her head.

THE END

I hope you've enjoyed this latest installment of the Devereaux Chronicles. I really appreciate the fact that you have invested both your time and your money in one my stories. It means a more to me than you'll ever know.

The Devereaux' will be back for more adventures, but it may be a little while before that happens. There are other stories that need to be told first.

Please be sure to check out my website or get on my mailing list so that you have all of the current information about my books that are, or soon will be, available.

Thanks again and keep on reading!

Debbie Boek

debbieboek.com
debbieboek.blog

www.ingramcontent.com/pod-product-compliance
Lightning Source LLC
Chambersburg PA
CBHW071604110726
47908CB00007B/2235